.1

Pease, Howard
    Shanghai passage. Illus. by Paul Q.
Forster.   Doubleday, c1929.
    301 p.   illus. (Tod Moran mystery)

I. Title

SHANGHAI PASSAGE

BOOKS BY HOWARD PEASE

Tod Moran Mysteries:

THE TATTOOED MAN

THE JINX SHIP

SHANGHAI PASSAGE

THE SHIP WITHOUT A CREW

WIND IN THE RIGGING

HURRICANE WEATHER

FOGHORNS

HIGHROAD TO ADVENTURE

THE BLACK TANKER

NIGHT BOAT

HEART OF DANGER

CAPTAIN OF THE ARABY

Other Books:

SECRET CARGO

JUNGLE RIVER

LONG WHARF

THUNDERBOLT HOUSE

BOUND FOR SINGAPORE

THE DARK ADVENTURE

SHIPWRECK

*Wu's eyes narrowed, his high cheek bones glistened in the light.
"We'd better wait until after the watch changes at midnight."*

A TOD MORAN MYSTERY

Shanghai Passage

by Howard Pease

Illustrated by
Paul Q. Forster

TOD MORAN
MYSTERY

j
c.1

DOUBLEDAY & COMPANY, INC., GARDEN CITY, N. Y.

BILL OF LADING

This cargo is consigned to:

MILTON S. ROSENFIELD

PALO ALTO, CALIFORNIA

CONTENTS

PART ONE
DEPARTURE

PART TWO
OUTWARD BOUND

PART THREE
THE TYPHOON

vii

CONTENTS

Part Four

PORTS OF ADVENTURE

Part Five

WRECKERS' LAMPS

PART ONE

DEPARTURE

WEST POINT

"There is no place . . . for excuses. A failure is never anything but a failure, and on
the battlefield is paid in
blood."

U. S. M. A. *Bugle Notes*

CHAPTER I

WILFUL MISSING

THE clear notes of a bugle sounded across the West Point parade ground. To Stuart Ormsby, sitting woebegone and grim of aspect in his room in North Barracks, the notes seemed to shout at him, "You're disgraced—disgraced—disgraced!"

Behind him his two roommates hurried into their long coats, without the unnecessary trouble of first donning a shirt. "I'm frightfully sorry that this has happened," one of them said quietly. "You won't leave until after parade?"

Stuart Ormsby did not turn his head. His gaze was fixed upon the street below, where the cadets were already falling into line. "No—I'll not leave till the six o'clock train." He muttered softly under his breath, then rose with a sudden movement. "They've never

3

been fair. They haven't given me a chance! That blamed woof-woof never did like me—said I was too fresh! And old bald-head policed me every chance he got."

Cadet Randall affectionately put his hand on Stuart's shoulder. "Poor old dead-beat Stew," he said with a wry smile; "you've had nothing but trouble ever since you came here. Always in the quill book—always getting demerits. You don't belong here. How did you ever happen to come?"

"If your father were a major in the Marines at Washington you'd know the reason, all right. Of course, I dislike to disappoint Dad—but don't think I'm sorry myself! No, seh—I'm mighty glad to get out of this prison."

"Why don't you take up engineering at Cornell?"

Stuart Ormsby laughed shortly. "I don't fancy it, that's why."

"What do you want to do, then?"

"Oh, I've got plans." He waved his hand in a vague gesture that attempted to imply his splendid and glorious future. "Yes, seh—I've got plans."

His roommates regarded him somewhat doubtfully as he sank back into the chair before the window.

A moment later they were gone down the stairs, and he was alone. Outside, the winter afternoon deepened toward twilight. Without moving he sat in the blue dusk of the window watching the line form, hearing the band strike up a gay march, seeing with misty eyes the cadets step out with rhythmic strides across the parade ground. This, he knew, was his last glimpse of the corps. He was through, finished, done with it all.

This last year and a half had been to him an ordeal of fire through which he had failed to come. The discipline, the hard duties, the ever-increasing studies which he had always consciously shirked—all were too much for him. From the very first day, when the upper classmen had called him "Mr. Dumbjohn" and had treated him as less than the dust beneath their feet, he had rebelled. And now he was dismissed, discharged for deficiency in studies and conduct. Free at last to go where he pleased without orders from a superior officer to guide him, he now began to doubt whether this freedom was what he really desired. Somewhere deep in his consciousness he knew that he didn't want to leave West Point. Not now—not in this manner.

Only for a moment did this regret hold him, then up surged the old rebellious feeling of injustice. Thank heaven, he was through with this military life!

He rose, donned for the last time his full-dress cadet coat, and picking up his headpiece, set the tarbucket firmly upon his closely cropped dark hair. In the mirror on the bare wall he saw regarding him a face lean and bronzed and clean cut. The jaw was firm, but about the mouth there was an unmistakable trace of unyielding pride. The keen brown eyes blazed scorn at him—a failure! The first defeat at the United States Military Academy in three generations of Ormsbys, who had served with Lee, with Roosevelt, with Pershing. His eyes closed for a second in anguish; then he drew himself erect. His right hand came up in a quick salute.

It was his farewell gesture to Stuart Ormsby, West Point cadet.

II

He dared not wait till parade was over and the men streamed back to quarters. In haste he changed to his one suit of civilian clothes, picked up his suitcase, and slipped like a shadow down through the twilight of the stairway. He was running away; he couldn't face his friends again.

In front of the gymnasium he encountered a khaki-clad private who stopped and questioned him. "Stuart Ormsby? A telegram just came for you. The C. O. told me to find you before you left."

With a trembling hand Stuart tore open the yellow envelope. His foreboding was correct; it was from his father in Washington.

Meet me Hotel Astor 8 PM stop from now on you take orders from me.

He crushed the paper in an angry hand. Yes, seh— just like his father! Never any understanding there, Dad always ordered him about as though he were a common private! He would be taken home in disgrace to his aunt in Mobile, where he had lived since the death of his mother twelve years before. Defiantly Stuart hurried forward with suitcase in hand, eager to leave the sound of the band behind him. He crossed the limit line with a relieved sigh, went down the steps to the river, and paused at the foot of the incline to glance back. The gray pile of stone rising from the Hudson brought an unexpected catch to his throat. Now that he was leaving was he to have regrets? No—no! He was glad, he told himself; he was hilariously happy to be free.

Crossing on the little ferry to the Garrison station, where lights were already gleaming, he felt a sudden sense of elation flow over him; but when the train had roared in from Poughkeepsie and he was seated at a window watching the shadowy river craft pass upstream the exhilaration gave way to a feeling of uneasiness, of bewilderment. He envisioned his father, Major Stuart Ormsby, United States Marines, waiting coldly, sternly in his hotel room for his explanation. And there was no excuse he could give.

When the train stopped at the One Hundred and Twenty-fifth Street Station his uneasiness increased; when the cars slid into Grand Central Terminal to debouch their stream of passengers his anxiety was almost oppressive. Nevertheless, he walked along the platform with eyes gazing straight ahead, his lips pressed firmly together.

Then he saw his father. Major Ormsby stood to one side, watching the passengers issue from the platform. No doubt he had just arrived from Washington and had stopped a moment at the Albany exit on the chance that

his son might come in on that train. In an instant all of
Stuart's resolve vanished. Panic seized him. Contem-
plating that tall military figure waiting there, thin
lipped and accusing, he realized he could never face the
older man. Stuart knew the very words his father
would use: "You have disgraced me! Dismissed from
the United States Military Academy! My son—an
Ormsby."

Stuart came to an abrupt halt. Passengers crowded
past him to the exit. With his heart pounding in his
throat he cast a tortured glance about him. Another
train was pulling into a platform on his left, and that
exit was now open. He rushed for it as though he were a
fugitive escaping the clutch of the law. Once lost in the
crowded space under the great vaulted roof he looked
about him with hunted eyes. Hurriedly he counted the
money in his pocket. Yes, seh—he had enough. He'd
leave this country which he hated; he'd go to a foreign
land and start anew. Anything, anything to get away!
But where? Eagerly his glance swept the long row of
ticket windows. His eyes lighted up in exultation at a
sign over a window which read *Montreal Express, 9
p.m.*

That was the very place! He'd get across the border.
He wanted freedom—he wanted air!

III

All night he watched from the window of his chair car
as the country swept past. As they neared West Point

he pulled down the window shade, raising it later to behold the Storm King looming dark and sombre across the river. At Albany he ate a sandwich while he walked up and down the platform to relax his chilled muscles. When they skirted Lake Champlain he perceived that winter was upon them. Bits of ice glistened near the shore; from crags high above, gaunt pines waved their tops. He dropped into an uneasy sleep, to awake in the cold dawn with a light snow falling against the car windows. Then a stop at a village near the Canadian line, the boarding of revenue officers in smart uniforms, the opening of luggage, the rumble of the train as it slowly crossed the St. Lawrence in the morning light.

Next came Victoria Station with its cold, echoing corridor. He crossed to the sidewalk and looked about. Montreal—freedom! Relief, too—no one knew him here. Stuart Ormsby and his old life were irrevocably left behind.

No sense of elation, however, rose to cheer him; instead, a feeling of forlorn depression weighed him down. He possessed one suit of clothes, a cap, and a suitcase filled with shirts and underwear. There was not enough money in his pocket to buy his meals even for one day.

He tramped along the street until he came to a second-hand clothing store. As he hesitated before the dingy entrance, a man emerged from the interior. "Monsieur desires something?" he asked, gazing inquiringly at Stuart.

"Yes, seh. I'd like—I'd like to borrow some money on my watch—and my suitcase."

"*Oui, monsieur.* I do a little pawn business on the side. Come in!" He smiled knowingly.

In the dim interior Stuart handed his watch and suitcase across the counter. After a moment of bargaining the man passed over a handful of coins and a ticket. "Sign here," he said, pushing forward a narrow book.

Stuart recoiled from that page of signatures; then with a trembling hand he wrote *John Rogers, Chicago*.

That was the beginning of the descent of Stuart Ormsby into the maelstrom of the lost and wilful miss·ing.

PART TWO

OUTWARD BOUND

CHAPTER II

THE VAGABOND

ALONG the Vancouver water front, where street lamps gleamed mistily through a driving rain, slouched the tattered figure of a youth. His hands were thrust deep into trouser pockets; between the wet coat collar and the dripping cap pulled low over the eyes the wan glow of the lamps revealed a face pinched and exhausted. At a windy corner opposite the great covered piers his weary steps came to an abrupt halt. Ahead of him a policeman and several seafaring men stood round two motionless upturned boots in the gutter. Like a person living outside the law the youth wheeled and tramped back again through the night and the rain.

For three months Stuart Ormsby had been running away. Penniless, depressed, alone in a foreign land and thrown upon his own resources for the first time in his life, he was finding his former high regard for freedom a childish illusion. He had eaten nothing for thirty-six hours; he had caught only a few minutes' sleep the night before when riding the blind baggage down the mountains from Banff. Now he had come to Canada's western terminal, and still ahead stretched a vagabond trail, leading he knew not where.

His immediate thoughts were of warmth and food. Where could he get something to quiet this gnawing hunger within him? Continued lack of nourishment and sleep had made him listless and confused of mind. Those hoboes, those blowed-in-the-glass stiffs, with whom he had travelled across country, would have battered a restaurant or a private house for a hand-out; but for Stuart Ormsby, a gay cat, an apprentice tramp, this method was a degradation he could not face. Yet this cold wind and rain, sweeping up the harbour inlet, sent an intense feeling of desperation over him. By Cæsar, he'd stop the very next passer-by and ask for help!

When the first pedestrian loomed out of the darkness his spirit failed him. The second figure went by unsolicited while the boy endeavoured to whip up his courage. The chill moments passed as he waited, shivering, beneath a street lamp on a deserted corner. Soon, above the steady beat of rain on the pavement, he heard footfalls coming toward him. He stepped forward, desperate, apprehensive, yet with a forlorn hope struggling within him.

"Excuse me, seh," he began. His lips moved tremulously; not another word could he utter. From somewhere deep in his consciousness came the voice of the Stuart Ormsby he had known in the dim past: "So you have come to this—you are a beggar." He closed his eyes in anguish and despair.

"Well," said a gruff voice, "whatcha want?"

The boy looked up. Facing him was the tall form of a man who stood with feet planted wide apart, as though upon the deck of a rolling ship at sea. He wore a blue pilot coat with its collar upturned; from beneath a cap which marked him as a ship's officer the boy observed in the lamplight a flaming thatch of hair.

"Nothing, seh. Excuse me." Stuart's mouth quivered with emotion.

Still the stranger did not move. "Hungry, eh?" The tone was loud and gruff. As Stuart turned away a hand reached out and grasped his arm. "Wait a moment, young man! Yuh want a job. Ain't it the truth?"

"A job!" Stuart whirled; a sudden hope welled up within him.

The man's glance swept the deserted corner; he lowered his tone. "Yeah. Would a watchman's job help yuh?"

"Anything," Stuart eagerly whispered. "I'll be mighty glad to do it."

"That's talkin'. I want yuh to help me bring my gear ashore from my ship. Come on."

Stuart followed. Glancing across his shoulder at the

rugged countenance of the man the boy decided that here was a person he could never trust. The eyes were keen and roving, the nose flattened, the mouth twisted into cruel lines, the chin square and unshaven. There was a disquieting air of mystery and intrigue about the man. Stuart sensed that the strands of a web, sinister and secret, were tightening about him. Hunger, however, drove him on.

Five minutes' walk along the docks brought them to a pier that was dark and silent. The rain was lessening; it now fell like a mist that half hid the buildings across the road. The man paused at a spot where a spur track led out over the water, glanced quickly up and down, and then went with a swaying stride toward the pierhead. Here the darkness was intense; the only sound was the gentle slap of water against the piles below.

"I want yuh to watch here," whispered the seaman. "I'm rowin' over to my packet yonder." He pointed to the round lights of a large cargo carrier moored to the opposite pier. "Don't make a sound; but if yuh hear anyone comin', whistle twice. Git that?"

"Yes, seh. I'll do it."

Stuart hung over the edge of the pier while the seaman went down the ladder to a waiting skiff. He heard the painter unloosed and dropped into the bottom of the boat, the soft sound of oars in the oarlocks as the black outline of the little rowboat vanished in the night.

A raw wind blew from the harbour; the misty rain continued. Stuart stood by an iron bollard while the minutes slowly passed. Surely the man had reached the ship by this time. Perhaps he was deserting and was merely going after his luggage. Still, this man was no common sailor; for his commanding voice, his bearing, his cap, all marked him a person of authority. The boy's thoughts were interrupted by the unmistakable sound of footfalls approaching from the street. He dropped to a crouching position beside the bollard; then, as the footsteps came nearer, he quickly let himself down the ladder and gained a hidden nook under the edge of the wharf on a crossbeam that ran between two piles. Here he was safe. With fast-beating heart he listened. Should he whistle a warning to the seaman?

The footfalls stopped directly above him, and he surmised that at least four men were standing there.

"Scatter along the dock," said a voice in a low, husky tone. "That dirty tramp tied up opposite is the *Nanking*. Pipe up if you see anyone coming from her."

Footsteps moved off quietly. Low murmurs still came from above. Stuart, straining his ears close to the planks, heard an oath as one of the men cursed the night and the cold. "Think we'll get 'em, Chief?" asked a low voice.

"Can't tell," came the response; "but the revenue officers at Seattle wired us to-day that nothing came ashore there and for us to be on the lookout. San Francisco is her home port, and they're suspicious of her, too."

"She's got a mighty bad name, Chief."

"She sure has. I was aboard her to-day, but couldn't find a thing. Gad, she's a dirty tub—that *Nanking!* I don't blame the crew for deserting when she hits port. Only the riffraff stay with her. I'd jolly well hate to ship out on her, myself. Ugh! she ought to be condemned."

The voices droned on, but now so low that the boy scarcely caught a word. Presently one of the men walked down the dock. The soft scuff of a shoe told Stuart that one other still remained.

Soon he, too, moved off; evidently he was patrolling this side of the pier. Stuart felt his heart beat in terror. Revenue officers! What would they do if they found him here, apparently in league with this seaman? He caught his breath at the thought of prison. Strange how some hated authority was always threatening him!

Overhead the footsteps of the patrolling officer came nearer, passed, and receded into silence. At that very moment he heard the soft swish of water near him. The boat! Tense and anxious he peered toward the sound; his eyes, however, could not pierce that wall of blackness. Should he whistle? That would warn the approaching man in the boat—but what of himself? He would be caught at the first sound; as an accomplice he would be thrown into prison.

From the darkness of the water came the vague outline of the prow of the skiff. The boy reached down and, catching hold, drew it under the wharf's deep shadow. "Quiet!" he whispered. "Men above. After you."

A hand reached out and pressed his arm. "Where?"

"Four men on the pier—patrolling."

Stuart heard a quick intake of breath. The grip on his arm tightened. "You in with them?" jerked out the man in a menacing whisper.

"No, seh! Ain't I warned you? They don't know I'm here."

"Get in, then, and shut up!"

With relief Stuart dropped to a seat in the stern. In the deep gloom he watched the man lift a package of indistinguishable size and place it on the crossbeam above them. Evidently he was not to be thwarted in his plan of getting this secret bit of cargo ashore, where doubtless a confederate would later pick it up in safety. Again from above sounded approaching footfalls. Breathlessly they waited. When the steps had passed and silence once more enveloped the pier, the seaman quickly drew out the oars and shoved off.

Stuart inwardly cursed himself for a fool. What had he let himself in for now? Yet, he admitted to himself, this was no new experience for him. Ever since he had pawned his suitcase in Montreal five months before he had been riding freight trains at night; more than once he had been chased by a railroad dick who was eager to pocket the fifty cents for the capture of a tramp in the yards. Step by step, he now realized, he had been driving himself straight into the hands of the law. He shivered slightly; his finger nails dug into his palms.

Out into the misty rain moved the boat; slowly the dim outline of the wharf receded. Just at the moment

when Stuart was beginning to feel that they were safe
from the officers, he heard a quick patter of running feet
and a harsh call: "Stop or I'll fire!"

The seaman grunted an oath and pulled with all his
strength on the oars. They were discovered now; there
was no need for further caution. A piercing whistle
shrilled out across the water. Stuart trembled. In a moment all four revenue officers would be on their trail.

Again came the cry from the pier: "Stop or I'll
shoot!"

Swiftly the seaman turned the prow of the little boat
toward the outer harbour. A second later a shot cracked
out. The bullet whined through the air above them.

Instinctively Stuart dropped to the bottom of the skiff
where the gunwale shielded him. He was dimly aware
that the tall seaman was dragging on his oars in great
steady sweeps, that they were swiftly drawing out into
the stream where they moved with a misty curtain enveloping them. Another shot echoed in the darkness.
Far to the left a faint splash sounded.

From the pier came shouts and muffled voices no
doubt planning a method of chase. The seaman snarled
in fury as he turned the boat sharply to the right. Soon
they glided under the stern of the tramp steamer, whose
bulk loomed above them sombre and mysterious.
The seaman, first shipping his oars with a practised
movement, caught something that trailed in the water
against the steel plates of the hull.

"Get up!" he ordered under his breath.

Stuart rose and grasped the swaying ropes of a ladder. Eagerly he climbed the wooden rungs. Once aboard this ship, he told himself, he would slip down the gangway to the safety of the other pier. At the top he jumped over the bulwarks to deck. There in the semidarkness he looked about him.

He stood on the deserted after deck of a rusty tramp freighter of perhaps four thousand tons. Across two covered hatches he glimpsed the lighted midship section rising against the black sky. A single funnel was belching forth a thick cloud of smoke to mingle with the falling rain. From the forward deck drifted the murmur of voices and the dull thud of hammers on wood.

A sound behind him made him whirl. His companion jumped over the bulwarks. The man leaned overside and drew up the Jacob's ladder. "We made it safe," he muttered with a grin. "I kicked the skiff loose. They'll never get us now. Ain't it the truth?"

A feeling of intense relief swept over the boy. In surprise he perceived that his knees were trembling and that sweat lay damp on his brow. As he rested a moment against a winch near the after rail, he saw the vague form of a sailor coming toward them. "That you, Mr. Bashford?" asked the man, as he came to a halt before them. "You're wanted on the fo'c'sle head, sir. We're pulling out."

Mr. Bashford made a curt gesture of acknowledgment, with a brief "Follow me" thrown over his shoulder to his companion.

Stuart hurried after him across the slippery steel deck.
Pulling out! By Cæsar, he'd better be getting ashore
mighty quick! This old freighter might be running down
the coast—and he surely didn't want to see the States
again. No, seh—not yet. He'd stick to his plan to beat
his way north to the salmon fisheries of Alaska, where
he'd earn a stake working through the summer.

He followed the man through a passageway of the
midship structure to the fore deck. Here all was activity. Men were battening down a hatch cover; others
were swinging in the gangway. Stuart noted these facts
with a sharp feeling of misgiving.

"How'll I get ashore, seh?" he urgently whispered,
drawing abreast of the seaman.

The man motioned him forward. "Yuh ain't goin'
ashore, see? I'm goin' to give yuh a job on this packet."

In dismay Stuart glanced about him at the littered
deck, the rusty bulwarks, the nondescript men who were
hawling on the cables of the derrick boom. "Is this a
British tramp?" he asked unsteadily.

"Naw—it's American. But yuh're from the States.
Ain't it the truth?"

American! A dull flush spread over the boy's face.
"No, I can't go," he blurted out in a tone of profound
conviction. "I've got to get ashore."

The man shoved him toward the wall of the forecastle head. "Yuh git down there to the seamen's
quarters," he snapped. "D'yuh think I'm lettin' yuh
git back to Vancouver where the bulls will ask yuh

things about this packet? Yuh can't fool with Shark Bashford. Git down there!"

He swung open an iron door, and now he pointed down a short flight of steps. "Stay there, kid. I'll sign yuh on the ship's papers later. Yuh rate an ordinary seaman's berth. And if yuh talk about what yuh seen to-night——"

Stuart leaned against the door jamb. "I can't stay," he remonstrated. Suddenly he raised his head. From high on the bridge came a shout: "Let go aft!"

That must be the voice of the captain. They were pulling out! He jerked away and fled to the bulwarks, ready to jump. The old tramp was drawing away from the pier; the water between the ship and the dock was slowly widening. A tug puffed alongside. As he stared, wide eyed, desperation driving him to jump into the water and swim for it, a hand wrenched at his shoulder. The tall red-haired seaman dragged him back.

"Run away, will yuh?" he snarled in rage.

"I'll call the captain or the first mate," Stuart challenged.

A laugh greeted his words. "Well, call. I'm the mate."

Stuart's dark beseeching eyes sought the other's face. In that forbidding countenance so close to him there was, however, no hint of compassion. The mate's thin face was distorted by hard, unreasoning anger. Stuart saw the man's right arm draw back for a blow. Before he could move, before he could even swerve, an iron fist flashed toward him. It thudded against his jaw and struck him to the deck.

He lay on his side with one arm outstretched, the roar of a wind in his ears. The square yellow light of the forecastle door wavered a moment, dissolved into blackness, and wavered again in a misty blur. Beneath him the deck seemed to toss and sway; a throbbing pain shot through him.

As in a dream he knew that he was lifted in arms that pressed him against the open doorway. "Put this seaman to bed down there," said a voice from a far distance. "He's drunk to the gills."

Then he was falling through space. Each iron step of the companionway caught him beneath the ribs as he rolled down into a black abyss. There, in the heavenly quiet of the forecastle, he lay with eyes closed. Above him a door slammed shut. Slowly he fought his way back to consciousness. Through a swimming vision he saw an electric bulb in the deck head swaying like a giddy moon from side to side.

He rubbed a hand across his brow, dragged himself to one elbow, and gazed around. He lay in a triangular compartment in the very bow of the ship, with a row of bunks two tiers high encircling it. For a moment he thought the place deserted, then he heard the loud breathing of drunken men.

From a bunk high above, the thin, pale face of a cockney seaman looked down at him in surprise. "Had a run-in with Shark Bashford, did yer? Gawd blimey, kid, that bloke is the worst bucko mate on the Pacific. Wot's wrong with yer?"

Stuart rose unsteadily, one hand braced against the forecastle steps. "I've got to get ashore." He repeated the words in a dazed voice, "I've got to get ashore."

"Ashore! Blimey, yer too late. We're pullin' out."

On the instant the boy knew that he wanted to get home; he wanted to get back to a decent way of living. Not this—not this! Because he knew too much the mate was shanghaiing him aboard this tramp steamer.

"I didn't sign on," he said as though to himself. "I didn't sign on."

"Yer not the first sailor ter be sent on the shanghai passage, kid. But nobody never got no rottener ship than this 'ere ole *Nanking*."

"Where—where are we going?" The words came muffled, from Stuart Ormsby's lips.

"Our first bloomin' landfall is Yokohama. We're bound fer the China coast."

CHAPTER III

SS. "NANKING"

"ALL hands on deck!"

Stuart Ormsby, seated on a bunk, looked wearily up at the doorway where a face was vaguely visible in the half light of the forecastle. "On deck, youse birds!" thundered the voice again.

"That's the bo'sun," whispered the little cockney seaman from the bunk above. "Keep quiet."

"Say, do youse guys hear your master's voice a-callin'?" went on the boatswain. "Are youse comin' up alone—or are youse comin' on my boot?"

In the silence that followed Stuart rose unsteadily to his feet, aware on the instant that his muscles were sore and bruised from his headlong descent of the iron steps. Glancing about, he saw that three men slept beneath blankets and that the small seaman who had been talking to him a moment before was now apparently deep in slumber.

An oath, low and obscene, came from the doorway; then the boatswain hurled his short form down the three steps. He drew up before Stuart in an attitude of menacing wrath. "Why haven't youse turned out?"

26

he fumed. "Git up there *pronto* and help the men lash the booms. We gotta git this old tub shipshape if we kin."

"I'm not a member of the crew," the boy hurriedly brought out.

The boatswain's weather-beaten face glowered. "Oh, youse ain't! Well, no dockside loafer can pull any stuff on me—see? Git on deck!"

Without waiting for a reply he crossed to a bunk where a huge seaman snored peacefully. "Rise and shine, youse lubbers!" he cried, jerking the blanket off the man. His most violent efforts, however, were of no avail, for the big seaman was evidently too far gone with drink even to move. Turning next to the cockney's berth he met a like response. But not to be outdone here, too, he dragged the little sailor unceremoniously from his bunk and dropped him to the floor.

"Youse can't fool me, Toppy," he snarled. "No 'possum in this fo'c'sle. Turn out!"

The seaman, thin and scrawny, rose and staggered against a bunk. "Wot yer want?" he yawned, aggrieved. "Cawn't a bloke get a bit o' sleep in 'is own fo'c'sle?"

"Can that stuff, Toppy! I know youse. Git on deck."

"Oh, Gawd, wot a ship!" Toppy went unsteadily up the steps, murmuring. "Sorry I ever left ole Lunnon. Blimey, yes."

Stuart followed with anger smouldering within him. On the third step he looked back to glimpse the boatswain still endeavouring to wake the other two men;

then he stepped over the high casing to deck. There in the darkness he paused to survey the ship.

The rain had stopped; beyond the square of light that slanted on the wet, glistening plates of the deck he saw dim figures moving about near the mainmast, no doubt still at work with the derrick booms. Across the two hatches rose the white superstructure with the yellow beams of its portholes piercing the night. High above on the bridge a faint light shone from the wheelhouse window, where the quartermaster stood at the helm. On the starboard wing burned a green light; on the port glowed the red eye of danger. Stuart crossed to the rail; under his hand he felt the bulwarks tremble with a faint vibration. The great iron heart of the *Nanking* was beginning its rhythmic, uninterrupted beat.

"Take yer larst bloomin' look at land fer a month," Toppy advised, coming up beside him. "Yokohama ain't so bad, though—but Shanghai's better."

Across the river red and green lights on the pierheads were reflected in the darkness of the water. Above them the dockside lamps of Vancouver winked through the night. Gazing at the brilliantly illuminated station of the Canadian Pacific Railway, which was now drawing abreast of them, Stuart was instantly overwhelmed by a sense of loneliness, of isolation. There was no hope now of his getting ashore. On this rusty tramp steamer, with its crew of deep-sea flotsam, he was being carried out of the harbour inlet into the strait; already he could

feel the long swells as the freighter breasted the open
water. There was a tang of salt air in his nostrils and a
sharp breeze on his face as the wind whipped the waves
into whitecaps.

His hand closed tightly on the curving steel of the
bulwarks. He had wanted to get away, he had wanted
never to see the States again; yet now that his wish was
about to be granted, a disturbing doubt struggled within
him. With every turn of the ship's propeller, his old life,
his home, were being left behind. What, he wondered,
lay ahead?

"There's the bo'sun," Toppy observed in a whisper.
"Thinks we'll work, 'e does. Come on—I know a snug
place where that bloke won't find us."

Glad of this opportunity to elude the authority of the
ship's officers, Stuart slipped with the seaman to the
port wing of the forecastle. Here the little Londoner
swung open an iron door and darted in. "Come on," he
whispered.

Stuart stepped over the high casing and closed the
door behind him.

"We ain't got no right 'ere," Toppy informed him
coolly; "it's the blarsted firemen's washroom. But the
bo'sun won't look fer us 'ere."

Stuart stood at the top of a short flight of ladder-like
steps leading down to a damp compartment, where a
youth of about his own age sat upon a stool, washing a
pair of overalls. At their sudden entrance he looked

up with a grin. "Hello, Toppy," he said. "Hiding?"

"'Idin' me eye!" retorted the other. "I'm orf duty. 'Ow's everythin', Joe Macaroni?"

"Fine, Toppy. I'm getting used to the engine room again. But this Black Gang is sure some rough crowd."

Toppy seated himself on the lower step and sighed heavily. "Wish I'd shipped below on this trip," he murmured sadly. "These bloomin' deck horfficers won't let yer sleep a minute." He pointed over his shoulder to Stuart, who had taken a seat on the upper step. "This 'ere's a lubber Shark Bashford just brought aboard. Don't yer feel sorry fer 'im, Joe Macaroni?"

The young man chuckled as he laid his dungarees on a bench and scrubbed them with a brush. Stuart, looking down on the fellow's engaging face, instinctively felt that here was at least one person with whom he could converse in his own language. He was a solidly built chap of eighteen or nineteen, with sandy hair, gray eyes, and a smiling mouth.

"My name is Moran—Tod Moran," the member of the Black Gang explained in a friendly tone. "But ever since I shipped with Toppy one trip as mess boy on the *Araby* he always calls me Joe Macaroni. I'm below deck now as an oiler."

"Yeh, goin' up yer are," said Toppy in a tone evincing whole-hearted pride and elation. "Mess boy, coal passer, fireman, an' now oiler."

Stuart smiled to himself. Did this young fellow really take pride in getting a position as an engine-room oiler on such a battered tramp as this *Nanking?* A feeling of pity, of commiseration for these men of the sea took possession of him.

"This is my first trip," he acknowledged a moment later, a faint trace of superiority in his voice, "and I'm mighty surprised to be here, too." He checked himself: certainly, he decided, he didn't want to confide too deeply in these men. He'd wait until he saw the captain.

"You from the South?" Tod Moran asked. "From Carolina?"

A slow flush spread over Stuart Ormsby's features. Here they were already—those dreaded questions. His hands moved nervously on his thin trousers as he answered, "I'm from Alabama—Mobile."

"Blimey, I know that port," Toppy broke in. "Put in there once on the ole *K. I. Luckenbach.* Wish I was back on 'er, too. She's got class."

"By Cæsar, seh," Stuart affirmed, eager to change the subject, "this surely isn't much of a ship!"

Tod Moran threw back his head and laughed. "The *Nanking?* Well, she might be worse—but I doubt it. I just signed on at Frisco a week ago." The smile left his lips; he dropped his dungarees into the soapy water and turned a serious face up to them. "Toppy, I'm sorry Captain Jarvis has become master of this steamer."

The little Londoner lighted a cigarette. "Aw, yer don't 'ave ter worry about Tom Jarvis. 'E's a rough 'un

— the skipper!—a little too rough fer the likes o' me. 'E kin take care o' 'isself."

"Sure he can—but have you heard what's happened on this old tramp the last three voyages?"

"Wot yer mean, Joe Macaroni?"

Tod Moran lowered his voice. "I've heard the men talking, Toppy. No skipper has made more than one voyage on the *Nanking*."

"I don't blame 'em, kid. One bally trip is enough fer anyone."

"But they've had no choice, Toppy. *Something has always happened to them.*"

"Gawd blimey!" Toppy leaned forward intently. "Wot yer know, Joe Macaroni?"

"Several months ago the captain of this ship disappeared in Hongkong when they put in for coal. They took a new skipper on for the homeward voyage, and he was found dead in his bunk one morning—strangled! There were marks about his neck where a rope had cut into the flesh. They buried him in Honolulu. The murderer was never discovered. Last trip something even more mysterious happened. Night after night the crew heard the captain cursing about something trying to get him. Finally he locked himself in his cabin, never coming on deck. When the ship docked at San Francisco he was put away in a lunatic asylum; but Singapore Sam and a couple of the other fellows say he wasn't crazy at all! ... Do you see what I mean? Captain Jarvis just took over the command in

Frisco ten days ago while his own ship, the *Araby*, is laid up for repairs. Now I'm wondering—*what will happen to him?*"

Over Stuart rose a sudden wave of apprehension that flooded his mind with an obscure dread. This freighter *Nanking*, with her rusty hull and her grimy

MAIN DECK + S.S. NANKING

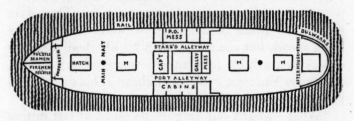

superstructure, was a ship with a strange and terrible past. What secrets lurked in her holds? What dangers stalked these decks at night to strike down the master on every voyage? And he, himself, was now a member of her crew. She was steaming west to unknown seas, taking with her a riffraff crew of officers and men, all dregs of the tropic ports of the Pacific. There could be no escape for him now. He felt the steady mounting beat of his pulse.

The little cockney was breathing heavily. "Gawd strike me pink!" he exclaimed. "I don't like it, Joe Macaroni—I wish I 'adn't signed on."

"Did you ever see a rottener bunch of officers?" Tod Moran continued. "Take that bucko mate, Shark

Bashford. He's been on this ship for two years." His voice droned on, but Stuart was not listening. Shark Bashford—the man who had shanghaied him aboard this steamer! This secret traffic with someone ashore was possibly even more serious than he had at first suspected. Was the first mate the man who was back of this series of mishaps to the *Nanking's* masters?

Stuart's hand clutched the step as the ship rolled to port and gently swung back to starboard. They were hitting the swells of the strait with the Pacific some miles ahead. For the first time in his life there was only a deck beneath his feet, and he was finding it unreal, unsteady. The tremor of the bulkhead at his side seemed to send a sudden tide of fear through his veins.

"What—what's our cargo?" he asked at last during a pause in the conversation.

"Medical supplies," Moran replied, turning back to his laundry. "Food, too, for some towns up the Yangtse Kiang. Civil war in China has led to famine there. This old tramp has been chartered to rush supplies to the American settlements. We loaded grain in Vancouver."

"Just wait till we hit the Bund at Shanghai," Toppy began with a reminiscent look; then, as the door of the washroom grated behind them, he turned his head, startled.

"Oh, here youse are!" sang out the boatswain. "Well, me lads, youse guys will hear from me this passage out."

"Did yer want us, Bose?" asked Toppy mildly.

"Did I want youse?" The stocky boatswain's vocabulary for the next full minute amazed Stuart by its variety of epithets. "I'll black your eyes if youse don't get up here!"

"We better git ter work, Alabam," Toppy announced casually to Stuart as he mounted the steps.

On deck the boy halted in surprise at the velocity of the wind which beat across the bulwarks and sang through the rigging above. By Cæsar, they must be heading right into a gale! He lurched close to the lee-ward wing of the forecastle, where Toppy and the boatswain were peering through a porthole. Cries and shouts came from the compartment.

"That's the blarsted firemen's quarters," confided Toppy with a wide grin. "They must be 'avin' a little fight. 'Ear 'em 'ittin' each other!"

In silence the three stood listening as the outcry behind the bulkhead increased to a mighty uproar. The next instant a door to the left of the seamen's fore-castle flew open, and a yellow glare flashed out on deck. From the doorway reverberated shouts and oaths, the scuffling and blows of infuriated men. Then up the lad-der tottered a dark form which crumpled to the plates of the deck.

"Cripes, they're killin' each other," muttered the boatswain. He put his fingers to his lips; a whistle shrilled out across the deck.

"What's the trouble?" Stuart asked uneasily.

"Now, don't get excited, Alabam," Toppy said cheer-fully. "That's just a friendly li'l' fight. That ain't nothin' ter wot 'll 'appen before this 'ere voyage is finished."

As the uproar in the Black Gang's forecastle still continued the boatswain hurried aft, no doubt to notify an engine-room officer of the trouble. A low moan came from the figure which had fallen to deck by the doorway. As the man attempted to rise and then fell back with a groan Stuart stepped forward. "That man's hurt, Toppy. We'd better help him."

Toppy put a restraining hand on the boy's shoulder. "Alabam, yer keep away from those blokes," he said earnestly. "If yer mix in their fights yer might get a bullet in yer back."

But Stuart had already torn himself free and was kneeling beside the prostrate fireman. "*Dio cane*," muttered the man. "I geet heem yet!"

He struggled to his knees, and Stuart saw that the man held a knife in his hand. In the light from the electric bulb burning in the deckhead just above the steps the steel blade glistened like an avenging dagger. "I keel heem—I keel heem!" shrieked the man, dragging himself back to the doorway. He was an olive-skinned Italian, short and sturdily built; his white, even teeth curved over his lips in anguish.

"Stay 'ere, Tony," Toppy admonished. "The bloody horfficers are comin'."

Stuart looked up as he heard quick steps approaching. Toppy drew him outside the range of light into the deep shadow of the washroom. "Keep outa this, kid," he whispered. "That's the skipper and the chief engineer. They'll 'ave ter hurry ter save Tony the Wop."

"We've got to put a stop to this, Mr. Rankin," said a voice, deep and vibrant, above the hum of the wind. "This is the second row in your fo'c'sle since leaving Frisco."

The chief engineer's answer was in a tone of hurt reproach. "Am I liable for the actions of this gang of cutthroats? They're the worst crew I've ever had. But you wait here, Captain Jarvis. I'll stop this."

The chief engineer reached for Tony the Wop and flung him aside; a second later his stocky form, clad in blue overalls and jumper, disappeared down the forecastle ladder. The commotion, however, did not cease.

The captain of the *Nanking* halted at the doorway and peered below. His back was toward Stuart, but the boy, gazing at that immense lithe form silhouetted against the square of light, thought that he had never seen a more magnificent specimen of manhood. Somehow, he had expected a captain to wear a blue serge suit with brass buttons and a cap with braid. Instead, this man was clad in dark trousers that covered a surprising length of limb; a white sleeveless singlet accentuated the broad shoulders and arms as muscular as a blacksmith's. Evidently the man ruled by his strength, by the force of his personality; for the poise of the head, with its tawny hair closely cropped, bespoke a commander of character and decision.

Captain Jarvis remained a moment in the doorway,

but as the cries, the shouts, the thuds continued, Stuart saw him bend his head and leap down the steps.

"Gawd blimey!" breathed Toppy at Stuart's shoulder. "Tom Jarvis is a-goin' inter action. Gawd 'elp those blokes down there."

From the firemen's forecastle came a thunderous voice. "Cut the rough, you men!" There was the sound of renewed blows, the thud of bodies hitting the floor, thin wailing cries that lingered in the air, curses that rose to screams of rage, and then a sudden falling off of the din, as though a rising gale had suddenly subsided.

Toppy tiptoed to the door and cautiously peered downward. His thin, mouse-like face was pale in the lamplight, his eyes wide and staring. Stuart saw his throat move convulsively as he muttered in awe, "Gawd strike me bline! 'E's done it."

The boy dropped to his knees beside Tony the Wop, who was moaning and cursing between his teeth. "Hurt?" Stuart asked.

"Not ver' much. Wait till I geeta these hand on Slim Morgan. He start thees—never keep his fires goin'— always leave his dirty ash pit for me to clean. Say, keed, help me into the washroom, yes? I don' wan' Captain Jarvees see me thees way."

As Stuart returned from the washroom, Mr. Rankin, the chief engineer, emerged from the forecastle, his bearded face twitching, one arm held close to his side as though in pain. Behind him the huge form of the

Nanking's captain blocked the doorway. There he swung about and spoke in a crisp, stern voice to the silent men below. "Any more o' this will mean irons for the lot o' you. You're at sea now, and I'm master. Do you understand?—master! If necessary, I'll lock you hellhounds below in the brig."

Silence ensued while that commanding presence stood there. Abruptly the man swung on his heel and strode aft. From the Black Gang's quarters drifted a low murmur of curses.

Toppy and the boatswain were conversing in undertones near the rail, evidently the best of friends. "Alabam!" shouted the little Londoner. "The bo'sun wants yer."

"Yes, seh?" Stuart crossed to them.

"Youse the new seaman?" asked the boatswain. "The captain sends youse his compliments. He wants to see youse in his office." He threw back his head and opened his mouth in a guffaw. "Better step lively, kid."

The captain! Stuart shivered. That display of strength and muscle had sent a feeling of awe and admiration over him. He felt repelled yet fascinated by the brutal personality which commanded this ship. Tod Moran had hinted that the last three masters of the *Nanking* had either been killed or had disappeared in strange circumstances. Well, he told himself as he went slowly toward the port alleyway, here was a man who appeared equal to any eventuality. There was no doubt that he commanded with an iron fist. And he, Stuart Ormsby, would be under that rule, feel that fist if he did not obey.

His breath came faster as he stepped into the passageway that ran athwart the ship between the port and starboard alleyways. "By Cæsar, what a crazy, outlandish ship!" he murmured aloud. He stopped before a white door marked *Captain's Office*, and raised a trembling hand. Could he face a barrage of questions from that deep, vibrant voice with its brutal tones? His hesitating knock echoed through the silence of the passageway.

"Come the hell in!" directed that vibrant voice through the door.

CHAPTER IV

CAPTAIN TOM JARVIS

SLOWLY Stuart swung back the door and stepped into the captain's saloon. At once he was struck by a faint yet unmistakable marine odour to the place. Opposite him, several portholes, hung with red plush drapes, opened upon the fore deck; directly below these ran a long settee of the same dark red material. Beyond the round centre table with a green baize top he saw the huge form of the captain sitting at a desk in the corner. Next to him, talking earnestly, was seated the first mate.

"This is the kid I just mentioned, sir," Shark Bashford was saying. "I found him stowed aboard. Aft he was, sir, in the stearing-gear room."

"A stowaway on this tramp!" The captain's deep voice rang out in mirth. "Suffering catfish!" He swung about to survey this strange phenomenon aboard his ship.

Stuart gave a quick start of alarm. A stowaway! So that was the explanation the red-haired mate gave as to his presence on the *Nanking*. The man hoped thus to shield his own secret actions from the vessel's master.

The boy raised his head defiantly; his cheeks were pale, his eyes burning. Shark Bashford returned his look with a gaze as hard and cold as steel.

Captain Jarvis took up a tobacco pouch and began filling a large carved pipe. "You chose a pretty poor ship to stow away on, youngster," he said in a low tone that carried across the cabin.

Speechless, disheartened, hesitant, Stuart regarded the man before him. The captain's face was rough hewn and squarely cut; his eyes, the boy thought, were the strangest he had ever seen: long and pale and mysterious in their depths, they gave the man a remote Tartar look. But as Stuart's glance strayed down to the immense, Herculean shoulders and arms he caught his breath in surprise.

The man was tattooed. Fascinated, Stuart studied the figures engraved on the rippling muscles. Beneath the thin singlet, taut across the shaggy, powerful chest, could be seen the faint outline of a Chinese dragon. Two evil heads, grinning broadly, emerged upon coiling necks to writhe upon his chest. There was something uncanny about that Oriental figure deftly tattooed in red and green. As the man breathed, the two heads seemed to dart and sway, the red eyes to flash fire and hatred. Around his left arm coiled a blue snake whose head lay flat on the back of his hand; and on the biceps of his other arm was a mass of stars like the quivering spiral of the Milky Way. By Cæsar, Stuart told himself, this was a mighty queer captain!

"What's your name?" The tattooed captain had fixed upon him a cold appraising glance.

Instinctively the boy drew himself up straight and tall. "Stuart Ormsby, seh."

"You're no Canadian. You from the South?"

"Yes, seh."

"Ever been in the army?"

A slow flush spread over Stuart's features. "No, seh," he answered in a low tone.

"You needn't lie about it," the captain went on calmly. "It don't make any difference. You're not the first deserter to go to sea."

A sudden rush of words came to Stuart Ormsby's lips. "I didn't desert, seh," he began; then he checked himself, nonplussed. What could he say, how could he explain? As his burning gaze swept the room in the anguish of uncertainty he met the malevolent eyes of the first mate. In that dark glance he read a warning: *Be careful what yuh say.*

Captain Jarvis struck a match, lighted his pipe, and settled back in the swivel chair. "Ever been to sea before, young man?"

"No, seh."

"I'm sorry for you, then."

At the words, at the tone of sympathetic pity, Stuart searched the other's face. Perhaps back of that brute force was a nature that had its moments of understanding kindliness. Perhaps he'd dare tell this captain the truth about his presence aboard, and about this mate, Shark

Bashford. He ran his tongue quickly over his dry lips. "I'm not a stowaway," he heatedly declared. "The mate knows that, seh. I came——"

"Shut up, yuh little liar," the mate cut in sharply. He was on his feet now, his thin face drawn into lines of bitter exasperation. He drew a hand through his flaming thatch of hair as he looked down at the captain with a conciliating glance. "Tryin' to lie outa this, he is, sir. Ain't it the truth? Well, we can fix him. We're short o' men on deck. I'll give him a job there."

Captain Jarvis observed the boy out of those strange Tartar eyes. With a shrug he swung about to his desk. "As ordinary seaman?" he asked.

"Exactly, sir," agreed Shark Bashford, leering triumphantly at the boy.

Stuart drooped. A pang of dread shot through him. He stretched out his hand and steadied it on the green baize of the table. He wasn't believed; now he would be at the mercy of the first mate. He closed his eyes at the vision of what the future held for him—pain and abuse, grinding labour and galling humiliation, poor food in the seamen's messroom, and a bunk in the forecastle with the scum of the world's water fronts around him.

His meditation was abruptly interrupted by the voice of Captain Jarvis. "Here—I want your address." He reached for a paper in his desk. "Where do you live?"

"My—my home, seh, was in Mobile, Alabama."

Shark Bashford grinned down at his superior. "Wonder what he did, sir, that made him leave home!"

Stuart's hand closed tightly on the edge of the table. His heart seemed to drop with sickening suddenness; his eyes grew misty. Would he never be allowed to forget his past? Would he hear these questions, these taunts, every day of the voyage out? They were like rapier thrusts to him, as though those sharp-pointed weapons with which he had fenced at the Academy were now piercing his flesh, probing into old wounds that still were raw.

"In case of accident," resumed the captain, "who shall I notify?"

Stuart's voice, when he answered, was strange to him, and thin. "My aunt, seh—Miss Millicent Ormsby." In the stillness he could hear the scratch of the pen.

"That's all." The captain swung about. "You'll take your place with the men and work your way. We can't put you back now, and you won't be allowed ashore in any foreign port. We'll land you back in the States where you belong. If you're wanted there for any reason —that's your own concern."

The boy looked with unflinching gaze at the bronzed face before him. "I'm not wanted, seh, for anything. Why—why do you say that? I'm not that kind."

His words were greeted by a laugh, harsh and guttural, from the mate. "Yuh sure are a little liar. And yuh're the worst specimen of dockside loafer I ever seen. Ain't it the truth, sir?"

Stuart felt the blood drain from his cheeks; he pressed his lips tightly together. They were accusing him of

looking like a dockside loafer, a wharf rat—him, Stuart
Ormsby! Were they making sport of him? He stared
at them unbelievingly.

Captain Jarvis puffed on his pipe, his great hand over
the bowl. "I'm afraid Mr. Bashford is about right," he
admitted. "What! You don't believe it? Sufferin' whale
oil! Take a look-see at yourself over there."

The boy turned his head and observed, above a sideboard where water glasses rested, a small mirror fastened to the wall. With deliberate steps, he crossed the
cabin and stood before it.

Through a swimming vision he saw the face of a
stranger staring back at him, a face thin and tired and
wan, with brown eyes deep in their sockets. The black
hair, long and unkempt, clung damply to the forehead.
He saw the eyes widen in amazement. By Cæsar, he
pondered, this surely couldn't be Stuart Ormsby. Why,
good heavens, this was a tramp!

A sudden tide of understanding, surging over him,
engulfed him in bitter waves of humiliation. No wonder
they treated him as an outcast, as a thief fleeing from
the law. How had he allowed all his self-respect to slip
away and leave him such an absurd scarecrow figure as
this!

Dimly aware that Captain Jarvis was speaking, he
turned with an unwilling step. "You better get a shower
in the washroom, young man—and clean up your
clothes. One of the men in the fo'c'sle can give you a
haircut. To-morrow you can get anything you need in

the way of dungarees and shirts from the steward's slop chest. We'll allow you that much." He gave Stuart a searching look. "If you're hungry, you'll find a hand-out in the messroom—that's all."

Stuart's throat moved slowly. "Yes, seh." Trembling, he brought up his right hand in a military salute, and, trembling, he left the cabin.

Outside in the passageway he leaned against the white woodwork, sick and faint. What had he done—what had he done! Saluted this tattooed captain as though the man were an officer at West Point! Given himself away. Was it any wonder they didn't believe him?

Behind him a door clicked faintly; then came the caustic, malicious voice of the mate in his ear. "Oh, here yuh are! Tried to tell, didn't yuh?" A hand grasped his arm until it bit into the flesh. "I'll pay yuh for that—for every damned word yuh said. Understand? Now go for'ard to your bunk, little boy!"

Stuart stumbled over the casing to the deserted fore deck. Under the clouds the night was black. Lurching to the rail, he took hold of the bulwarks with both hands. Fool—he had given himself away! They would think him a deserter from the army, for he could never, never tell them he had been dismissed from West Point.

The thought brought a stab of pain. West Point! . . . He remembered, with a catch in his throat, how the Hudson flowed around the point and then swept on between green hills toward the bay. He could see the gray pile of stone that was the Academy rising like a castle above the river. He could see his own room, with the table by the window covered with his rarely opened books. Outside was the parade ground with the corps marching in rhythmic stride. He could hear the band playing, see the colours flying in the breeze, feel his quickly mounting pulse. And there was Stuart Ormsby in full dress, tarbucket on head, stepping out proudly in the line. . . . His face fell forward into his arms on the bulwarks.

Presently he raised his head. Not a star above—nothing but blackness ahead. A biting sea wind sang through the rigging; it stung his cheeks and brought to his nostrils a salty tang that promised glimpses of tropic ports across the world; of crowded harbours beneath flashing sunlight, of Oriental water fronts swarming with a slant-eyed populace, of Chinese coolies poling sampans up a yellow river. . . . At that moment something deep within him stirred. He listened. Around him was the soft eternal music of the sea.

CHAPTER V

TOD MORAN GIVES A WARNING

DURING the night, the *Nanking*, that time-worn little tramp, steamed steadily south through the inland waters of British Columbia. She threaded her way among innumerable islands and, soon after dawn, swung her blunt nose southwest around Vancouver Island, with Esquimault Harbour on her starboard beam. Under a gray sky she took the south passage through Juan de Fuca Strait. Low rugged hills rose from each shore. A slender ocean liner came up behind, drew abreast, and passed with a smiling jeer from a passenger leaning over a white rail. Between the two ships, gulls wheeled and swooped with raucous cries. Far ahead a long oil tanker appeared and presently went by to port with a thin ribbon of smoke trailing above her churning wake.

Stuart Ormsby, ordinary seaman on the second mate's watch from twelve to four, was given work in the entrance to the starboard alleyway. Seated on his haunches, he chipped the dirty white scale from the steel plates of the superstructure. The steady thud of the small, edged hammer rang through the passageway. It was not exhausting toil such as the men experienced below deck in the stokehole, but his arms soon ached from the continuous exertion; and the hours, dragging their weary way across the afternoon, seemed endless. Toward four o'clock, Cape Flattery lifted and fell astern. Ahead lay a gray expanse of ocean. His heart leaped within him at the sight—his first glimpse of the broad Pacific!

The *Nanking* rolled gently; her forecastle head climbed the swells beating in from sea and plunged downward with sharp, quivering movements that gave the new member of the crew an uneasy feeling in the pit of his stomach. Gazing across the rail he saw a fog bank looming ahead. As they sluggishly drew abreast of Tatoosh Island the heavy blanket of mist was upon them. Fog hazed like spindrift across the deck and blotted out the crow's nest on the mainmast high above. With it came a dampness that beaded Stuart's lashes with moisture. At once the steamer's whistle blared a long note of warning.

From somewhere off the port beam an answering blare came like an echo out of the mist; and, after a short interval, a great gray shape passed to one side in the gloom. An unfathomed feeling of apprehension shot through Stuart. In this dangerously crowded lane of world shipping they might collide with some mammoth vessel entering the strait. He looked about him with a nervous glance. There was no unusual commotion on deck, however; evidently the officers and men accepted this hazard as part of the day's work. Yet, as he listened, he heard above the steady throb of the engines the muffled clang of a gong from the engine-room entrance. Almost immediately he was aware that the *Nanking* was slowing down to half speed; she was nosing her way with the utmost caution through the thick, damp atmosphere.

When eight bells sounded the end of the watch, he drew a deep breath of relief, dropped his tools in the store closet, and crossed the slippery plates of the fore deck. He had an hour in which to clean up and rest in his bunk before evening chow was served. From the seamen's quarters he obtained a galvanized-iron bucket, filled it with fresh water from the hydrant outside the port alleyway, and returned to the washroom. At five o'clock the ringing beat of the mess boy's triangle summoned the men to supper.

The messroom lay between the two alleyways, just abaft the galley. The members of the deck crew took their places at the starboard end of the long table, the engine-room gang at the port. Stuart noticed among the seamen a sullen air of resentment.

"Blimey, do we 'ave ter work like this every bloomin' day o' the voyage?" Toppy querulously remarked as he speared a huge slice of bread. "An' that bo'sun, now— ain't 'e the narsty bloke! 'E thinks 'e's 'ard-boiled." The last words were muffled as Toppy shoved a knife heaped with stew into his wide mouth.

"Yah, Toppy, for once you're right," agreed Swede

Jorgenson across the table. "An' lookit this grub. Slum —the first day out!" He reached unsuccessfully for the salt, then looked at Stuart. "Pass Lot's Wife, Alabam— will you?"

"We got a rotten steward," added one of the firemen. "I bet he's makin' a rake-off on the grub money. Ain't it so, mess?"

The Filipino mess boy, grinning in reply, shoved a pot of coffee at the man. As he turned to the sink in the corner, he stopped short, his dark face fuming with indignation. "Get out!" he cried. "This is not place for animals."

Stuart, following his glance, saw a small, long-armed monkey leisurely pulling himself over the high storm step. There in the doorway he hesitated for a second while he flashed a bright glance at the seamen. With surprising swiftness he leaped to the end of the table where he sat with an owl-like expression upon his solemn face.

"Hullo, Ming," exclaimed Singapore Sam, a tall, rawboned sailor whose weather-beaten face was always wreathed in a broad grin. "Hungry, huh?"

The monkey scratched himself on his shaggy chest, while his eager eyes searched the table in quest of a choice morsel of food. As his little almond eyes rested upon Toppy's dish of bread pudding he jumped joyously up and down on his haunches. Quick as a flash, a slim, hand-like paw shot out and secured a raisin from the sticky mass.

At once Toppy was on his feet. "Yer bloomin' thief!"

he shrilled. "Git outa 'ere! Strike me pink if I won't wring yer blarsted neck!"

The monkey fled in panic down the table, leaving a trail of disaster in his wake. A pannikin of stew slopped over, a tall pile of bread crumpled as though stuck by a typhoon, a can of condensed milk rolled to the floor, spouting liquid at every turn. The messroom was promptly in an uproar. Toppy's scream of rage was augmented by the cries of the Filipino mess boy. Others at the firemen's end of the table voiced their defense of the monkey's rights.

"Let him alone, mess."

"Git that dirty brute outa here!"

"Blimey, I'll kill 'im!"

"Say, none of youse guys is goin' to touch Ming— see?"

A banana swooped through the air, and Ming, with a dexterous movement, caught it and sprang to the safety of the opposite doorway. There he sat on his haunches while he swiftly peeled it and stuffed half into his mouth at once, his blinking eyes roving over the firemen.

Toppy dropped to his seat with an aggrieved air. "Lookit my puddin'. The little blighter took the only bloomin' raisin in it. Ain't that luck fer yer? Gawd blimey!" He wrinkled his nose over this delicacy, tasted it gingerly with a finger, and then, apparently finding it unspoiled, stuck a spoon into it with great gusto.

"Whose pet is that monkey?" Stuart inquired.

"The dirty beast belongs ter Wu Sing, the cook. 'E got 'im in 'Ongkong last trip. Wu say 'e brings good luck. Blimey, not ter me, anyhow." He took a gulp of coffee, frowned slightly, and proceeded to dump half a dozen spoonfuls of sugar into his cup. "I don't like that monk. 'E's too bloody 'uman. Don't 'e look just like a Chink?"

Stuart, gazing at the little gray beast, admitted to himself that in truth there was a distinct resemblance to an Oriental. The eyes were slanted; the hair, growing beneath his chin like a beard, made him think of a Chinese merchant sitting silent and inscrutable in the doorway of his shop in Pell Street. Certainly Toppy was right in this observation.

A moment later Stuart pushed away his plate of food; he couldn't eat any more. The great dishes of greasy food, the smells, the steam, the clatter of tinware, all were too much for him. Hurriedly he rose and went on deck.

A cry followed him down the passageway. "Wot's the matter, Alabam? Seasick?"

Too ill at the moment to reply, Stuart lurched to the rail. The chill mist touched his cheek with a welcome caress. Desperately he fought to free himself from those waves of nausea that threatened to rise and engulf him He trembled, wiped a hot hand across his moist brow, and step by step guided himself along the rail to the bow of the ship.

Down the ladder to the deserted seamen's quarters

he stumbled. The hot, close air of the place smote him like a blow. He circled the shadowy tier of bunks till he came to the apex of the triangular compartment and, climbing weakly over his bunkboard, sank exhausted upon the straw mattress. Flat on his back he lay. His breath came in deep gasps, his stricken eyes closed with a sigh of thankfulness. In his ears roared the crash of a wave as the steamer buried her nose in a swell; then came the hissing splash of water skidding along the starboard strake.

Safe now in the haven of his bunk, his mind ran back over the events of the last three months. He recalled his hurried flight from West Point, the face of his father as he stood, stern and unyielding, in Grand Central Ter-(minal, and his own quick resolution to escape from the country; then the train ride to Montreal and the vagabond journey across Canada. The outcome of all this was his present unenviable position. Why, this ship was ten times worse than the Academy! Here were the same military discipline, the same aloof officers, the same orders; yet in addition there was a rough way of living which he had never before experienced: food that sickened one at the sight, sleeping quarters always thick with cheap tobacco smoke, always filled with the odours of unwashed bodies and soiled clothes.

The opening of the iron door made him shift his weary eyes that way. The men were coming back from mess; cursing, laughing, jesting boisterously, they descended the steps to their quarters, where they were allowed to smoke at will. Singapore Sam reached up and switched on the electric light over the narrow table.

"Lookit!" came Toppy's high falsetto above the hum of talk. "Alabam's sick."

"Poor li'l' boy," Singapore Sam remarked loudly. "Is he a-goin' to die, d'ye think?"

"'E's fair green about the gills. Blimey, in two days we'll be lettin' 'is body slip off a bloomin' plank on the taffrail while the Ole Man says a prayer like a mission bloke. Gawd, ain't it pitiful?"

"Toppy's always got his fly trap open," drawled Swede Jorgenson. "Let the kid alone. Ain't this ship bad enough——"

"Shut yer marf, yer bloody squarehead," cut in the little cockney with venomous fervour. "Cawn't a bloke pass a remark in 'is own fo'c'sle?"

"Aw, pipe down, you scurvy limejuicer! Give us a rest," called a voice.

Toppy, however, was not thus to be silenced. "Maybe the Swede is right," he said in a sad tone; "if this blighter is a-goin' ter die we better be nice and quiet."

The little cockney's mouse-like face appeared for a second above the bunkboard. "If yer leavin' us ter-night, Alabam, don't yer make too much fuss about it, will yer? We gotta sleep." His yellow fangs showed in a wide grin as he reached up and pulled the light-curtain across the bunk, shutting out the glare of the electric bulb.

Stuart turned his face to the darkening porthole.

Toppy wasn't so bad, he acknowledged to himself. To hide a friendly gesture, he would be sure to cover it with a taunting phrase. The boy smiled wanly as he closed his weary eyes.

He was roused by a hand on his arm, and the voice of the watch saying softly, "Eleven-thirty, kid. Time to turn out."

Stuart sat up and rubbed his eyes. A green night bulb burned dimly in the deckhead. Just below him Toppy was muttering sleepily as he pulled on his dungarees; across the compartment Singapore Sam was tying his shoes. Quickly the boy slipped into his clothes, buttoned his coat, and pulled his cap down over his eyes. The deck would be wet and cold, he knew, for every three minutes the fog whistle was punctuating the stillness with its warning note.

"My blarsted trick at the wheel," Toppy grumbled. "It ain't no fun on a thick night."

A moment later the three seamen climbed noisily up the steps to deck. At once they were lost in a world of rolling mist. The sky, the deck, the sea were invisible. All about them was the impenetrable obscurity of the fog.

"Come on, Alabam," growled Toppy. "We'll get a bit o' coffee before we go on watch."

From the darkened galley they procured a pot of coffee left by Wu Sing on the huge range, and then in the messroom they made sandwiches of cold, slightly green meat, which they munched in silence. The mem-

bers of the Black Gang soon joined them, three firemen with stupid faces and muscular bodies, and a coal
passer of pasty complexion. Stuart left first, determined
to get his orders before eight bells sounded on the
bridge.

In the dimly lighted passageway he met Tod Moran
emerging from the petty officers' messroom. "Hello,
Joe Macaroni," Stuart flung at him.

"Hello, Alabam," the oiler replied. "How goes it?"

"Oh, I reckon it might be worse."

"By thunder, I surely don't envy the deck crew to-
night."

"It must be good and warm down below," Stuart suggested.

"Most of the time it's too hot, Alabam." Tod looked
about quickly, came closer, and spoke in a lowered
tone. "Say, have you—have you seen anything funny,
anything strange about this tramp steamer?"

"No—what do you mean?"

"There's something mighty queer going on, that's all.
You want to watch your step. I got a tip from the skipper. He's looking for trouble ahead."

"Trouble with the crew?"

"Yes; they're divided. The old gang has been up to
something."

"Dope running?" Stuart whispered.

"Oh, not that! Every ship on the Pacific smuggles in
dope. This is something deeper, something that makes
it worth their while to get rid of the captain. Just keep

your eyes open and don't mix. There's a tough crew aboard."

Stuart nodded. "You bet—I know that."

From the engine-room entrance issued the sharp clang of a bell. "Ten to twelve," Tod noted hurriedly. "Where are they putting you on watch to-night?"

"I'm to relieve the lookout on the fo'c'sle head."

Tod regarded him in surprise. "That's queer," he said reflectively. "An able seaman is usually in the bow. Who placed you there?"

"The second mate."

A low whistle came from the oiler's lips. "I'll bet Shark Bashford's behind that. Well, watch out, Alabam. So long!"

Stuart stood there a moment in silence, pondering the oiler's words. At length, puzzled, uncertain, he went slowly down the passageway to the exit, which was blocked by a wall of fog. He shivered slightly as he stepped on deck. Through the black obscurity of the night the whistle on the bridge was sending out its mournful note of warning.

CHAPTER VI

OUT OF THE FOG

"LIGHTS burning brightly, seh!"

Through the night and the fog Stuart sang out the routine words to the officer of the watch. Placed an hour and a half earlier as lookout on the forecastle head, he stood now in the profound obscurity of the ship's bow, his back to the windlass drum. The deck, the rail, the sea had vanished; the thickening mist enshrouded his little world in folds so dense that the sensation of being lost in boundless space crept over him.

Listening intently, he heard with relief the soft swish of water from the steamer's bow as it cut through the broad Pacific. At intervals there came from aloft the low muffled blare of the whistle. Stuart shivered, wiped a hand across his damp face, and moved forward with the utmost care to the rail.

Were they out of the danger zone yet, he wondered, or were other vessels drawing in on the converging routes of the chart, endeavouring to enter the channel of Juan de Fuca Strait? Alone here since midnight, with the chill of the fog invading his tired muscles, a sense of grievance had been stirring within him until his whole spirit grew aflame with rebellion. Why should he stand

watch on such a night when he was probably the only
green hand aboard the tramp? He wasn't familiar with
the ways of the sea; he hadn't asked to go on this
voyage in such a battered freighter, to live with those
swine in their reeking forecastle, to eat with them in
their messroom alive with cockroaches. By Cæsar, the
officers weren't treating him squarely, either; they were
just like those military authorities at West Point. Well,
Stuart Ormsby had never yet allowed himself to be a
goat under the tyranny of such discipline. He wouldn't
do a bit more work than was absolutely necessary!

Through the encompassing blackness, he felt his way
aft to the companion rail and swung down the ladder
to the main deck. In the corner where the washroom
wing joined the firemen's quarters, he found a spot warm
and protected. Here he crouched, chilled and depressed,
his arms about his knees, his eyes directed upon the
misty glow of the red and green lights on the bridge.
There was no sense at all, he argued to himself, in his
keeping a strict lookout above. No eye could pierce that
nebulous wall of gloom; and if any steamer drew near, a
person would surely hear her whistle long before her
lights became visible. His weary head nodded. Drugged
by exhaustion, lulled by the murmur of the sea and the
faint tremor of the deck beneath him, he dropped into an
uneasy sleep.

Some time later he awoke with a start. Instantly,
his drowsy mind leaped awake, aroused by the impression that someone had bent over him. He took in at a

glance the fog-swept deck, the black bulkhead of the forecastle rising above him, the ghostly sheen of the companionway rail. Surely it was not the whistle which had wakened him, for that, blowing every three minutes, had woven itself into his dreams. If the hour had struck on the bridge and he had failed to respond with the ringing of the bronze bell in the bow, then without doubt his absence had been detected.

In a panic he rose and climbed the ladder to the deck above. At that moment, two o'clock sounded on the bridge. Relieved that he had slept only half an hour he hurried forward and answered with quick, even taps on the bell: *one*, *two—three, four* ! As the soft echoes drifted aft on the heavy air, he swung about, quivering in every muscle. Directly behind the windlass a scuffling noise was audible.

"Who's there?" he asked in a breathless whisper. "Who's there?"

Utter silence greeted his words. The thought went through his mind that he had allowed his fancy to conjure up an imaginary sound. The next instant, however, he froze to the spot. Not five feet from him a scream, shrill and uncanny, tore through the air.

His heart gave a leap of terror against his ribs; sweat stood out on the palms of his hands. His throat moved convulsively. "Who—who's there?" he breathed.

No answer came. Slowly he went forward and, touching the rail with a trembling hand, circled the small, triangular deck.

A door slammed sharply on the bridge. "What's wrong, lookout?" called the second mate.

Stuart raised his voice. "Nothing—nothing, seh!"

"Any drunken bums down there?"

"No, seh. I'm alone—I don't know what that noise was."

A pause ensued; then the mate resumed, "Keep a good watch ahead. It's a thick night."

"Yes, seh."

Stuart let his glance sweep out into that dark abyss of rolling fog. Had something happened while he slept? Stories he had heard that day in the seamen's quarters floated to the surface of his mind, stories of the *Nanking's* past history: of a collision while entering the Golden Gate one morning in a fog, of a weird meeting in the South China Sea with a junk, deserted yet full-rigged, of a strange unearthly cry heard at night from a sea bird, which presaged disaster for the *Nanking's* captain. Desperately thrusting these reflections away he kicked the deck with one foot. That sodden thud on the steel plate seemed his only contact with reality.

The next moment he remembered the pocket flash which had been given him when he took over the watch. His fingers closed eagerly upon it. In an attitude of acute attention, he pressed the button—a cone of light leaped outward. It revealed through the hazy gray atmosphere the blurred outline of the companion steps and the black pile of cable near the hawser chock. By slow degrees he swung the beam to the left; his eyes endeavoured to pierce the enveloping gloom. All at once his fingers trembled. The light wavered, vanished for a second, and flashed on again, as he stared, amazed.

Facing him in that translucent cone was the startled form of a Chinese. Stuart knew on the instant that the white coat and loose trousers covered the slim figure of the cook, Wu Sing.

"What—what are you doing here?" the boy challenged unsteadily.

The cook's yellow features, with the skin drawn tight across high cheek bones, broke into a smile of humble supplication. His long eyelids narrowed; his white teeth showed plainly as he chose his words in halting pidgin English. "Ming gettee loose. You sabbee? I take look-see roun' deck."

"You mean the monkey?" Stuart flung at him, a hint of disbelief in his tone.

"Yes"—with a sibilant hiss. "You see him, maybe?"

"No. Was that cry from the monkey?"

"No can tell. You puttee that light out, sabbee? I no likee the mate see Wu here."

Stuart loosed his pressure on the electric torch, and the night closed down about him, more intense, more impenetrable than before. The cook moved closer; his blurred outline became visible; a faint Oriental odour drifted to Stuart's nostrils.

"Li'l' boy," went on the sibilant murmur, "you say nothin' what you see here, sabbee?"

"Oh, I understand," Stuart hotly acknowledged

"You mean, I suppose, that I'm not to say anything about your being here. Well, I don't care in the slightest what goes on in this dirty ship. As far as I'm concerned, the crew can do anything they like. Let 'em fight, let 'em murder, let 'em mutiny——"

He checked himself and stepped back with a quick movement. A hissing breath followed him. Issuing as from tightly closed teeth, the incisive whisper brought a warning, a menace that made his hair softly stir. "S-s-s! Be still!"

Distinctly audible from the iron steps of the ladder was the faint scuff of approaching footfalls. Wu Sing's blurred outline merged into the velvet darkness; as silently as a shadow he disappeared.

Stuart strained his eyes toward the companionway. What secret actions brought these men in the dead of night to the forecastle head? There was a deep undercurrent of mystery, he knew, circulating through the holds of the *Nanking*. Was he to be drawn against his will into this stream of unlawful activity? Not if he knew it first, he told himself with tight-drawn mouth.

With relief he heard a second later the husky voice of Shark Bashford. "Where are yuh, lookout?"

"Here, seh—by the rail."

"Good." The man came nearer, but he remained only a voice in the night, a low throaty murmur that sent an apprehensive chill through the boy. "Yuh can go below for a spell," continued the mate. "I'll stand yer watch fer awhile."

Go below! Surprise silenced the words that rose to Stuart's lips. The tone of the voice had been friendly, too, almost as though the man were unwillingly begging a favour of him. "Yes, seh," Stuart stammered at last. "Yes, seh."

"I'll call when I wants yuh." A hand grasped the boy's wrist. "Are yuh on the skipper's side?"

"I—I don't know what you mean. That tattooed savage! Why should I be on his side?"

"Tha's all right, kid. Yuh go below and turn in. Hold yer tongue. When anyone talks too blamed much on this here tramp somethin' always happens. Get me? But I don't think yuh'll say much. Oh, no—not since I seen yuh asleep on watch!" He laughed shortly; his tone turned hard. "Yeah, I seen yuh there all right— asleep by the fo'c'sle door. Ain't it the truth?"

"Yes, seh."

Frightened because the mate had seen him asleep on watch, slightly bewildered at this mysterious order, and dubious as to the advisability of carrying it out, Stuart reluctantly crossed to the ladder and descended to the main deck. When he swung open his forecastle door and glimpsed, in the twilight of the interior, three seamen furtively slipping into their clothes, he was seized by a sudden resolve. With a barely perceptible clang, he shut the door and remained on deck.

A vague suspicion was now taking definite form. Shark Bashford was using him for his own foolhardy purposes. Perhaps the mate might even blame him later to the captain for leaving his post. Well, he'd been caught asleep once; that was enough. He vowed to himself that he'd keep his eyes open this time; none of these officers should find him easy bait.

He stepped to the bulwarks and peered ahead. The fog swept round the spread of the forecastle with such velocity that every now and then he had to wipe the moisture from his eyes. As the minutes dragged by he became aware of other men seeking the seclusion of the forecastle head. He heard their stealthy footsteps come forward and climb the ladder. The door nearest him opened to emit three dark figures which also climbed above; and a second later he discerned a similar exit from the firemen's quarters.

He wasn't surprised at this secretive meeting, he said to himself; he wouldn't be surprised at anything that happened on this old tub. He counted the men as best he could, however, and made out that at least nine had joined Shark Bashford on the deck above. Low murmurs drifted aft to him, surly voices hushed as in hidden conclave. Sharp disagreements rose which were silenced by two authoritative voices. The first was the mate's, and the second—could it be the chief engineer's?

He recalled Wu Sing's presence on the forecastle head and the man's feeble explanation. Was the Chinese cook up there now? The longer Stuart pondered the question, the more he became convinced that the cook was playing a game of his own, certainly without the knowledge of the first mate.

Once a strange phrase, "Wreckers' lamps," came down to him, and a well-known voice saying, "We got him easy—ain't it the truth?" Once he heard a seaman's harsh words of protest, "But this is mutiny, sir," and the mate's command for silence.

Stuart's hand moved nervously on the rail. Mutiny! Was that the storm that was brewing around this old tramp? Were these men planning to get command of the ship from their new captain? Tod Moran had been right, then, when he had sensed danger. The oiler and that crazy little cockney, Toppy, might be the only friends Captain Jarvis had aboard.

Stuart, wearily glancing ahead, distinguished the vague glow of a light on the water. So hazy was it, so dim, so unreal, he thought for a second it must be a figment of his imagination. He stared, wiped a hand across his eyes, and stared again. It was still there, coming nearer—the faint red glow of a vessel's port light.

Had it been seen by the men on the forecastle head? Evidently not, for the low mutter of their undertones still floated down. By Cæsar, they must have failed to post a lookout! A tide of sheer terror washed over Stuart; then, quick as a flash, he jerked himself about. With all his might he shouted up to the bridge: "A ship —on the sta'b'd bow!"

Almost at once two quick warning blasts roared from the *Nanking's* whistle. On the approaching craft a startled foghorn answered. Stuart's gaze swept out

again into the encircling gloom. Aghast, he beheld the
red gleam steadily, unswervingly advance. Second by
second the ruddy glow deepened. Suddenly a radiant
white light spread in widening circles from the new-
comer's deck, revealing huge sails that soared aloft like
phantom wings to merge into the obscurity above. A
sailing ship, unwittingly about to cross the very path
of the old tramp, had kindled a flare-up torch in the
desperate hope that the steamer would note her position
in time to avert a crash.

Out of the mist, however, a bowsprit and jib sail were
already pressing toward the boy. A wooden bulwark
took form; a windjammer, two masted and full rigged,
loomed above him. Appalled, he staggered back from
the rail.

The old tramp gave a vicious lurch to port that sent
him sprawling to deck near the forward hatch. Bells
signalled *full speed astern* to the engine room. The faith-
ful iron heart of the *Nanking* seemed to stop beating for
a breathless moment; then the deck quivered and
strained and groaned as the immense propeller, with a
reverse movement, churned the waves astern.

A gull-like cry flew over the water. The flare winked
out—night closed down.

A crash sounded as wrenching timber thudded
against the *Nanking's* bow. Voices drifted down to the
boy where he struggled to his feet. On the instant he
realized what had happened: the jib boom and bowsprit
had swept across the forecastle head, tearing away the

gear, the rail, the men who stood in its path. Under the impact of that blow the old tramp rolled sharply to port, then rolled sluggishly back again.

Stuart glimpsed overhead a nodding sail dip toward him. For the duration of a dozen heartbeats it hung there before it swung back and dissolved in the night. The two ships, steamer and windjammer, thumped alongside with a grinding reverberation, while curses screamed through the air. Slowly they drifted apart; a wall of fog imposed itself between them.

Stuart stood braced against the coaming of number one hatch, as erect and immobile as a stanchion riveted to deck. He saw as in a dream the forecastle doors swing open and two yellow squares of light slant across the plates. Directly before him, in the light from the seamen's doorway, lay the crumpled body of a man, fallen from the deck above.

The tense, menacing voice of Shark Bashford pierced through his daze. "Keep quiet about this—understand?"

"I will, seh—I will." He repeated the words without knowing what he promised.

The moments that followed were confused and obscure to Stuart. Dimly he was aware that the whole ship was alive with half-clad men, that from the bridge a great search light was playing a strong beam upon them, that the shouts, the running feet, the excited cries were quieted, silenced by one voice which was terse and commanding—the voice of the *Nanking's* master.

"It ain't nothin' serious, sir," said Shark Bashford presently, as if from a remote distance. "The blamed brig shoved her nose right into us. But no harm done to either ship, sir. The skipper o' the brig yelled that they was O. K. Only one of our own men hurt—Slim Morgan. He musta fell from the deck above and broke his neck."

"He's dead?"

"I think so."

There ensued a long pause during which Stuart knew the two officers were kneeling beside that still form on the deck. "Gut me if it ain't a fireman!" exclaimed the captain in surprise. "What was he doing on the fo'c'sle head, Bashford?"

"Don't know, sir. I dare say he was sleepin' there."

"On a night like this!" There was a look of keen distrust on the captain's face as he rose to his full height. "Who was on watch forward?"

At the question a pang of dread went through Stuart. He felt as though he were submerged in deep water and were vainly trying to fight his way to the surface. In his mind a question hammered madly: *Am I guilty of this? Am I guilty?* What if this had occurred when he had been asleep on watch? Should he have allowed the first mate to relieve him when he was on the second's watch? He quivered as though struck when he heard the mate answer the captain's inquiry—"Ormsby was the lookout, sir."

The silence seemed to beat in waves about him. All eyes, he knew, were directed his way.

"Young man," said the captain in his low, vibrant tone, "come over here."

"Yes, seh." His leaden feet dragged on the steel plates. All the blood in his body seemed drumming in his ears.

"The quartermaster tells me you reported a ship off the starb'd bow—but not soon enough. Where were you standing?"

"At the sta'b'd bulwarks, seh."

Captain Jarvis gave him a long, searching look. "What happened?"

Stuart's lips moved soundlessly. What should he say —what should he say? If he followed the menacing be-hest of the first mate he would be aligning himself defi-nitely, irrevocably with the mutinous element aboard. Yet could he tell the truth—all of it? Admit that he had slept on watch and then been relieved by the first mate? In a moment of bitter illumination he realized that it was not the mate who had sprung this trap for him: it was his own actions. He felt himself sinking into the depths of a fathomless sea; like a drowning man he looked round for something to grasp, something to weigh him up.

He swallowed, beat his way up to the surface, and brought out with an effort, "It—it was so dark, seh, so foggy that the sailing vessel came up before I knew it. I shouted to the bridge as soon as I saw the light. The ship was almost upon us before she blew her foghorn."

"Ormsby, who placed you on watch to-night?"

"The second mate, seh."

"Was this fireman talking to you?"

"No, seh." The words came, stifled, from the boy's lips.

Captain Jarvis glanced across at his first officer. Evidently the master of the *Nanking* realized that there were depths here that were yet unsounded, but for the present he asked no more questions. For a long moment of suspense the two men regarded each other with glances as cold as frozen seas. Stuart then perceived that the men had moved into two groups; taking sides behind their leaders, they faced one another across a narrow width of deck.

Behind Shark Bashford stood the bearded chief engineer, the fat steward, Wu Sing the cook, and at least six seamen, together with four of the engine-room gang. With that tense, silent group supporting him the mate stood triumphant, with chin outthrust. Beneath wide reddish-brown eyebrows his pale eyes looked forth from his bronzed face with a deep glint of malice.

At Captain Tom Jarvis's back were only three adherents—Toppy, wide eyed and staring, Tod Moran, tight lipped and alert, and Swede Jorgenson, whose stolid features indicated that he failed to take in the import of this attitude of suppressed defiance.

Stuart alone stood outside these two factions which so bitterly faced each other. And the mate was calling him! Though no word was spoken, Stuart caught the look of meaning which the mate threw his way. He was telling the boy in silence to come to his side. Stuart realized that if he did this, he would have no explanations to face, there would be no questioning into his past or future movements. They would accept his lack of seamanship, his sleeping on watch with a grin of sly complicity. Suddenly the conviction seized him that, if he chose the mate's side, he would be lost. Only the captain and Tod Moran could save his self-respect, his own integrity. He grasped at that thought as a drowning man at a life ring in the open sea.

He stumbled across the few feet of deck and took his place behind the captain. There he raised a pale, defiant face to Shark Bashford and his group of men.

The mate's hands clenched at his sides; his eyes glittered with evil malice. To Stuart the man's silence was more significant than bitter denunciation.

"Gawd blimey," breathed Toppy at the boy's side. "Wot's it all about, Joe Macaroni?"

"Keep still, Toppy," the oiler whispered. He cast a look of affectionate approval at Stuart. "Hello, Alabam," he added in an undertone.

"We'll look further into this matter to-morrow," announced Captain Jarvis in cool, ringing tones. "Bashford, relieve this boy and place an able seaman in the bow. Two of you men carry that fireman's body up to the hospital cabin. I'll take a look at the fo'c'sle head. Scatter, you men!"

Stuart stepped back to the bulwarks outside the beam of light. A feeling of loneliness, of infinite bitterness weighed him down. Distrusted by both sides, he was separated from the mate by his open refusal to join him, and from the captain's and Tod Moran's friendship by his own actions. Would they ever accept him as a seaman? Him? . . . Why, he had slept on his first night watch; he had raised no outcry at treachery toward the captain of his ship. The boy's finger nails bit into the palms of his hands. His wall of pride was crumbling into fragments about him.

In silence he stood there while the ship got under way. He heard the bells in the engine room ring *half speed ahead*, felt the quiver of the deck as the first thresh of the propeller sent the old tramp on her way, saw the rolling fog wraiths glide slowly past as she ploughed through the seas ahead. He was an outcast in this mass of deep-sea flotsam—and he wanted now with all his heart to take his place as a trusted member of the crew.

The western shore of his homeland had dropped astern of them; they were twenty fair-weather days from their first Oriental port of call. Not even the blue light of a star was reflected in his deep pool of loneliness. . . . Would he never himself make port?

PART THREE

THE TYPHOON

RADIO REPORT
8 P. M. JUNE 28

Nanking — British Columbia for Oriental ports. 3453 miles from Vancouver.
Seattle *Post-Intelligencer*

CHAPTER VII

SHIPMATES

GULLS followed them out to sea. They circled above the churning wake as the *Nanking* emerged the next morning from the last trailing gust of fog. Clear sunlight beat down upon a sea of emerald green. Whitecaps leaped in the breeze; the unbroken expanse of the Pacific extended on all sides to a far horizon.

At eleven o'clock the old tramp's engines were stopped. Stuart dropped his tools in the alleyway and joined a little group of men who stood with uncovered heads in the very stern of the ship. Captain Jarvis, tall and straight, his head slightly bowed, intently scanned a tiny book that was lost in his hands. Before him the flag-covered form of a motionless body lay upon a plank one end of which rested on the taffrail, the other in the hands of two seamen. The captain's voice sounded deep and solemn in the utter quiet of the morning. The men bowed their heads. Stuart felt the steady mounting beat of his heart as the voice repeated the burial prayer for the dead at sea. "We therefore commit his body to the deep . . ."

There was a gentle whisper, less than a sigh, and all that remained of Slim Morgan of the Black Gang slipped from the taffrail to the silent depths below. Shrill cries pierced the stillness as the screaming gulls swooped low over the water. Nothing was there, however, save a widening circle of ripples that slowly spread and dissolved.

Captain Jarvis raised his hand in a signal to the mate on the bridge. The *Nanking's* deck began to quiver. Once more the tramp steamed on her way, with the patent log on the taffrail clicking off the nine nautical miles an hour.

As the dull routine of a ship at sea descended upon the officers and men, the days slipped imperceptibly astern. To Stuart this was a period of grateful contentment. He stood no more night watches, but instead worked a straight eight-hour day shift. The steady toil of cleaning up the battered freighter, of chipping the rusty scale from her superstructure and painting it a shining white, so drained his mind of energy that no impulse remained to brood upon his own troubles. At night he climbed to his bunk, pulled his light-curtain across the forward part, and dropped at once into a dreamless sleep.

The evenings after five o'clock mess, however, brought moments of intense loneliness. The men in the forecastle left him strictly to himself. Though no mention was made in his presence of the events of that foggy night, he was aware by the sullen glances cast his way that he was distrusted as well as shunned. No one greeted him with a cheery smile; no one invited him to join the little groups of three or four men who smoked and chatted on the forecastle head while night closed down. Seated alone on number one hatch he would catch snatches of sailors' talk that kindled his imagination. A man was recounting his experiences on the beach at Singapore, that meeting place of the riffraff of the seven seas; another was denouncing in no uncertain terms the Seamen's Hospital in Shanghai; a third was telling of his adventures aboard a schooner cruising between Palawan and the Solomon Islands. Stuart longed to approach these groups, to listen to the details of their narratives; but, fearing their contempt and slurring remarks, he always avoided the ladders that led to the little deck above.

Often he saw Toppy and Swede Jorgenson slouching on the iron bitts in the stern of the ship in conversation with the oiler, Tod Moran. Stuart never joined them. Indeed, he took pains to keep out of their way, for he wanted no questions thrown at him. They would be sure to ply him with queries as to his past history, as to the events that led to the crash with the brig. All this he wanted to forget.

One evening, more depressed than usual, he descended to the twilight of his deserted forecastle and threw himself flat on his mattress. Looking up at the crossbeams so close overhead, he saw a cockroach scurry quickly away into the shadows. Low murmurs drifted down from the men on the forecastle head. Now and then from the firemen's quarters on the other side of the bulkhead came loud laughter and boisterous voices. He raised himself on an elbow and gazed through the open port. It was the moment of sunset, and a low bank of clouds was aflame with a ruddy glow. The mirror-like sea was devoid of any passing craft, just as it had been for days on end. He dropped back to his pillow; his hand moved wearily across his eyes.

This was loneliness, he perceived—homesickness, call it what you will. He was like a buoy broken loose from its moorings, floating aimlessly. Yet an instinct he unerringly recognized as right had brought him to this pass. Did the fact that he was working with his utmost ability mean nothing to those on board?

He was lying there in the darkness when the men drifted back to their quarters. The light flashed on in the deckhead. A game of Khun Khan was started at the narrow table; the donkeyman and Chips, the carpenter, began rolling bones on the floor. The air was soon blue with a rising haze of cheap tobacco smoke.

"Blarst 'is 'ide," he heard the little cockney snarl; "'e's always three sheets in the wind, an' 'e bullies us like a bally slave driver."

"Aw, pipe down, matey," admonished the Swede.

"Shut yer marf, yer squarehead!" snapped Toppy. He heaved a dismal sigh. "Lor', wot'll 'e do next, I arsk yer—wot next!"

"Shush, Toppy. Yoost wait a minute. Here Boats is now."

"Hello, bo'sun," sang out Singapore Sam. "Want to join our little game? No? Aw, you're gittin' just like that toff in the bunk yonder. He don't never say a word."

Stuart turned on his side and looked down at the men. His face flushed with sudden hope. Say a word? If they'd only give him a chance!

Toppy swung about from the table where he was watching the men at cards. "Yeh, Alabam. Wot's wrong with yer?"

"Oh, nothing, Toppy." A wistful smile played about the corners of Stuart's mouth. "I reckon I'm not quite used to the sea yet, that's all."

Singapore Sam looked up from his cards. "Kid," he brought out slowly, "you won't never be a seaman; I kin tell you that. You ain't got the proper cut to your jib."

"I didn't know," Stuart returned, "that you had to look just so in order to be a sailor. What's wrong with me?"

Toppy immediately spoke up. "Yer works too bloomin' much—that's wot's wrong, Alabam. Every time the bo'sun gives us an order yer jumps ter it right away. That ain't the way a real seaman acts."

"Key down, Limey," cut in the boatswain. His stocky form whirled to face Stuart. "Don't youse listen, kid, to this here limejuicer. He don't work a-tall."

"Wot! Gawd blimey, arfter all I've done on this blarsted tub——"

The boatswain's hairy paw silenced Toppy's further remarks. "Youse don't work half enough, kid," the man went on calmly to Stuart. "Always soldierin' on me, youse are."

Stuart gazed down in surprise at this petty officer who bossed the men on deck. "Why—why, I've sure tried to, bo'sun!"

"Say—call me 'sir.' Understan'?"

"Yes, seh."

A series of guffaws came from the men at the table. "You certainly got the kid goin', Boats," one of them said.

With a lithe movement Stuart swung himself to the floor. His cheeks grew crimson. These men were making sport of him!

"Now where youse goin'?" snarled the boatswain, blocking the boy's way.

"On deck," Stuart mumbled.

"Oh, youse only think youse are!" The man's dark face, blue where the beard showed through, slowly twisted into lines of pretended fury. "Yeah, the mate he told me I'd have to watch youse. Well, youse got to obey—see? An' call me 'sir.' Get me?"

Stuart turned his face away. Though his throat moved

convulsively no retort passed his lips. For a moment
utter silence enveloped the forecastle. Chips and the
donkeyman rose and gazed in eager glee at the boy; the
men at the table put down their cards, intent upon this
scene before them.

"Are youse gonna call me 'sir'?"

Stuart looked the man squarely in the eye. "Do these
other men call you that?"

"Gawd strike me bline," shrilled the cockney; "the
kid thinks 'e's already got 'air on 'is chest! 'Ear 'im
sass the bo'sun!"

Singapore Sam threw back his head and laughed.
"Oh—ho! So you gotta take that sort o' stuff from a
kid, Bose! You sure are easy."

A slow flush spread over the boatswain's face. "I'l'
show this lubber!" His eyes narrowed; his chin shot
forward. "Think youse'll git fresh with me, huh? Take
that!"

His fist caught Stuart squarely on the jaw. Under the
impact of the blow the boy's head flew up; he stumbled
back against a bunk stanchion.

"You bane too rough on the kid, Boats." It was
Swede Jorgenson speaking in his slow drawl.

Stuart's hand moved up to his throbbing chin.
Through blazing eyes he saw the boatswain regarding
him, not with that mocking, taunting expression, but
with a look of bitter enmity. The boy's fists clenched
at his sides. Deliberately he took a step forward. "Cow-
ard—bully!" he challenged in a low, tense tone. "I

don't intend to take anything like this from you, bo'sun!"

"Oh, youse don't! We'll see about that."

Stuart drew his right arm back for a blow.

"Better be careful, kid," the boatswain sneered. "Do youse know what it means to attack a superior officer at sea? It's mutiny! Understand? . . . Mutiny!"

"Yeh. Key down, Alabam!" Toppy's voice was suddenly filled with friendly apprehension. "The bloomin' bo'sun will 'ave yer locked in the brig if yer don't look out."

The brig! Stuart felt the blood drain from his face. So he dared not fight back! He must take all the taunts, all the insults that the boatswain took a fancy to inflict upon him. Into his consciousness surged a feeling of utter impotence that dispelled the anger which had mounted to his brain. So this was what he could expect on the *Nanking* ! . . . He turned, went round the table, and without a backward glance strode to the iron steps. Although no word was flung his way he was aware that the eyes of every man followed him as he climbed to deck.

Coming out into the starlight he crossed at once to the bulwarks, where the night breeze cooled his burning cheeks. Beneath strange stars the tramp freighter was steaming southwest across a sea of tranquil loveliness. Off the port beam a full moon hung low in the sky; a path of silver flashed toward him across the water. From the stokehole fiddley sounded the rattle of the ash buckets; the end of the four-to-eight watch was near.

Stuart's hands clenched on the rail. His mouth, quivering with suppressed emotion, took on a bitter twist. Just when he had hoped to make friends with those on board, to be accepted by them as one of the crew, this had happened! This, then, was their answer to his overtures of friendship. Bitter thoughts welled up within him.

Footsteps sounded on the steel deck as someone approached from amidships. Stuart did not turn his head.

"Oh, it's the Alabama 'possum, huh? Well, now what's wrong with mamma's li'l' boy? I bet he's homesick. Ain't it the truth?"

As Stuart did not answer, the taunting voice went on: "What? Yuh ain't got even a word to say? Look here, kid, yuh don't git away with that stuff on this here ship!" A hand, gripping his arm, swung him about till he faced the mate.

"What—what do you want?" Stuart demanded.

Shark Bashford thrust his hands into his trouser pockets and, standing with feet wide apart, swayed slightly on the tips of his toes. "Ain't yuh learned yet how to address an officer?"

"Yes, seh. I reckon I know."

"Well, now, that's better. What's the matter with yuh, anyway?"

"What's the matter?" Stuart blurted out the words with swift intensity. All his pent-up rage burst forth against this man who had shanghaied him aboard the ship.

The mate listened with a steadily widening smile; now and then he nodded. When the boy had finished, exhausted by this quickly passing storm, the man threw back his head and chuckled. "God, yuh're funny, kid! What d'yuh expect on a tramp steamer? And is it my fault that yuh're here? Didn't I get yuh out o' that trouble at Vancouver?"

"Trouble for you—not for me," Stuart flung back at him.

"Oh, is that so!" The mate's tone turned hard as steel. "Any more remarks like that, kid, and yuh'll be sorry I didn't let the bulls get yuh. This is how yuh repay me for all my pains. And I don't forget that yuh took sides against me, neither. Well, take my word for it, I'm watchin' yuh. Yeah—I told the bo'sun to keep his weather eye on yuh, too. Yuh better watch your step."

Stuart moved aft along the bulwarks. "All right, Shark Bashford, I'll watch my step!"

"What did yuh say?" With a swift stride the man caught up with him.

"All right, seh. I understand."

"Now, that's better. Yuh sure are learning." The mate, laughing shortly, swung about toward the bow of the ship.

Stuart went slowly aft across the moonlit deck. Eight bells began striking on the bridge: *one, two—three, four—*

five, six—seven, eight. But he didn't raise his eyes. He wanted to get as far as possible from the seamen's quarters.

In the port alleyway he met the firemen emerging from the fiddley after their four-hour watch down in the bowels of the ship. Stepping aside to let them pass, he took them in with a curious glance—weary men stripped to the waist, their glistening bodies streaked with coal dust, black sweat rags twisted round their necks. When they had gone forward he continued along the alleyway, only to be brought up short again by a stocky figure coming from the engine-room entrance.

"Why, hello, Alabam." It was Tod Moran's engaging voice.

Stuart nodded and, without a word, passed on to the dark after deck. He didn't want to talk with anyone— not just now. He wanted to be alone, to think this out by himself, to see wherein he had failed.

Footsteps followed him. A hand touched the sleeve of his shirt. "I haven't hardly seen you for a week, Alabam. I've wanted to have a talk with you."

Stuart sank down upon number three hatch. One hand strayed along the canvas cover as he made a hurried effort to collect himself. Had Tod Moran seen his face there in the passage, seen the bitter expression of pain upon it? Thankful that here the midship structure cast a shadow across the moonlit deck he raised his head.

Tod halted before him. "I've meant to go forward and see you," he confided, "ever since that night. But

I've been working overtime so much on these rotten engines that I generally turn in as soon as I get up to deck. Come and see me some time. I bunk amidships in one of the P. O. cabins."

"You're a petty officer, then?"

"That's an oiler's rating. I share one of the cabins with the bo'sun."

"The bo'sun!" Stuart gave a snort of disgust.

Tod sank down beside him. "What's the matter, Alabam?" he asked in an urgent tone. "That bo'sun been razzing you?"

"Maybe you'd call it that."

"Don't take him too seriously. He's only a petty officer."

"But he's over me, isn't he? He's the one who gives me orders."

"Have you worked enough?"

Stuart shook his head despondently. "I don't know, but I was doing my best."

Tod put his hand on the other's shoulder. "This isn't much of a ship, I'll admit," he brought out slowly; "but we've got a good skipper—one of the best on the Pacific. He won't allow any of his officers to lord it over the men any more than he can help. What's happened?"

Stuart leaned forward, his elbows on his knees. "I reckon I don't fit in," he murmured. "I don't know why, either. I've tried."

"A fellow can't expect to fit in right away with those fo'c'sle bums, Alabam. I heard Captain Jarvis say that the *Nanking* seems to have picked up only the refuse of the West Coast ports. And they're up to some underhand business, too. Swede Jorgenson and Toppy are about the only ones who appear to be loyal to the captain."

"But I don't even get along with those two."

Tod Moran chuckled softly. "Toppy—well, he just likes a little fun. He's O. K. And the Swede is a good sort, you know; he's slow, but you certainly can depend upon him. Most of the time, though, his mind makes me think of a vacuum tube back at school."

Stuart looked searchingly at the youth beside him. "You're going to school?" he asked, interested.

"Sure thing. I'm a student at Palo Alto—at Stanford University. I ship out with Captain Jarvis now and then to earn money to keep me going there. A seaman gets his board and room—such as it is—so his pay is absolutely clear. Yes, I'm going back to college after this trip."

"I sure envy you, then." Stuart spoke sincerely. "I— I've got no place to return to."

"Why—what do you mean?"

"I've flunked out of school, that's what." He paused, caught his breath sharply, then rushed on with the whole story. "You see," he presently ended, "I'm through—finished. There's no more studies for me, no more football, no more Saturday-night hops. And I can't even make a living. I don't know a trade—I'm not worth a cent to anyone." He rose and crossed to the bulwarks. His gaze, sweeping out over the water, came to a stop at a glistening point where the silver radiance marked a wave crest.

Tod followed him. "Listen here, Alabam—you and I ought to be friends."

Stuart turned. "You mean it?" he said in a low tone.

"Sure thing. It wasn't very long ago that I took my first trip to sea. I know what it's like. But you'll get over this—you'll pull through. You'll even get to like it."

"Like this life at sea?"

"Sure. Don't let the men razz you. Kid them back—they like it. Come on with me, now. I'm going to take a shower and clean up. I sure need hot water and soap when I come up from the engine room."

"All right, Moran, I'll come."

"Moran! . . . Say, don't be so formal. You're not at a West Point prom with one of those Vassar girls." Tod turned toward the alleyway.

Stuart threw back his head. His eyes shone. "All right, Joe Macaroni."

"Now, that's something like it!" Tod grinned over his shoulder. "We're shipmates, aren't we? . . . Say—how about a little hand-out from the P. O. mess!"

CHAPTER VIII

THE FIRST ATTEMPT

DAYS and nights dropped astern. Stuart now no longer dreaded the lonely evenings. If Tod Moran came on deck at the end of his twelve-to-four watch Stuart would join him immediately after mess; if the oiler worked overtime on the engines, which were always in danger of breaking down, Stuart would wait in the stern of the ship, hanging over the taffrail to watch the log line sink into the foaming wake fifty feet astern.

Sometimes Toppy also strolled aft, and the three would watch the sun go down off the port beam in a blaze of splendour. "It'll be 'otter ter-morrer," Toppy never failed to remark. "See that bloomin' red sky? I'm glad I don't belong ter the Black Gang, Joe Macaroni."

Neither the little cockney nor the oiler endeavoured to learn from Stuart more of what had happened that night on the forecastle head. Yet all three knew that the air was charged with suspense. If the mate and his gang were biding their time the captain was ignoring the situation, and in his steady driving of the men seemed intent upon his one purpose—to take his ship successfully to Shanghai and back.

One evening, immersed in the twilight, the three friends sat on a hatch of the after deck while the stars came out one by one. " 'Ave yer been in the army, Alabam?" Toppy innocently inquired.

Stuart flushed as he replied, "No, but I've been to a military school." He sighed; it seemed as though years had elapsed since he had left the Academy at West Point.

"Yer sure jumps aroun' when the bo'sun gives yer a bloomin' order."

"I want to draw some dungarees," Stuart hastened to announce; "the slop chest should be open mighty soon."

Toppy immediately pointed out the dangers of drawing unnecessary gear. "If yer chalk up too many shirts or dungarees against yerself, Alabam, then yer don't 'ave no allowance ter draw at the first port o' call. I know from bloody hexperience. I gets sixty-two-fifty per month, an' I'm allowed ter draw 'arf at every bally port; but if I don't like the ship and jumps 'er, then I leave part of my bloomin' pay be 'ind. Ain't that 'ard luck fer yer?"

"But then you have plenty of money when you get back home again," Stuart rejoined.

Tod Moran threw back his head and laughed. "Yes, and every cent that Toppy slaves for during a four months' voyage always disappears the first night ashore."

Toppy gave him a hurt look. "Wot's wrong with yer,

Joe Macaroni? Shut yer marf and quit larfin'. Blimey, on this trip I'm savin' so I kin stay ashore a few weeks."

Stuart glanced up at the deck above. The round face of the steward appeared in the upper half of the Dutch door to his cabin. Already two other members of the crew were drawing their needed gear. Tod led the way above.

"Whatcha want to-night, boys?" greeted the affable steward. "Socks, singlets, shoes? I got some fine shoes. I mean they're good ones, the best I could get in Frisco. What'll it be—dungarees? Well, I'm afraid I ain't got just your size. I mean I couldn't get all the sizes I needed, but I'm sure these'll fit the cut o' your jib, and anyway, when you wash 'em, if you ever do, it won't make no difference, they shrink so. Yes, you better git 'em plenty big."

Toppy blinked. "Didn't I tell yer, Alabam, it wasn't no use ter draw no gear? 'E ain't got nothin' yer want."

"What! Nothing this big boy wants? Why, I got as nice a little store here as you'll find on the Embarcadero in Frisco. What I mean is you can't get no better outfit for a seafaring man than I can give you right here. What's a little difference in a few sizes when this ain't no ocean liner with females strutting the deck and officers wearing gold braid and sitting down to mess with the ladies—what I mean is, it don't make no difference, for this is just what he wants, though maybe he don't know it yet, and anyhow it's time I closed the slop chest. I mean you gotta hurry."

Stuart, dazed by the flow of words and the amount

of goods shoved across the narrow counter of the door, chose a pair of blue dungarees and several singlets. He realized that he might as well batter a smooth hard wall as try to get in a word with the steward. The man, short and paunchy, wore an ingratiating smile on his well-shaven face; he moved restlessly about his cabin, which was piled high with boxes. Sitting atop a shelf was Ming, the monkey. The little beast was busily eating a stick of candy and only looked up to blink in a casual way while he chewed on the hard confection.

"Aw, Gawd, let's get outa 'ere," Toppy murmured as he moved away. Tod remained with Stuart while the necessary paper was signed. The prices, the boy noted, were equal to any shop on Fifth Avenue.

Tod grinned as he drew Stuart away. "That bird's got some line, Alabam. He's a sly one, too."

"I didn't have a chance to put in a single word," Stuart said ruefully. "And did you see that monk——"

He checked his words as Tod halted just ahead of him, opposite the entrance to the port passageway. Before them stood the huge form of the *Nanking's* captain. The man beckoned them in mysterious silence.

Tod stepped into the passageway. "Did you want us, sir?"

"Not so loud, Joe Macaroni," Captain Jarvis returned in a low tone. "I want to see you—quietly. Bring that Mobile friend of yours along."

Stuart, momentarily elated to see that the captain had taken notice of him, followed the two past the closed doors of the engineers' cabins to the end of the passageway. Here Captain Jarvis swung back a door and motioned them into his sleeping quarters.

The room lay directly beneath the wheel house and over his office, all three cabins being connected by a small inner staircase. Stuart took in the place at a glance. In one corner above a long chest of drawers was the bed spread with white linen—quite different from a seaman's bunk. Two portholes opened forward, and opposite these a green plush settee ran along the wall. Captain Jarvis waved the boys to a seat.

Tod dropped into a chair by the small round table, and Stuart slid along the settee into the corner. Both looked up expectantly.

"I've called you two boys in here to tell you both to watch your step. We're beginning to sail close to the wind."

"You mean, sir," Tod brought out, "that there's trouble ahead?"

Captain Jarvis nodded as he dropped into a seat facing Stuart and leaned across the table. His eyes, pale in his bronzed face, glittered with suppressed feeling. "There are plans being made on this old tramp," he said quietly, "that I can only guess at. I want to warn you. I realize as well as the men that you two have taken sides with me. If this storm ever breaks I don't want anything to happen to you on my account."

"We're not afraid, seh." Stuart spoke impulsively.

The captain scrutinized him appraisingly. "I know

you're not. I've been watching you, young man, since you first came aboard. There's nothing to complain about, either. But you're not afraid because you don't know what you're up against. Well, I do! Gut me if I don't have to admit that this is the worst crew, barring none, that I've ever sailed with. They're up to devilment."

Tod leaned forward. "What do you mean, sir?"

"Simply that I'm alone on this ship." The man's voice grew tense. "You know how I took over this command as a stranger to those on board. Half of this crew have made other voyages on this freighter; the other half are riffraff that I couldn't trust in a storm. You realize what happened to the last three masters of the *Nanking*. Well, the same thing has started with me."

"What's happened, Captain Tom?"

"Nothing that I can lay my hands on, Joe Macaroni. Perhaps I'm imagining things—yet I've never been one to do that. For days I've been aware of eyes following me in every part of this ship—even when I'm locked in my cabin. Yes, I've had to lock myself in here! For the last three nights I've heard footsteps stop outside my door, as though someone stood there listening. Last night, toward seven bells, I switched on my light and saw my door knob turn silently. I jumped up and, unlocking the door, flung it open. The passageway was empty. . . . To-day when I came down from the bridge during the afternoon watch I found that my cabin had been searched. Oh, not much was to be seen; yet a sign here, a touch there, told me that strange hands had ransacked my belongings. I went at once to my desk and took out my automatic. It was empty; every cartridge had disappeared!"

Stuart felt a tremulous wave of fear pass over him. Though the captain had not mentioned his officers, the boy knew that even those men were not to be trusted. Nervously he glanced about the little cabin. Over the captain's shoulder the two portholes showed wanly in the deepening gloom.

"You have other cartridges?" Tod asked.

"Plenty of 'em. I had them locked in a drawer."

Tod moved his clenched fist along the table. "What can we do?"

"Do? Sufferin' seagulls, Joe Macaroni, there ain't nothing you can do. Only don't take my side when you hear the men talking. Lay low and don't mix."

"But I want to do something. Stuart and I will both help. Won't we, Alabam?"

"Yes, seh. Just tell us how."

Captain Jarvis rose and switched on the electric bulb in the deckhead. The white glow gave Stuart a feeling of safety, of comfort. He drew a deep breath as the man dropped into his seat again.

"You boys want to help? Then watch everything that goes on. It won't do to let this gang know we're working together, so you better report to me secretly."

"Yes, seh—we'll do it."

"But what's it all mean?" Tod cried, puzzled.

Captain Jarvis's mouth tightened into a straight, hard line. "I don't know," he confessed; "but with everything in China in an uproar, with civil war raging for months along the Yangtse Kiang, it might mean anything." He looked about him. "It's getting mighty hot already; I'd better turn on the fan."

He half rose from his chair and reached for the electric fan on a shelf in the corner near him. Stuart heard a sudden hissing breath and a low thud near his hand that made him draw back from the table in surprise. A cry escaped his lips. At the very spot over which Tom Jarvis had been leaning a moment before now quivered a long-handled knife, its blade embedded in the wood.

For an instant the three did not move. Their eyes were intent upon that deadly steel blade before them. All realized that only his sudden move toward the electric fan had saved Tom Jarvis.

Tod Moran sprang to the wall. There was a faint click as the room was plunged into darkness. Stuart saw that the porthole on his left showed a reflected glow from other lighted ports of the superstructure, but the one over the captain's shoulder was obscured. Someone was blocking the porthole, peering into the room!

The boy felt the blood drain swiftly from his face. The next instant the dark object drew aside; the port showed wanly in the black bulkhead.

"Quick," came the captain's alert voice through the darkness. "We'll get on deck and catch that thrower."

He switched on a light above the inner stairway, and

the three rushed headlong down into the office below them.

"Lock the door behind us, Alabama!" ordered that deep voice again.

Stuart paused at the door just long enough to be sure that the lock had caught, then he hurried after his two friends, who had disappeared into the starboard alleyway.

When he joined them, they were standing in the darkness of the fore deck, gazing upward. The straight high wall of the superstructure rose to the bridge unobstructed by any object. There was nothing there to show how a person could possibly have thrown the knife through the porthole. By Cæsar, thought Stuart, the man must have stood like a phantom in midair to fling that knife into the captain's cabin with such unfailing accuracy. He looked around him in bewilderment.

The night was still. A faint breeze hummed in the rigging; the ship was ploughing ahead through a quiet sea beneath the star-flung vault of heaven.

"Let's go back," Captain Jarvis said shortly.

Without another word they retraced their steps through the deserted alleyway. At the door of his office the captain fitted a key into the lock, and they entered after him. He nodded toward the little stairway, and they quickly mounted to the cabin above. Tod Moran, in the lead, switched on the electric light. As Stuart turned to the table, an exclamation of amazement rushed from his lips.

"Look, seh, the knife is gone!"

In the silence of that moment of stunned surprise the three turned their eyes upon the table. Nothing now remained there but a small cut to show where the knife had bitten into the wood.

"It must be on the floor," Tod said in a tone of easy assurance, as he dropped to his knees. A second later he turned a pale face up to them. "It's gone."

"Someone sneaked in and stole it, seh."

Captain Jarvis shook his head. "Every door is locked. I've been taking no chances since this afternoon."

"Then someone has a duplicate key," Tod pursued.

"Impossible, Joe Macaroni. I had new Yale locks put on my cabin doors in San Francisco. I was looking for trouble ahead." His quick glance swept the confined space of the cabin. "Careful, boys! Someone must be hiding here!"

Tod and Stuart looked at each other in consternation. The sudden thought that they were being stealthily watched by a hidden assassin who was concealed perhaps in the shadowy stairway leading above to the wheel house sent an unmistakable quiver of dread through them. As they stood immovable, Captain Jarvis strode to his desk and whisked his automatic from a drawer. Holding it poised for action in his hand he crossed to the little stairway and went cautiously upward.

Stuart heard him turn the knob of the narrow door. It

was locked. He returned with an expression of puzzled uncertainty upon his face. Without a word he stepped to the door of his bathroom and suddenly swung it open. "Empty," he murmured. "Gut me if I can understand this. Search the cabin for that knife."

The two boys at once went into action. With minute care they looked under the rug on the floor, searched the shadowy corners, explored the staircase, and even investigated the bunk. There was no knife to be found.

"It had a straight slender blade, seh," Stuart said reflectively, remembering how the knife had appeared as it quivered in the table. "The handle was long and engraved with figures."

"It's not here," Captain Jarvis said at last. He turned his keen, pale eyes upon the two youths. "You asked me how you could help. Well, gut me if this ain't your chance. Find that knife—and find its owner! The storm is already breaking."

CHAPTER IX

BY WHOSE HAND?

TWO evenings later Stuart knocked upon the screen door of Tod Moran's little cabin. It lay just across from the engine-room entrance in the port alleyway where the petty officers were berthed.

"Come on in, Alabam," invited Tod.

Stuart found his friend lying on his back in the upper bunk, a pencil in one hand, a paper tablet held in the other against his upraised knees. Below him in the other bunk the boatswain was reading a much-thumbed magazine, on the cover of which a cowboy riding a bucking bronco was silhouetted against an orange-red sun.

"Hullo, youse," sang out the boatswain. "Find a chair."

The space between the bunks and the bulkhead was only a little more than two feet, and in this crowded nook, where clothes swayed on pegs, Stuart found a narrow seat fastened to the wall.

"It's sure getting hot," he remarked, disconcerted for the moment by the presence of the boatswain.

"Aw, this isn't hot yet," returned Tod. "You ought to be below, where the thermometer is climbing to a hundred ten and going higher every day. You're lucky to be on deck in these waters."

"When do we hit Yokohama?" Stuart asked.

"In four days if these rusty engines don't bust," the boatswain volunteered, "an' if we don't run into no storms. We'll hit the Japanese Current in a couple o' days, about the beginnin' o' typhoon season, too. Believe me, if youse guys git a taste o' one o' them hurricanes, youse'll wanta be back home again." The man's wide mouth broke into a grin. "Youse looks kinda worn out, Alabama. What's a-matter? Too much work?"

Stuart wearily shook his head. "Oh, I'm all right— but painting overside all day in this sun isn't any joke. A fellow gets mighty tired by night time."

"Kid," said the boatswain, as he slowly crawled from his bunk, "youse is pretty lucky not to be down in the bunkers or the stokehole. That's where a stowaway generally goes. And believe me, they work down there." He threw back his head in a yawn, scratched his chest, which showed dark matted hair beneath his singlet, and thrust his bare feet into a pair of Japanese straw slippers. "Guess I'll go on deck awhile. It ain't so hot there now the sun's gone down."

"So long, Bose," Tod called after the departing figure.

When the slap-slap of the slippers had receded down the alleyway Tod leaned over his bunkboard. "Close the door, Alabam," he said quietly. "Good. We don't want anybody to hear us talking."

Stuart looked up as he took his seat again. "Anything new?" he asked.

Tod shook his head. "Not yet, but that's because Captain Tom is careful. He's taking no chances now. We've only got our suspicions."

"What do you mean? You've discovered something?"

"Not a thing. And I can't understand what became of that knife."

"Well, we can be sure of one thing," Stuart put in. "Somebody knows how to get into the captain's cabin and knows how to do it in a hurry. No ghost took that knife."

Tod grinned. "You're telling 'em, Alabam. But who took it? And how did this unknown person get into the cabin and out again while we were on deck? We couldn't have been outside more than two minutes."

"It's got me, too," Stuart acknowledged. "But what I'm wondering is how this person managed to throw the knife. Those two portholes open onto thin air."

"Any sailor could drop a rope from the bridge deck, and swing down. It'd be simple."

"Who was on the bridge that night?"

"The second mate. But, according to Captain Tom, he doesn't amount to much. He's probably under the hand of the first mate."

"You think it was Shark Bashford?"

"I don't know," confessed Tod. He scanned the paper on which he had been writing. "I've been putting down a few notes." He paused, and then went on to explain. "Captain Jarvis always says that working out a problem should be done with calm, mathematical precision. That it's like weaving a pattern into a rug. Take all the threads and weave them together. When you're finished, the answer to the problem should stare you in the face."

"It sounds simple," said Stuart, without conviction. "But where do you get your different threads?"

"I've got them, I think. I've put down on this paper the name of every man who has sailed on this ship the last two voyages! Ten names are here—about one third of the crew. I'm taking these and making notes on all we know about them."

"Go on," said Stuart, interested. "Tell me what you've got."

Tod Moran leaned over, his eyes on his notes. He lowered his voice almost to a whisper. "Let's begin with Captain Jarvis. We know that he came aboard at San Francisco two days before I did, just as much a stranger as I am, or you. He was aware of what had happened to the former masters, so he prepared for trouble. He had new locks placed on his cabin doors; he kept the keys in his pocket. Nothing happened until the night after we left Vancouver; then we collided with a brig of the Alaska fishing fleet. Slim Morgan of the Black Gang was killed, and that brought out the fact that a certain group of men were holding a secret meeting on the fo'c'sle head. Oh, you didn't have to tell the captain that, Alabam! He was wise to that meeting."

Stuart moved uneasily. "I—I'd like to tell him all I know about it," he began. "You see, I—I slept on watch that night."

Tod regarded him in surprise. "You slept on watch— on a foggy night?" There was disbelief in his tone.

"Yes," Stuart went on, with dogged determination. "I crept down to the lee of the starboard wing. I didn't realize the danger—I went to sleep. Something roused me, but I didn't know what. I went above, and the mate soon joined me there. He had seen me asleep. He told me to go below for a while; he'd take my watch. I thought it was mighty strange, but I went down to the main deck again. I was getting suspicious so determined to find out what was going on. I saw the men slip forward and climb to the fo'c'sle head. There were at least nine of them. While they were there talking I saw the light of that sailing ship coming toward us through the fog. You know what happened then."

Stuart stopped and turned his eyes out the single porthole which was now only a gray blur of sky. In the little cabin, shadows were invading the corners.

"You can check up the names of the men I've got here," Tod said slowly. "Let's take Shark Bashford. He's been first mate on this ship for two years. He has a master's certificate but he's never been promoted. I suppose the Company doesn't think much of his ability nor of his honesty. Anyway, we can surmise that he's been disappointed more than once in not being given the command of the *Nanking*. Is he the one back of all this trouble? Undoubtedly he's mixed in it, but we can't be sure that he's the leader. Captain Tom doesn't believe that Bashford is guilty of murder. He's merely the tool of a stronger personality. That ringleader is the one we want."

"I'm not so sure you're right," Stuart mused. "Bashford is leader enough for these men."

"Perhaps. But it's doubtful if the mate would commit a murder simply to get a higher post when another ship on another line might advance him without any risk whatever. But he's always remained on this old *Nanking*. Now, why?"

Stuart looked blank. "I don't see the point of his remaining here. Unless, however, he is up to some secret business which brings him more money than the command of another ship."

"You've said it, Alabam! But what is this secret business you speak of? When he brought you on board ship in Vancouver he might have been smuggling dope ashore; but that can be done on any ship on the Pacific. In fact, it is done on most of them. This must be something which makes the *Nanking* profitable to his work, something which makes it necessary to silence the captain when he discovers the secret. When Captain Jarvis learns what is behind these attempts on his life, then the efforts to silence him will be tripled."

Stuart nodded. "It looks as though the nearer we get to China the more dangerous it becomes for the captain."

"Which means," Tod pursued, "that we've got to work faster. We've got to solve the mystery before it's too late! Now, let's take up the other deck officers. The second and third mates are both young fellows and comparatively new to this ship. That rules them out. But the bo'sun is an old hand."

"The bo'sun!"

"Yes. He's my cabin mate, and I've had a chance to watch him. I can't make out a thing against him. He's either not in with this gang very deeply or he's more sly and secretive than I think. But let's move on. There's the steward."

"He's a funny bird," Stuart put in.

"Not only funny. He's making a nice little pile of money on his slop chest and on the eats, too. He's been on this ship for nearly two years."

Stuart smiled. "The trouble with this ship is that every man aboard her appears guilty of something. Is every ship like this?"

"Most of these old tramps are," Tod explained. "When a fellow wants to disappear he changes his name and goes to sea. I'll bet that one third of the men aboard this tub have signed on under assumed names. You may be sure that many of 'em are wanted back in the States for forgery, or robbery, or murder—or perhaps they want a divorce or are merely running away from their families. Make friends with them some time and you'll hear enough stories to make a book."

"Do they tell you the truth?"

"Hardly ever. But let's get back to our notes. Next we'll take up the chief engineer."

"Mr. Rankin," Stuart said thoughtfully. "I haven't seen much of him."

Tod made a wry face. "Well, I have! He's a bully and a slave driver to the gang in the engine room. The Black Gang hate him. He's been on this tub longer than any of the officers; but that doesn't prove anything, of course. Was he on the fo'c'sle head that night?"

"Yes, seh, I'm sure he was! I heard two voices that seemed to command the rest. One was the mate's and the other must have been the chief's."

"Could you swear to it?"

"No," Stuart confessed; "I couldn't."

"None of the Black Gang has been on this ship for more than two trips. They won't work under the chief, especially in the heat of the China Sea." Tod paused. His eyes ran over his notes again. "That's all. We haven't got much to work on; but we have managed to narrow our suspects down to four men."

Stuart looked up quickly. "Haven't you forgotten someone?"

"I don't think so. Who do you mean?"

"The cook, Wu Sing."

"Oh, he's all right." Tod spoke in a tone of easy assurance. "This is only his second trip out of San Francisco."

"Well, don't be too sure about him," Stuart protested. "I was alone on the fo'c'sle head about two o'clock that night when I heard a cry. It gave me the creeps. I pulled out my pocket torch and flashed it round the deck. Wu Sing was there, hiding."

Tod leaned over his bunkboard. "Go on. What did you do?"

"I asked him what he was doing there. He said he was searching for Ming, his monkey. That was only an excuse. There wasn't any monkey there."

"Yet it might have been true," Tod said reflectively. "The little beggar climbs all over the ship when he gets loose. But what about that cry? Did he explain that?"

"He didn't get a chance. He told me not to say anything about his being there; and just then we heard the mate coming up the ladder. Wu disappeared quick as a flash."

"Oh, Wu Sing is all right," Tod announced. "I like him."

"Like him!" Stuart echoed.

"Yes. I've known Chinese in California all my life. They're trustworthy, good workers, and loyal friends. Wu is like them. He's O. K."

"I don't trust him a bit," Stuart insisted. "By Cæsar, he's one of those slick Orientals who——"

"Hush!" Tod raised his hand in warning. He was gazing intently at the closed door.

Stuart listened. As silence ensued in the little cabin, he heard the faint scuff of feet outside the door.

"Someone's been listening to us," Tod whispered. "Quick, he's moving away. See who it is."

In two strides Stuart was at the door. Flinging it
open, he saw through the screen door that the alleyway
beyond was empty. Cautiously he peered down the
passage. He just glimpsed a flash of light-blue overall
vanishing to the after deck.

"I can't tell who it was," he whispered. "Wait."

The next moment he was in the passageway, sliding
quickly aft. There in the entrance he came to a halt.
The bo'sun was sitting on number three hatch, apparently engrossed in watching a school of dolphin
swimming away from the ship on the starboard beam.
Wu Sing was taking down his laundry from a line strung
between the seamen's messroom and the derrick boom.
Upon his dark ivory countenance was an expression of
ineffable tranquillity. Puzzled, Stuart returned to Tod's
cabin.

"I don't know who it was," he admitted, chagrined.
"The bo'sun was sitting on a hatch, but he was altogether too far from the alleyway. That Chinese cook was
taking in his blamed laundry just a few feet from the
entrance. It must have been Wu all right."

"I don't believe it," Tod announced with decision.
"You're taking your ideas of Orientals from a lot of
cheap movies. You've got plenty yet to learn about the
Chinese. But didn't you see anyone in the alleyway?"

"Just a glimpse of a leg disappearing round the corner.
I think whoever it was wore light-blue dungarees."

Tod smiled ruefully. "And practically everybody on
this tub wears 'em, from the chief engineer to the cook.

Dungarees always look that colour when they've been washed. Well, Alabam, we sure let something be put over on us this time. Whoever was listening there could have heard nearly every word we said. And that means he knows just what we're up to."

Stuart gave his friend a long searching look. As he took in the expression of restrained alarm upon Tod's pale countenance he realized with a sudden rush of fear that they had exposed themselves to a precarious future. "This means, I suppose," he brought out at last, "that we're in danger?"

"Danger!" Tod echoed. "By thunder, Alabam, we're sailing close to the wind."

CHAPTER X

TYPHOON WEATHER

SAY, youse, shake a leg down there! Hell's bells, we gotta git this ship painted before we makes Yoko. Believe me, if youse keeps soldiering on me like this I'll have youse put down in the stokehole!"

Stuart, seated in a bo'sun's chair which was swung overside the midship structure, went on with his steady work without replying. He dipped his large brush into the can of white paint and splashed it along the steel plates of the cabins. Every now and then he paused to push back the old white sailor hat which Tod Moran had given him and wipe the sweat from his face. The air about him was heavy, hot, and moist.

That morning at dawn, beneath a sky spotted with red and violet tints, the *Nanking* had shoved her nose southwest across the thirty-eighth parallel. Three days from her first landfall, she was now ploughing through long swells that made Stuart grasp the ropes of his little platform. He was getting used to sitting thus in midair with the water flooding past the hull just below him. By Cæsar, he told himself with an unexpected sense of elation, he was becoming a regular sailor! Let the boatswain rave every half hour: he didn't care. He **was** making a good job of this. For his part, he didn't intend the *Nanking* to look as though she were painted by lubberly hands.

Toward five bells of his morning watch he became aware that the ship was losing headway. His feet, pressed against the cabin wall to steady his platform, no longer trembled from the faint vibrations of the steamer's engines. He glanced toward the after deck in surprise. The chief engineer hurried aft and disappeared into the scuttle of the shaft alley. Stuart vaguely wondered if the propeller shaft had broken.

The tramp began wallowing in the swells. A shout from the boat deck high above made him glance up. In sudden panic at what he saw, he grasped the ropes with both hands.

Down the side of the superstructure crashed a huge plank. With a resounding thud, it hit the wall just above his head and, as it swung past him, struck his left leg a numbing blow.

As he closed his eyes, his lips tight-drawn to keep back a cry of pain, he heard the plank plunge into the water and thump against the hull. His head swam with a dizzy feeling. He swayed.

"Say, yuh squarehead," a remote voice high above was calling, "whatcha mean by droppin' that plank right onto a seaman! Yuh mighta hit Alabam down below. Ain't it the truth?"

Stuart leaned against the ropes until his head cleared.

Thankfully, he realized that his hands had not loosed their clenched grip. Looking up he beheld the baleful face of Shark Bashford peering down at him.

"Are yuh hurt? Ludwig the Dane made a little mistake, that's all. When the ship rolled he lost his balance and let the blamed plank fall."

A moment later the little cockney came around the corner of the cabin deck, a dripping paint brush in his hand. "Wot's wrong? Blimey, yer leg's bleedin', Alabam. 'Old tight!"

"I'm all right," Stuart remonstrated. "Somebody dropped a plank on my left leg, that's all." Though he spoke in a steady voice a swift rush of fear swept through him. A straight blow from the timber would surely have knocked him into the water below; dazed, he might never have come to the surface. Had it been dropped by mistake, or was this the first attack in a campaign to silence him and Tod Moran? This thought, rather than the throbbing pain just above his knee, flooded him with this mounting sense of terror.

"Yuh better git down to the hospital cabin," called the mate. "I'll tell the steward to fix up that leg. Yuh'll be all right by noon."

Stuart carefully let himself down to the rail of the cabin deck. When he felt the safety of the deck beneath his feet, he leaned for a moment against the wall. His face was cold and clammy. Looking down he saw a long rent in his dungarees through which the flesh showed scratched and bleeding. He limped slowly aft to the hospital cabin, which lay next to the steward's slop chest.

While he waited there he glanced about. The old tramp still wallowed in the swells. He heard the captain calling peremptorily down to the chief engineer. Evidently serious trouble had occurred to the engines, for the two voices rose in a fury of altercation.

"Well, well, here's another man wants fixing up," said the steward, appearing from the port passageway. He unlocked the door of the cabin marked *Hospital* and turned to the boy. "Come in, kid, I'll make that leg feel better in a jiffy; I mean it don't take me long to bind up a little scratch like that."

Stuart, entering, saw two white bunks against the wall and a medicine cabinet in the corner. "Here we are—plenty of gauze and mercurochrome. Just roll up that dungaree and I'll get busy; when it comes to doctoring up these men here there ain't a better little fixer than Bill Sanderson, the steward. Yes, sir, I ought to 'a' been a M. D. and I would 'a' been if I'd had half a chance to go to school and college; I mean I'd know how to wear a moustache and goatee and tell the ladies how sick they was when they wasn't at all. Say, this is kinda bad. Hurts, too, don't it?"

Stuart compressed his lips while the man probed the cut with an applicator, spread a mass of jelly-like substance over it, and bound it with a roll of bandage. All the while, the smooth flow of words went on. Stuart smiled to himself, hardly listening. His leg already was soothed.

"You're the third man I've had to fix up since we left Vancouver—Tony the Wop, and then the chief, and now you. Though Tony got more than his share, I'm thinking. Two nights running he had to come to me for help. The last time he had a nice bunch of scratches around his neck."

Stuart's interest was abruptly roused. "Around his neck?" he said. "What happened to him?"

"Don't know for sure, but if you ask me I think it's a mighty queer place to have a rope go sliding. He said he ran into a cable on deck. Where was it, I ask you. He was lying to me as plain as day."

"When did that happen, Mr. Sanderson?"

"The night we hit that blamed brig. Oh, it wasn't that what did it. This was at least half an hour earlier. Well, funny things happen on this old tramp."

Stuart left the man with a word of thanks, his mind absorbed by a suspicion. Was there any connection between this injury to Tony the Wop and that strange cry on the forecastle head that night? Now that he thought of it, that muffled cry had sounded as though a man were screaming in agony while fingers pressed into his throat. The boy came to a sudden decision. He'd see Tony and attempt to learn what had happened.

He limped slowly down the ladder to the after deck and turned forward into the starboard alleyway. Opposite the engine-room entrance Toppy was leaning over the drinking fountain.

He raised his head when he saw Stuart and drew a

deep breath. "Gawd blimey, but this 'ere ice water is the best bloomin' thing aboard this tub. I 'opes the ice machine don't go on the blink like the engines."

"What's wrong with them?" Stuart inquired.

"Aw, some dumb oiler let one o' the shaft bearings burn out."

"You don't mean Tod?"

"Naw, it ain't his watch." Toppy wiped a hand across his mouth. "Gotta get to work now before that blarsted bo'sun sees me. We're in a nice fix if we don't get goin' before night. The barometer's fallin' every minute, and Sparks got a radio report sayin' there's a bloomin' typhoon comin' our way. Ain't that luck fer yer?"

"A typhoon!"

"Yeh. I was in one of 'em once on the China Sea, an' it wasn't no joke, Alabam. If the skipper's wise ter 'isself 'e'll run outa its way. But 'ow kin we without the screw goin'!" Toppy turned disconsolately away.

"Wait a minute," Stuart said hastily. "Toppy, do you know a fireman named Tony?"

"Yer mean Tony the Wop? Sure."

"What sort is he? A friend of the captain?"

"Oh, 'e's all right, Alabam. 'E's outa Frisco with Tom Jarvis 'isself. Sure, 'e likes the Ole Man."

Stuart left the Londoner and, emerging from the alleyway, looked across the bulwarks to the far horizon. The sky was hazy. Around the sun a ghostly halo was visible. The air was utterly still, and the heat even more oppressive than an hour before. He limped to the forecastle, where he noticed, with an uneasy feeling of apprehension, that the leaden sunlight cast strangely pale shadows on deck.

The sweltering quarters of the Blank Gang were similar to those of the seamen; the only difference was an accumulation of black greasy dungarees and shirts which flapped on their hooks at each sluggish roll of the ship. A lone occupant lay on his blankets, half naked and sweating, one arm hanging limply over the bunkboard. Stuart recognized him as the stocky Italian fireman.

"Hello, Tony," he said eagerly.

"How you, keed?"

"Pretty hot, Tony. Are you off watch?"

A flood of oaths came from the fireman's lips. "I go below again at noon," he explained. "The chief he maka me work for week when I seeck. Slim Morgan giva me knife slit in my side so I can hardly shovel coal into furnace. But I gotta work jus' same." He sighed, and Stuart saw that his usually florid face was pale and drawn. Beneath his thin singlet a gauze dressing could be seen plastered over a lower rib.

"Keed, what happen to your leg?" Tony asked.

"I got a little scratch. I'll go on duty again after lunch."

Stuart caught his breath. His gaze was fixed on the Italian's neck. Around it were deep scars, as though fingers had pressed mercilessly into the flesh. The boy, dragging his eyes away, asked in a casual tone, "You hurt your neck, too, Tony?"

Tony's dark flashing eyes regarded him in silent distrust. "Yes," he finally admitted, wiping a hand across his damp face. "You frien' of the captain, no? Well, I tell no one yet what thees mean. What you think? I tell you!" He lowered his voice to a husky whisper. "You remember the night when we get rammed by sailing ship? Well, that night my side ache ver' much so I cannot sleep. I go above to fo'c'sle head. Then when I stan' there in dark I hear two men fighting. I hear Slim Morgan say, 'Don' keel me! Don' keel me! I promeese I won' tell the skipper. Put 'way that knife!' Then I get ver' much afraid. I theenk, 'Tony, thees no place for you.' I start to go down ladder when I hear you cross deck and reeng four bells. Jus' then I hear Slim Morgan scream. Ah, I never forget that!" Tony broke off. His twitching face indicated the intensity of his emotion.

"Slim Morgan!" Stuart cried. "Then he was the one who cried out!"

Tony nodded. "I stan' there, not able to move one leetle bit—you understand?—when you ask, 'Who's there?' A minute after, the secon' mate call out to you from bridge; and while you talk I hear someone draggin' a body pas' me. I move, queeck, but thees man hear me. He grab me aroun' my neck, and he say, 'Who is thees?' I answer, 'Tony.' Then he say, 'Tony, leesten! Wot you do here? You get below and say notheeng.' When I go down my neck hurt so much I go aft to get the steward to put mediceene on it."

"Did you see who the man was?" Stuart asked, breathless with interest.

"No—I don' stop to see notheeng. When I reach my bunk I theenk maybe it is the mate that did it. But then I say, 'Tony, you're wrong. Shark Bashford is tall, and thees man is short.'"

"Could it have been the cook, Tony?"

"That Chink? No, no! Wu Sing is not leetle man, either, and thees fellow spik good English." Tony shook his head in despair. "Leesten, keed—you wait—thees old tramp is in for much trouble. I know."

"You're not afraid, Tony?"

Tony the Wop turned on his side with a suppressed groan; his glance darted in fear toward the forecastle door. "Yes, keed, I'm 'fraid—an' you know why? Because Singapore Sam he come an' tell me, 'Tony, the mate say you keel Slim Morgan!'"

"But that's absurd," Stuart remonstrated. "Slim Morgan was killed when the bowsprit of that brig tore across our fo'c'sle head."

"Oh, so you theenk that?" Tony looked searchingly at the boy. "Keed, I tell you the truth! Slim Morgan was keeled when we hear him cry out. Yes—he was knifed through the heart jus' one hour before that sailing ship hit us. Now wot you theenk of that, huh?"

Stuart stepped back against the opposite bunk. "You're crazy, Tony!" he cried. "That couldn't be."

Tony the Wop drew his mouth into a snarl. "Oh, you don' believe me, wot? Well, I spik the truth. Slim Morgan had knife-cut in hees back. I know. And now Shark Bashford say I do it!" His voice rose to a shrill scream of protest. "I no keel him—I no keel him! An' when we get to Yoko they'll put me in jail. Wot I do, keed—wot I do?"

In astonishment Stuart gazed at the man. Could Tony be telling the truth? If he were, then that would account for that terrified scream. There was no doubt but that the Italian believed it. His face was convulsed with fear, his lips moved tremulously, his hands dug into the blankets.

"Does Captain Jarvis know this?" Stuart brought out at last.

Tony nodded. "I theenk he know. But he say notheeng —he don' like hees officers. Tom Jarvis is no fool. You don' put notheeng over on him." Tony threw himself back on his pillow. "Tha's why I stay down here instead under awning above. I see mate look at me jus' like he say, 'Tony, you guilty as hell.'"

Stuart turned quickly as the forecastle door swung open. The boatswain's short thick form blocked the entrance. "Say, youse Alabama 'possum," he called down in wrath, "git up here on deck. Youse ain't sick."

"All right, Boats," Stuart answered. "I'm coming."

He spoke the words without a hint of bitterness, his mind intent upon this problem which Tony had brought forth. Had Slim Morgan really been knifed in the back and then his body thrown to the deck below in a desperate attempt to keep the truth from the captain? If so, Stuart had no doubt but that Captain Jarvis was aware of all that had occurred, yet was acting his part for reasons of his own. And how innocent was Tony? Had he told everything that had happened to him that night on deck? Perhaps; but Stuart could not be sure. In any case, there was a deadly assailant on board. And who was it? If that unknown man who was sought aboard this ship by Captain Jarvis and Tod Moran and himself were not the mate, were not the cook, then who was he?

Still pondering the problem, he stepped on deck. A fine misty rain that seemed to grow out of the very atmosphere was falling to the hot plates of the deck. The ship rolled helplessly in long, oily swells. Off the port beam a low, rugged cloud bank appeared like distant land, and from it a squall was diverging and coming their way.

"Hurry up, youse!"

Stuart gave a start. Like a flash his mind leaped back along the line of his problem. A man who was not too tall! Could this unknown assailant be the boatswain?

CHAPTER XI

AT THE HELM

A T EIGHT bells Stuart went above for a trick at
the wheel. Elated at an unexpected order from the
captain, which gave him an opportunity to walk the
Olympian heights of the bridge, he hummed a little
tune as he climbed the ladder. So intent was he upon
the consideration of his new duties that he gave only a
passing glance to the dark cloud bank off the port
beam. The *Nanking* was now sluggishly moving ahead
at half speed; at every slow turn of her propeller a loud
thump issued from the shaft alley.

As Stuart emerged from the companionway, the first
mate, standing in the lee of the starboard wing, eyed
him with a look of distrust. "Whatcha doin' here?" he
snapped. "Don't yuh know yuh ain't allowed on the
bridge?"

The ship gave a vicious lurch, and Stuart grasped the
rail for support. "Captain Jarvis ordered me up, seh.
I'm to take over the wheel."

Shark Bashford removed his officer's cap and wiped
his perspiring forehead with a handkerchief. His eyes,
beneath their wide red brows, continued to follow
Stuart with a beady glance.

"Come in, youngster," called out Captain Jarvis from the wheel-house window.

Stuart threw open the little door and limped over the storm step. The quartermaster stood at the helm before the open window. Captain Jarvis, clad in blue serge trousers and white singlet, surveyed the barometer fastened to the wall. From the height of this square cabin Stuart noted that one commanded a view of the ship both fore and aft.

"Ever stood a trick at the wheel before?" inquired the captain.

"Oh, yes, seh. I helped steer a yacht from New London to Bermuda one summer during a race. Seven of us took turns for five days, seh—and we won!"

The grizzled face of the quartermaster broke into a skeptical grin.

"Well, you'll do for a couple of hours," went on the captain. "Until this storm hits us, anyway. It's early for a real typhoon—though I don't like the looks o' that sky, nor the way the barometer is falling and jumping about. Quartermaster, give the boy his bearings and see that he keeps her on the course. I'm going out with the mate to shoot the sun."

For the next fifteen minutes, under the vigilant direction of the quartermaster, Stuart stood with feet braced before the wheel. "If ye can't steer no better than this," grumbled the man, "ye'll put us into Manila instead o' Yoko." He glanced out of the window that opened aft onto the boat deck. "My God, our wake looks like a

snake crossing the ocean! Ease the helm! Now, that's
better. Hold her steady." He heaved a deep sigh.
"There ain't any seaman on this ship what knows
enough to take the wheel in a storm. Well, I'll leave ye
now, 'cause I gotta git back here at four bells. If things
git any worse, I'll relieve ye before then."

Alone at the wheel, Stuart gazed down at the swaying compass card beneath the binnacle glass. By Cæsar,
the ship was still on her course! He took a spoke, raised
his eyes, and gazed through the window before him.
Captain Jarvis and Shark Bashford were talking together in the port wing. Straight ahead, the mainmast
with the crow's nest near its top cut squarely across his
vision. He could see the boatswain and three seamen on
the forecastle head hurriedly taking down the awning.
Beyond them long, heavy swells bore down upon the
port bow in a rapid succession that made the ship
pitch and toss. Whenever she plunged her nose into a
great oily wave Stuart eased the wheel and glanced
down at the compass card.

The strange yellow light that hung over the sea
abruptly vanished. The sky darkened. Large drops of
rain pattered upon the decks. Stuart sniffed the air with
rapture as a breath of wind came out of the southwest.
It steadily increased in volume until it hummed around
the bridge, then fell swiftly away again. The rain
stopped; the sky grew blacker. Stuart lost his sense of
elation. In its place came an excited feeling of awe and
suspense. Why, even a lubber could tell they were in for

it, with these sudden squalls breaking away from that cloud bank, with the sea turning that dark green colour, with the sky pressing down seemingly upon the very masts and funnel of the ship.

He heard the first mate descend the companion to the chart room under the bridge. A moment later the captain reëntered the wheel house.

"Well, young man, how you making it?"

"Very well, seh."

Captain Jarvis regarded the barometer in silence. At length he crossed to the speaking tube and whistled down to the engine room. "Ask the chief how long it'll be. Fifteen minutes? Make it shorter. We want full speed in a hurry. Every minute counts."

The boy at the wheel could sense the man's uneasiness beneath the calm tone of command. The captain's strange Tartar eyes turned to contemplate the deepening blackness of the sky and the steamer's bow as it wallowed in the trough of the sea. Already spray was hazing across the forecastle head and the fore deck taking water.

The rear door of the wheel house suddenly flew open, and the radio operator flung himself into the cabin. "Just got a report from the *West Atalca*, sir. She says this is the worst typhoon in years. She's trying to run out of it. We're right in its path."

Sparks of the wireless, Stuart noticed, was a young fellow of twenty-three or -four, the only person aboard ship who continued to dress in a spotless uniform. His pale thin face now brightened at the cool assurance in the captain's voice. He departed with a lighter tread for the radio shack.

A whistling sound issued from the speaking tube. At once Captain Jarvis turned to it. "Yes, yes. Rankin? Good. Keep 'em going, man."

He stepped to the telegraph dial and swung up the indicator to *Full Speed Ahead*.

Stuart felt the wheel strain under his grip as the steamer increased her speed. He eased the helm, took a spoke, his feet braced to meet the roll of the ship. A relieved sigh seemed to emanate from the old tramp Under black clouds she surged eagerly ahead.

Captain Jarvis opened a locker against the after wal' and brought forth his oilskins. "Ormsby," he said in a low tone, "I ordered you up here because I wanted to tell you to keep to your fo'c'sle when off watch. Don't be alone! Tell Tod Moran the same. With heavy weather about us, somebody might get a notion this was a nice chance to get rid of you. If anyone went overside, we'd naturally think a wave had done it. Get me?"

"Yes, seh."

"Seen anything of that knife yet?"

"No, seh, but we haven't given up looking."

The captain thrust his tattooed arms into the coat and buttoned it across the dragons on his chest. "I'm thinking we'll never see that knife again," he mused. "By this time it's probably overside."

Stuart swung the wheel to port. "Tony says the men

are talking, seh, about Slim Morgan. They say he wasn't killed by the bowsprit of that brig. He was knifed in the back instead."

"Oh, they know that, do they?" Captain Jarvis looked intently out of the window. "Well, it's true. Someone had knifed him before that ship ever hit our bow. Then his body was thrown to the main deck in a desperate attempt to hide the truth." He hesitated and took a turn across the confined space of the wheel house. "I'm not letting on I know. I want to catch the man responsible for all these crimes aboard the *Nanking*. Now do you understand why I tell you to be careful? I trust no one aboard this tramp except Tod Moran and you."

Stuart trembled. Trust him? The words brought a pang of shame. He had slept on watch, he had started his work aboard this ship without a thought of the responsibility that it entailed; and now the captain told him that only he and Tod could be trusted. He bit his lip sharply.

A moment later he raised his head with a resolute look. "You've no reason to trust me," he blurted out. "I was brought aboard this ship by Mr. Bashford. I slept on watch; that was probably why we know so little about this Slim Morgan affair."

Captain Jarvis gave him a searching glance. But Stuart did not falter; once started he intended to tell all that he knew. His words rushed forth without hesitation. He told of his meeting with the mate in Vancouver, of their flight from the revenue officers, of Shark Bashford's actions in forcing him to stay aboard. He told of his watch that night on the forecastle head, of his falling asleep on the main deck, of the meeting of the men in the still hours of the night.

When he had finished, the captain remained silent for a moment. "Youngster," he said at length, "I guessed some of your story. Now forget all of that. That's behind you. Strike out like a real seaman. This is your chance."

At the tone of sympathetic understanding in the man's voice, the boy's eyes grew misty. He choked on the words that refused to come from his tightened throat. Looking ahead he suddenly stared off the port bow in amazement. His heart leaped in terror. "Look—look, seh," he cried. "That wave!"

A mountainous wave was bearing down upon them. Its dark green height and white crest loomed high above the forecastle head. In an instant the captain was at the wheel. "Ease her! That's right. Steady."

The *Nanking* buried her nose in that sea. With a quivering movement she slowly rose; her forecastle head stood poised for a second against the black sky; then she plunged downward. The ship strained and groaned. A shudder went through her. Stuart's thoughts were now intent upon the wheel. He all but lost his grip as the ship rolled far to port and swung back again with a twisting, corkscrew motion. She trembled under the impact of tons of water falling onto the main deck.

With appalling swiftness the sky turned black. The

darkness of night closed down upon the ship and the sea. Then came the wind.

It advanced like a great hand rushing through the darkness to strike the old tramp a tremendous blow. First a distant hum that increased to a whine, a scream, it struck the superstructure with a bellow of rage that wrenched every loose object from the decks. The wheel house was filled with its clamour and fury. Stuart, half blinded by the gale, heard the captain cry out and saw him in the gloom frantically jerking the plate-glass window across the opening. In the little wheel house it now seemed utterly quiet; but outside the world had gone mad.

Great booming seas dashed over the bulwarks. The tumultuous uproar of the storm smote Stuart's ear-drums with a deathly fear. This was like nothing that he had ever imagined. All the dark elements of the eternal sea were screaming about the little cabin, beating at the door, shaking the windows and threatening to break the glass before him. The *Nanking* was in an agony of distress. Every bulkhead, every steel plate and rivet laboured and groaned beneath the shock of those towering waves.

A flash of lightning illuminated the decks for an instant, and Stuart glimpsed seamen running forward to the safety of the forecastle or aft to the security of the midship structure.

After the lightning came thunder. It detonated around the ship like the vast rolling beat of an im-

mense military drum. Stuart shivered at those con-
tinual explosions, at the thundering concussions around
him. He stood with the captain at the helm, easing it,
taking a spoke, swinging it free and bringing it up
again. Neither uttered a word.

As another flash illuminated the decks, Stuart momentarily forgot the wheel at what he saw. Climbing high
up the rigging to the mainmast was a small dark form.
In that instant when the white light played upon the
sea, the deck, the mast, he glimpsed Ming, the monkey,
scurrying into the crow's nest.

For a moment his mind remained intent upon a question. What was the little beast doing up there? He
remembered being told that Ming at times climbed into
the rigging, yet he could not recall ever having seen
him loose on deck. The thought struck Stuart that perhaps Ming was in the habit of exploring the deck after
dark when only the night watch was on duty. Now, with
this unearthly darkness descending upon them, the
monkey may reasonably have thought it night time.
But what was his interest in the crow's nest, that small
basket-like platform high on the mainmast?

All thoughts of Ming slipped from his mind a second
later when the rain struck them. It came like a cloud-
burst, as though a vast waterfall had suddenly dropped
from the heavens, pouring tons of water upon the puny
tramp steamer. The noise was deafening. The wheel
house was enveloped in Stygian blackness. Only the
dim glow of the binnacle light shone faintly upon the

rugged countenance of the captain at Stuart's side. The boy's arms ached; his breath came fast. His mind grew numb from the appalling shriek and whine of the wind, from the thud and splash of the rain.

A gust of wind swept up behind them as the rear door opened to admit the quartermaster. Moving up beside the wheel, he shouted into the captain's ear, "Came—at once—didn't expect——"

Captain Jarvis's deep voice boomed out above the din of crashing seas, "Close—shutters—windows—break!"

The man turned away. He struggled and fought with the door to the bridge. With all his might he pressed against it. Then in a sudden lull it opened outward and at once the wheel house was filled with the whistle of the gale. Spray dashed against Stuart. It was on his hands, his face, his hair. The door closed quickly. The ship rolled far over to starboard; the wheel whirled. A great wave pounded upon her decks, and the boy felt the whole ship shudder under the impact of a tremendous blow. He sighed with relief when the quartermaster returned in safety.

Captain Jarvis gave up the wheel; the quartermaster took his place at Stuart's side. . . . Those four hours that followed stretched across the boy's memory like an endless black corridor filled with unknown terrors. Three puny mortals were pitted against a merciless foe that brought to bear upon their tiny craft all those dark eternal powers of the sea. With the bridge deck swinging unsteadily beneath their feet, with the wind howling about them like a malignant spirit in the darkness of night, with the pound of mountainous waves which plunged over the bulwarks and covered the *Nanking* with lashing spray from stem to stern, the hours dragged on through the afternoon. Only the occasional flash of the captain's torch on the chronometer showed the weary men that the hands still pointed to the hours of day. Day? To Stuart it was endless night.

Toward five o'clock the first mate staggered up the little inner stairway to announce that the port lifeboat had been carried away. Soon after, the steward, ghostly in his white coat and trousers, arrived with coffee. The men drank the hot liquid in great gulps. A word flung across the cabin was lost in the din about them.

The chronometer on the wall had just pointed to six o'clock when the wind fell away with a last dying cry of derision. The ship grew steady, the waves no longer pounded on deck. A strange stillness descended, as though the enemy had withdrawn for a moment of rest before a more stupendous final attack. Far off could be heard the hum and whistle of a great wind.

Stuart pressed a tired hand against his eyes. He wondered vaguely if they had come through to safety.

Like an answer to his thought came the weary voice of the *Nanking's* captain speaking as if to himself. "Look at that barometer! It's lower than I ever dared to imagine. We've ridden through to the centre of the

typhoon. There's a wall of whirling death around us."
He strode to the door and flung it open. A pale, weird
light filtered into the wheel house. "When she hits us
again, God help us! . . . We're in the very heart of
danger."

CHAPTER XII

THE HEART OF DANGER

YOU can go below now, Ormsby," said Captain Jarvis. "Better go through my cabin; you'll find the doors unlocked. And send up London Toppy to relieve the helm."

"Yes, seh."

Stuart dragged his tired legs across to the inner stairway and lurched downward, his hands clinging to the rail. His brain was drugged with exhaustion. After all those hours of storm this unnatural stillness, seemingly drumming like waves against a windward shore, penetrated his mind with a sharp feeling of suspense. Surely, surely the old *Nanking* would never be able to withstand another siege. From this cyclonic centre of the hurricane, could she ever beat her way through to safety? He realized with a touch of surprise that he was not afraid; rather was he filled with an overpowering desire for rest. Just let him stretch himself in his bunk and sleep.

He was crossing the captain's cabin when he became aware of angry voices raised in expostulation. Evidently two of the ship's officers were having a little set-to in the office below. As he descended the second flight of steps in the gloom words came to him loud and clear.

"Yuh're always slinkin' round these cabins—an' the decks, too. Ain't it the truth? Now, don't lie to me, yuh dirty yellow Chink!"

"No, no, Mr. Mate. I no movee roun' deck. I go find Ming—sabbee? I lose him. He gone—maybe overboard."

"Good riddance if he has. I don't see why the skipper lets yuh keep that beast on board. I hope he fell overside, all right." There was a deep laugh, then the voice went on: "Boats told me what yuh did, an' it don't go, see?"

As Stuart emerged into the lighted office the talking ceased. Wu Sing stood near the open door to the passageway, unconcernedly facing the first mate. Shark Bashford turned a startled gaze toward the boy. The man was clad in dripping oilskins; his eyes remained fixed upon Stuart's face. Suddenly he shrugged, drew a hairy fist across the red bristles of his jaw, and flung himself out the door without a word.

Wu Sing smiled. "Him belly bad man," he said softly. "I keep 'way from him." He closed the door and came forward to Stuart.

The boy saw those yellow eyelids narrow to slits, saw the long ivory hands brush the buttons of the white coat. "You tellee mate?" the cook asked in a sibilant whisper.

Stuart looked at him uncomprehendingly. "What do you mean?"

"You tellee Shark Bashford that Wu was on fo'c'sle head that night in fog?" There was a tinge of menace in the deep intensity of that hissing tone.

"No," Stuart answered, "I didn't say a word to anyone. What makes you ask?"

"Oh, if you no tellee, that's allight. You good boy. I givee you piece cake from the officers' mess. You likee cake?"

"You bet." Stuart's face grew radiant in anticipation. "By Cæsar, Wu, I haven't tasted cake for months. But"—and his voice faltered—"do you think we'll make it through this typhoon?"

The cook's eyes showed sudden fear. "I no likee this thunder, this lightling, this lain. No—I no likee. But we got fine master, this Captain Jarvis. He bringee us to Shanghai. Don't you be 'fraid, li'l' boy. You come Wu's galley to-night for cake. Sabbee?"

"Sure thing."

Wu Sing opened the door. "Allight," he whispered, and disappeared a second later down the passageway.

Stuart gazed after him with a feeling of distrust. This sly Oriental, he decided, no doubt wanted him as a friend for certain reasons of his own. Well, Stuart Ormsby wasn't going to swallow any line and sinker just for a slice of cake. By Cæsar, no!

He thoughtfully made his way to Tod Moran's little cabin. It was after six o'clock, and the oiler should be off watch. He found his friend stretched on his bunk, the porthole clamped shut, and the electric light burning in the deckhead. In the boatswain's berth lay Toppy.

"Hello," said Tod. "I see you're still alive."

Stuart turned his weary eyes to the little seaman. "Orders for you, Toppy," he said. "The skipper wants you on the bridge to relieve the wheel."

"Oh, Gawd," yawned Toppy, "don't I get no rest a-tall?"

"Captain Jarvis said he wanted a real seaman at the helm," Stuart pursued; "you and the quartermaster are the only ones he can rely upon during such a storm as this."

Toppy jerked himself erect. "W'y didn't yer say so at first? There ain't a skipper on the whole bloomin' Pacific wot knows 'is stuff like Tom Jarvis." With a swagger to his rolling gait he left the cabin.

Tod raised himself on an elbow. "Close the door, Alabam." A nervous smile flitted across his face. "This is a mighty bad typhoon. That four hours in the engine room was the worst watch I ever stood. I slid all over the steel plates; and the poor firemen were always getting burned when the ship pitched. How'd you make it?"

Stuart sat down wearily on the seat in the corner. "I never knew a storm could be like this," he admitted. "I expected the ship to go down any minute. And the worst is ahead."

"Aw, if she made it once, she'll make it again. There's

not much a fellow can do, either. But given a seaworthy tub and a real captain a steamer generally makes port. By thunder, the old *Nanking* has taken a worse beating than I ever thought she could stand." He drew a hand through his sandy hair. "Better keep off deck, Alabam. It's dangerous."

Stuart nodded as he leaned forward. "You're repeating Captain Jarvis's very words, Joe Macaroni. Only he said that something besides a wave might wash us overboard."

Tod glanced at him quickly. "Well, I've got a little job to do to-night, but it won't take me on deck." He paused, and his gray eyes flashed. "Alabam," he resumed in a lower tone, "my notebook has disappeared. It's been stolen!"

"What notebook?"

"The one I made those notes in about this ship. Remember I told you how I looked up the records of everybody on board? Well, I jotted down all I knew about each one—from Shark Bashford to the cook. I was trying to weave my threads into a pattern. And now it's gone from under my pillow. Someone is surely interested in what we're trying to figure out."

Stuart looked at the empty lower bunk. "Do you suppose the bo'sun took it?"

"I don't know—but this cabin is never locked. Anyone could come in here." He smiled grimly. "Well, Alabam, we don't seem to be getting anywhere with our mystery, do we? No knife found, and now my notes stolen.—There goes the mess bell. It's late to-day. Come in after chow. I want to tell you about this little detective job I'm planning to carry through to-night."

Stuart went down the alleyway to its end, where a steel door now blocked the passage to the fore deck. "Alabam," called Tod's voice after him, "don't go on deck."

"I want to change to dry clothes before mess."

"You're crazy to cross that deck now. If we dive into this typhoon again while you're in the fo'c'sle you won't be able to get back."

Stuart pulled down the iron cleat of the door. "Oh, it seems mighty quiet now. I'll hurry."

He stepped to deck and swung the door shut behind him. Night had closed down. Stars shone high above, but all round the ship rose a black impenetrable wall of cloud from which came the distant whine of the rotating gale. The deck was steady; beyond the bulwarks he vaguely discerned a choppy sea.

Halfway across the slippery deck he stopped. He raised his head and looked up at the mainmast. Far above he dimly made out the dark outline of the crow's nest. He remembered that he had forgotten to tell Wu about seeing the monkey climb above. Was the impish little creature still up there? He recalled how the storm had swept over the ship just as Ming had gained the safety of the lookout's platform. Pity surged through Stuart. Quickly he looked about. It occurred to him that if he hurried he had time to climb into the rigging and descend before the full force of the storm was again upon them. The quietness of the ship as it steamed through the darkness gave him a false sense of security.

He ran to the bulwarks, took hold of the cable with both hands, and, springing upward, drew himself atop the rail. He started up the ladder. It was solid to his touch; a sense of assurance swept through him. He raised a hand carefully above him, gripped the cable, and then lifted his right foot till it rested on the rung of the ladder. Slowly, with the stiffness in his left leg hindering his progress, he went upward.

Near the bottom of the ladder, where its cables were fastened to the bulwarks, the rungs were wide, but as he climbed they narrowed perceptibly. He soon noticed that it was momentarily becoming more difficult to keep his balance. He paused once to glance downward. Below him was a dark void; the red glow of the port light was now even with his shoulder. A puff of wind touched his cheek. Was the distant roar of the gale drawing nearer, or did he only imagine it? At any rate, he was two thirds up the mast: he must go on.

With more caution he continued to climb. The ladder grew steeper; it was now narrower than his body. Once, losing his balance, he swayed out into the darkness; but his hands gripped the cables and he pulled himself back, flat against the rungs. While he rested there, with the blood beating wildly in his ears, he acknowledged to himself that this was no place for a lubber: only an able seaman should be climbing the rigging in the dark. He was already higher than the bridge. He could see the glow of the binnacle light reflected in the wheel-house window.

Looking up, he distinguished near at hand the outline of the crow's nest black against the stars. He climbed on. A moment later the ladder narrowed to the width of a few inches, and, reaching up, he touched the wooden floor of the lookout's perch, which was riveted to the mast. In the little deck there was an opening like a half moon, and through this he struggled.

When he stood upright within the basket-like structure he discovered that a board was fastened between the stanchions of the sides to serve as a seat. Sitting there with his arms across the steel rail, his feet on the floor and his knees against the encircling canvas, he found it a place of safety and quiet in a world of black obscurity. Above him he saw a single star suddenly wink out.

At that instant something brushed against his leg. He looked down eagerly and whispered, "Ming—Ming!"

The little monkey jumped to his lap, whimpering in fear, and pressed his rain-sodden body against Stuart's shirt. The boy knew that Wu Sing's pet was seeking help and protection.

"Ming, you little imp," Stuart said half aloud, "this serves you right. What made you climb up here?" He drew a hand across the wet fur. "Well, you certainly are a mess. Quit shivering! You needn't be scared now."

Ming clung still more tightly, and Stuart settled the little creature into the crook of his arm. Two small round eyes, each a dim green glow, stared up at him. The eyes blinked twice quickly, and the boy felt the trembling cease.

Stuart looked upward. Not a star now shone above. In every direction lay solid blackness. From the height of his perch the round yellow lights of the forecastle portholes were small and remote. He twisted his body and looked down upon the wheel-house window and the lights on each side, the red to port, the green to starboard. As he turned back to the rail before him his foot struck a loose object. He reached down to investigate.

His fingers found an apple core almost wholly eaten, a banana peel, a small leather book. His heart gave a sudden leap. Tod's notebook! A smile drew down the corners of his mouth. Of course, he might have guessed the truth—Ming was the thief.

Into his mind, however, drifted a doubt. Why should the little monkey steal a notebook? Could his owner, Wu Sing, be responsible for this? Having read the notes, could not the Chinese have induced his pet to secrete the book in this hiding place? A second later Stuart's fingers touched something that rested in the corner where the deck met the curved canvas side, something sharp and hard and smooth. Involuntarily his hand jerked away. Could it be? . . . Cautiously he explored again. His fingers closed about the handle of a knife.

THE HEART OF DANGER

On the instant he knew that it was engraved—engraved with Chinese characters!

Wu was back of this, as he had suspected. Tod was altogether too gullible. Just wait till he got down and showed this find to him and Captain Jarvis! Quickly he wrapped the blade in his handkerchief and thrust the knife safely into a dungaree pocket. Into another went the notebook.

So immersed was he in his discovery that he was startled a moment later by wind beating furiously against the crow's nest. With a steady whine that rose and fell and rose again it bore against the ship with such force that she trembled as though in terror. With a thunderous roar a sea poured down over the port bow. Ming, whimpering again in fear, pressed closer. Stuart grasped the rail for support, for the old tramp swung over to starboard until the boy thought she would never stop. The mainmast with the crow's nest secure at its top was tilting in a great arc across the sky. Almost thrown from his perch, Stuart clung to the rail and the stanchion, while his heart pounded madly in consternation. Directly below him now was water.

For a long moment the canvas basket remained poised above the sea; then it quivered and pitched back through space, while the boy felt every ounce of breath driven from his lungs. By Cæsar, he'd better get down mighty quick! The typhoon was upon them again.

Ming whined in sudden terror. Hurriedly Stuart unbuttoned his collar and made a snug refuge for the little creature between his old blue shirt and his white singlet. With Ming thus secure, the boy dropped to the floor and, holding to the seat, let his feet slide down through the opening. When they touched the ladder he drew a breath of relief.

It was dangerous, he knew, making these first few steps. As he paused there to secure a foothold, the wind came whistling out of the southwest with renewed fury. He felt the ship rise beneath him as the forecastle head mounted a wave. With a twisting corkscrew motion the *Nanking* plunged. The crow's nest again swung furiously to starboard in a soaring arch above the deck. Stuart's feet dangled in midair.

Terror stricken, he clung to the seat while the encircling rim of the opening cut into his ribs. He felt the mast tremble, sensed the wide swing back to port. His heart seemed to stop beating. Lightning split open the heavens; he glimpsed the inside of the crow's nest for a second with its pile of refuse on the floor. The next moment thunder exploded all round him in great vibrating concussions, as though the enemy were beginning a second stupendous attack.

Blinded by the lightning, deafened by the noise, he yet managed to draw himself up till his feet were safe on the platform. There he crouched, facing aft, his hands about the seat, his back against the stanchion that held the canvas, his feet braced against the mast just above the opening to the ladder.

Now he realized why the monkey cried out in fear, why the little fellow shivered and clung to him in an agony of distress. With a sickening suddenness that made the boy's heart drop within him the mast swept far to one side; there it remained for the duration of a second or two before swinging back again. And all about him in the darkness was the wind! It screamed with demoniac fury, it swept up through the opening as though to tear loose his hold, it took the very breath from his lungs. But he held his place, held it even when the rain poured upon him like a torrent, sluiced about his platform, and splashed down to deck eighty feet below. To deck? . . . No—the crow's nest was now tilting far to starboard over the open water.

He was drenched to the skin; his dripping hair clung to his forehead; water was in his eyes, his nose, his mouth. He bowed his head low over his chest; Ming moaned and trembled against him. His hold on the seat remained as immovable and strong as the riveted stanchions themselves. "Ming," he murmured, to keep up his own courage, "you were caught here once and managed to live through it. I suppose we can do it again."

He had not counted, however, on sickness. Those up-sweeping curves through the air soon overwhelmed him with nausea. First slowly, then in increasing waves of absolute illness, it rushed over him, until his arms grew limp, and he wondered if he cared whether he held or not. Through his numbed mind drifted the thought of a safeguard. If only a rope were handy with which to tie himself there! It suddenly occurred to him that his belt would do as well. Desperately, yet with infinite caution, he moved his left arm; his fingers unfastened the buckle. During the intervals when the crow's nest stood upright, he slipped the belt between the canvas and the stanchion behind him and fastened it again securely about his waist. There was little chance of his being jerked from his perch now, unless—unless the mast itself went overboard.

Strange ideas took possession of him; his mind rambled. His fear-burdened thoughts floated back to the security of the Academy at West Point. He was in his room again, studying the art of war, the manner of firing those great artillery guns. This was the zero hour when one was attacked; it was the enemy who now stormed the trenches, who continued to fire those immense shells that whistled through the air and exploded with deafening blasts. He was wounded; he knew he was dying. Yet deep within him some smouldering spark made him hold on, made him put forth just one more effort.

All through that night of storm and terror, with the elements gone mad, the old tramp plunged groaning and straining through the seas. To the boy clinging to the crow's nest it seemed an eternity of noise and horror. Great waves dashed upon the deck; from stem to stern the *Nanking* was enveloped in flying spray. Yet with dogged determination he clung to his perch, thankful for the protection of the platform and the canvas cover that threatened to rip to shreds about him. In the wheel house, he knew, stood a man whose keen intellect strove against appalling odds to carry his ship through to safety, and on that man every soul on board must rely.

When morning came the wind abated; the typhoon went swinging northeast along the Japanese Current. The *Nanking*, battered, woebegone, yet triumphant, still rode the swells toward the west. Out of the sea astern of them the sun rose and flooded the decks with a warming radiance.

A boy then crawled from the crow's nest and crept slowly down the rigging. In the crook of his arm clung a monkey with chattering teeth and flashing eyes. A seaman, crossing the deck to the forecastle, stopped to gaze aloft in surprise. The figures of two men came from the wheel-house door and leaned over the bridge rail to stare in amazement.

"Gawd strike me bline," shrilled a voice. "It's Alabam!"

"Bring that lad into the office," boomed the deep tones of Captain Jarvis. "He needs help."

Hands reached up and assisted him down to deck. He swayed there for a moment before being led aft.

"Blimey, wot 'appened?" asked Toppy in a breathless whisper. "We thought yer'd been lost overboard."

He was in the captain's office now, with Toppy holding him up, the monkey still clinging frantically to his arm, and Captain Jarvis at the foot of the stairs eying him with the utmost concern.

"I've found it," Stuart murmured. "The knife . . ." He held out the weapon in his hand.

The captain stepped toward him. "Have you seen Tod Moran?"

Stuart roused himself with an effort. "Tod? . . . What do you mean?"

"He can't be found. Shark Bashford said he went overside from the after deck."

"No—no." Stuart forced himself to remain erect while over him, like a rising tide, swept fatigue and numbness and pain. "He can't be. He told me—he was doing—some detective work on his own but he wasn't going on deck."

"They've got him then!" The words came, muffled, from the captain's lips. "They've hidden him some place on board. I'll find him if I have to tear every rivet from this ship—and the truth from every man!"

Before the boy's eyes a white light wavered; there was a roar of wind in his ears. He put out his hand. "Captain Tom——" He staggered.

"Here—catch him, Toppy! He's all in!"

The arms of the little cockney received him as he fell.

Part Four

PORTS OF ADVENTURE

Yokohama Harbour
Foreign and Offshore Vessels
in Port

Arrived July 2, Am. Stmr.
Nanking; Jarvis—18 days
from Vancouver.
Tokio *Japan Times*

CHAPTER XIII

THE SECOND ATTEMPT

YOKOHAMA! Blimey, that's the place fer a sailor lad.—'Old still, Alabam! 'Ow can I cut yer 'air if yer keeps movin' all the blarsted time? Gawd, won't the little Japs think yer a gay young seaman!"

"But I'm not going ashore, Toppy."

"Wot! Yer ain't goin' ashore at Yoko? Gawd strike me pink, then w'y do yer keep me in this fo'c'sle where it's 'ot as 'ell?"

"Because I need a haircut—badly."

Toppy heaved a sigh of resignation as he clipped the scissors dangerously near Stuart's ear. "All this bloody beauty-parlour stuff fer nothin'."

"Yoko ain't no good no more, anyway," declared

Singapore Sam from his bunk. "Since that last earthquake there ain't nothing left but dirt an' ruins."

"Do yer ever see anything else in these blarsted slit-eyed ports but dirt an' poor ruined seamen?"

Swede Jorgenson turned from the cracked mirror before which he was laboriously shaving. "Yiminy, let's go on to Tokio. It's only forty minutes by tram. Yah, Alabam, you better come along, too. We're gonna take on a full cargo o' booze."

"But a stowaway isn't allowed to land at a foreign port," Stuart explained.

With a professional air Toppy stepped back and surveyed the product of his skill. "There yer are, Alabam. Yer finished."

"Yeah, he's finished all right," grunted Singapore Sam. "I sure hope none o' his friends see him like that."

"Yer big stiff! Wot yer mean by that remark?"

"Not a thing, Limey. Only you don't catch me letting you cut my hair."

"I don't cut no bloke's 'air wot don't wash an' shampoo it even onct a year."

"Shut your fly trap, you scurvy limejuicer!"

Stuart hastened to interpose. "Thanks, Toppy," he said gratefully. "You're certainly a first-rate barber."

The little cockney showed his yellow fangs in a self-conscious grin. "Oh, I've saw worse ones," he admitted. "Now, if Tod Moran was only 'ere I'd feel blarsted gay, I would."

The words brought a pang to Stuart. Thoughtfully he climbed the steps to deck. It was four o'clock in the afternoon, with Yokohama two hours distant. The *Nanking*, battered and woebegone of aspect, her decks cleared of wreckage from the typhoon, was now passing from Uraga Strait into Tokio Bay. Low hills covered with verdure rose on the starboard beam. The beauty of this first landfall was lost to Stuart, however; his mind was dwelling upon the strange disappearance of his friend.

Four days had passed since Captain Jarvis had brought his ship safely through the typhoon, yet as far as the forecastle knew, nothing more had been learned of Tod's disaster. At mention of the boy's name, the men sadly shook their heads; they took it for granted that at the height of the storm a wave had washed the oiler overboard. Stuart, however, knew better. He had met Captain Jarvis in the port alleyway the day after the typhoon, and to his questioning glance the man had replied, "Don't worry, Alabam. Tod is safe on board. But play your part as if you thought he'd gone overside. Get me?" Although Stuart had nodded acquiescence he still failed to understand. He could think of no place where Tod might be hiding. Certainly his friend was not in the captain's cabin, for that was now unlocked. Yet the boy wondered if this very fact might not be an effort of Captain Jarvis to throw their enemies off the course.

As Stuart now stood disconsolately at the rail Shark

Bashford came up beside him. "Goin' ashore, kid?" he asked.

"No, seh. I'm to stand watch at the accommodation ladder to see that no peddlers come aboard."

"Yuh feel kinda down-hearted. Ain't it the truth?"

Stuart nodded.

"Too bad about that friend o' yourn bein' lost overside." There was a tinge of mockery in the man's tone.

Stuart flashed him a look of bitter hatred. The mate, lean and tall, slouched over the rail. His red hair was plastered with sweat against his forehead; his wide mouth curved in an ironical smile. Stuart, gazing at him with repulsion, felt a torrent of words flooding his throat. Biting his lip sharply to keep back a heated reply he shrugged and walked rapidly aft.

At six o'clock the *Nanking* anchored outside the Yokohama breakwater. Around her immediately swarmed sailing sampans like huge, grotesque water beetles seeking prey. A strange jargon of words rose loudly from the boatmen. Stuart, listening intently at the top of the accommodation ladder thrown overside the fore-deck bulwarks, soon perceived that the Japanese were bidding in English for passengers to take ashore. Excited seamen rushed about the steamer's decks. Men with satisfied smiles on their faces emerged from the captain's office, counting their rolls of bills. Others had formed a line outside the steward's slop chest in a belated effort to draw new gear. Unclad firemen hurried from the shower room to the forecastle:

their voices rose boisterously in anticipation of their first night ashore.

To Stuart it seemed as if he alone took no part in this gaiety. He had lost all desire to leave the ship. If Tod were here, he reflected, it would be different. The two had planned to go ashore together and hunt up one of those Oriental chocolate shops where American ice-cream sodas could be obtained; for after three weeks of ship's diet they found an overpowering hunger for sweets luring them shoreward. Stuart's hands gripped the rail. He had not expected his first landfall to be like this.

Acting under orders he allowed two wrinkled "sew-sew" women to climb the steps to deck. These aged Japanese mended the seamen's clothes in return for a few pennies; for ten cents they gladly did a month's laundry, taking away with them half the cake of American soap, which they furtively hid in the folds of their kimonos. They went about the decks on stockinged feet, their singsong refrain issuing from toothless mouths, "Sew-sew? Sew-sew?" They were Stuart's first intimate glimpse of Japan.

As twilight deepened the men left in groups of three or four. They rushed down the accommodation ladder to the little platform, where they hurriedly bargained for their fare ashore. The cheapest boatman received the group, at which the remaining sampan men raised their voices in shrill cries of protest. The seamen waved back gaily to Stuart, who stood alone at the rail. He saw Toppy and Swede Jorgenson depart together.

"We're goin' ter get soused ter the gills," the little cockney called out as the sail of his sampan was raised. Singapore Sam, Tony the Wop, and two firemen clambered into another boat. Shark Bashford and Mr. Rankin, the chief engineer, soon followed.

The old tramp at length lay quiet as though deserted. Only a thin spiral of smoke rising from her funnel indicated that a stoker still remained below on duty. Night closed down; stars came out. A flooding tide washed softly against the hull. Inside the breakwater, where ships of all nations rode at anchor, portholes gleamed through the darkness. Glittering lights extended along the Yokohama water front.

Stuart, leaning over the rail, sniffed with delight the mingled fragrance of the land. Directly above his head a shaded electric bulb threw a cone of light upon him. Presently the tall figure of the captain emerged from the darkness of the fore deck. He wore a white duck suit and canvas shoes; his tawny head was bare.

"Everybody gone?" he asked Stuart. "Good. Get a sampan quietly—and have it wait below."

"Yes, seh."

Stuart swung himself over the bulwarks and went down the steps to the small square platform which hung a foot above the quiet waters of the bay. There he called a boatman who lay off to one side and ordered him to wait for a passenger. He glanced up as he heard footsteps coming down the ladder. Two figures were moving toward him.

"Tod!" he exclaimed in surprise and relief. "It's you."

"Quiet there!" ordered Captain Jarvis over Tod Moran's shoulder. "Get in quickly, Joe Macaroni. Let no one see you. We'll pick you up at Moji in three days."

"Yes, sir." Tod stopped before Stuart and grasped his hand. The oiler was dressed in a dark suit; a cap was pulled over his eyes. "Captain Jarvis will explain, Alabam." He lowered his voice in a hurried whisper. "I'm going ashore to follow Shark Bashford! So long!"

In a moment Tod had departed alone. Stuart stood beside the captain watching the sampan's sail swing aloft and slowly dissolve in the darkness. So quickly had Tod come and gone that Stuart found a hundred questions tapping at his mind as he climbed to deck.

Beneath the white cone of light Captain Jarvis halted, a smile on his bronzed countenance. "Sufferin' fish hooks, I'm glad that's over," he announced in his deep vibrant voice. "Don't let anyone know, kid, that Moran is safe and gone ashore. This is an opportunity we'll never get again to discover what's ahead of us."

"Tod is all right, seh?"

"Sure. He's fit as a stanchion. I didn't dare tell you what had happened for fear the fo'c'sle men might see by your manner that Moran was safe aboard. We don't want them to know——"

He checked his words as soft footfalls approached from the alleyway. Wu Sing, dressed in a Chinese suit and slippers of dark-blue satin, passed them with a nod. "I go ashore, Mr. Captain. I likee see frien' in Tokio."

"Don't forget we want breakfast in the morning," reminded the *Nanking's* master.

Wu pattered down the steps. "Oh, yes, sir. I comee back late to-night."

Stuart saw Captain Jarvis gaze intently after the Chinese. "Do you trust him, seh?" the boy asked.

"I trust none of this crew." Suddenly he looked at Stuart. "Did it ever strike you that Wu Sing's pidgin English is a little—well, childish?"

"But don't all the Chinese talk that sort of English, seh?"

"Sufferin' halibut, no!" The captain shook his head, obviously puzzled. "Wu's talk is almost too good to be true. Perhaps, though, I'm altogether too suspicious, but that Chink was the cause of Tod's mishap."

"I never did think much of that cook," Stuart ventured. "He's too sly to suit me. And that knife I found in the crow's nest must belong to him. It's engraved with Chinese characters."

"I know. That knife is a clue that points directly to Wu. If he weren't the cook I'd lock him in the brig on suspicion—but what would the crew do without their chow? It might hasten a mutiny."

"You think, seh, that it's mutiny the men are planning?"

The captain doubtfully shook his head. "I don't think so, for they have nothing to gain by that. For a while I

suspected them of carrying guns and ammunition il-
legally to these Chinese Nationalists, but I went over all
the cargo in our holds and found that I was wrong.
No—we haven't yet discovered the secret."

"I'll bet Wu Sing knows a thing or two!"

"You're right, lad. And I'm just waiting a chance to
make him talk. It was your suspicions, too, that led
Tod into trouble. But he learned something—something
extremely important!" Captain Jarvis paused and
leaned over the rail. His rough-hewn profile was turned
to Stuart, and the boy saw his brow knit in a frown. The
man passed his hand slowly through his closely cropped
hair, as though he were vainly trying to comprehend the
meaning of some secret action.

"That night of the typhoon," Captain Jarvis went on
in a lowered tone, "Tod decided to look into Wu's
affairs. He watched the cook's cabin and saw the bo'sun
knock softly twice, then enter. He was certain now that
the bo'sun and Wu could give him valuable information.
If only he could hear their conversation! The alleyway
porthole of the cook's cabin was clamped shut; becoming desperate, he decided to risk the boat deck in an
effort to hear through the cabin ventilator."

The captain's voice became tense. Breathless, Stuart
hung on every word. "Tod went out to the after deck
and climbed the ladder. He felt his way across the boat
deck to the ventilator which he judged must come from
the cook's cabin. But the wind and waves made such a
noise that for some time he couldn't hear a word. Then

in a sudden lull he caught a single phrase in the bo'sun's voice: '*Sotoko's in Moji.*' A wave crashing over the decks drowned out the rest of the sentence. As he hung there in the darkness, dripping wet, someone grasped him from behind. He was held in such an iron grip that he had no chance in that utter blackness to recognize his assailant. The scoundrel waited until a big wave loomed up on the port beam, then he dragged Tod aft past the lifeboats. And gut me if he didn't throw the lad down to the after deck—the blackguard!"

The man's hands closed on the rail till the knuckles showed white. "Oh, Tod wasn't hurt badly! But the only thing that saved him was the wave which at that moment fell over the bulwarks and plunged across the deck. It eased his fall and flung him against the opposite rail. In desperation, he clung there, while the water sluiced through the chock and fell away around him. When he rose he found himself at the very stern of the ship near the after house. He knew he would be trusting providence too much to attempt to cross that deck again; so he managed to pull down the cleat of the store-room door. Once safely inside, he threw himself upon a pile of rope. He was bruised; the breath was knocked out of him; he said he felt as though he'd swallowed half the Pacific Ocean. Anyway, he was safe, and there he remained through the rest of that night o' storm I found him next morning."

Captain Jarvis broke off. Gazing shoreward, he rested his elbows on the rail.

"And Tod was hiding there all the time?" Stuart blurted out in surprise.

The captain nodded. "Yes. This was an opportunity, I decided, that we mustn't lose. I locked him in there for three days and secretly carried him food. To-night I gave shore leave to every man we could possibly spare. Thus Tod was able to slip out unnoticed. 'Sotoko's in Moji!' That's where Joe Macaroni is going—and if I'm not missing my guess the mate or the bo'sun will fail to show up here in the morning. We're to suppose they're drunk, but in all probability they'll be taking the train south for Moji. That's our next stop. Are they picking up something there to take on to Shanghai, or are they meeting some outside person with whom they're in league? Well, that's Tod Moran's little job ashore. I know I can trust to his discretion and intelligence to find out." Captain Jarvis drew a tobacco pouch and pipe from his pocket. Still leaning on the rail he absent-mindedly filled the bowl.

"When do we leave, seh?" Stuart asked.

"To-morrow noon. We're remaining here just long enough to take on some steel netting. I don't intend to enter the Yangtse Kiang without making the upper decks safe from mutineers or marauders."

Stuart looked across at the lights that twinkled along the city quays. Certainly, he mused, this tattooed captain took every precaution. Knowing that the ship would be prepared for trouble when they steamed up the river through the war zone to Shanghai the boy felt suddenly safer. This master of the *Nanking* was a man to be reckoned with, a man who was ready for every emergency.

"Well, youngster, keep this to yourself," cautioned the captain. "Tod made me promise to tell you. We knew we could trust you, and that's why you were ordered to take the watchman's place here to-night. Let's hope——"

Abruptly he stepped back with a cry of warning. Stuart whirled in startled surprise. A pistol shot echoed in the night. A bullet spat past them and thudded against the steel plate of the superstructure directly behind.

"Quick! Get out of the light!" Captain Jarvis snapped out the words with an oath.

Two other shots followed in rapid succession. Stuart leaped to the safety of the starboard alleyway. An instant later the captain joined him. The man's face was pale. There was a rent in the left sleeve of his coat where a bullet had clipped it. "We were a couple of fools," muttered the captain, "to have stood beneath that light."

"The shots came from a sampan," Stuart said with a tremble in his voice. "Are you hurt, seh?"

"No—just a scratch." He winced as he moved his arm.

In spite of the words of assurance Stuart gazed wide eyed at a spreading blood-stain on the white sleeve.

Captain Jarvis held himself erect. "Oh, I'm all right, Alabam. I want you to watch that accommodation ladder closely. Better sit in the darkness of number two hatch. If anyone except a member of the crew tries to come aboard yell out for me. I'll be in my office. It's the skipper of this ship that devil is trying to get."

"Who—who could have fired those shots?"

"Who?" The man's voice was deep with passion. "That shot was fired by the man we want. I hope to God he didn't see Moran go ashore."

Stuart looked out across the dark water toward the riding lights of the vessels at anchor. Was the sampan containing their assailant now nosing its way shoreward? And who was this man? Suddenly a thought flashed into his consciousness—why shouldn't he give chase? He swung about to the captain; eagerly his words rushed out.

"Let me go after that sampan, seh! I might be able to follow it, catch that man!"

Captain Jarvis instantly acquiesced. "All right, Alabam. I don't dare leave my ship, but you may go. Get one of those skiffs at the accommodation ladder and give chase. But you've got to promise one thing: You're only to find out the identity of the man who fired those shots. Understand? No attempt to fight; no effort on your part to bring him back to the ship. Just get the name of that cowardly blackguard."

"Yes, seh. I'll do it."

"Here's some money for the boatman. Quick! Don't lose a moment. After him!"

"Yes, seh," the boy threw over his shoulder. He was already running for the ladder.

CHAPTER XIV

THE CHASE IN THE SAMPAN

ON THE platform of the accommodation ladder Stuart came to a breathless halt. A shout from a boatman, "Go 'shore? Go 'shore, mister?" brought a gesture of acquiescence from the boy.

"Quick!" he urged.

A moment later the stem of a sampan grated against the platform. Stuart jumped in. "Hurry," he said in an undertone to the Japanese boatman; "I'll pay you well."

"Yes, mister." The man spoke with a swift intake of breath.

Stuart stood in the prow, his weight against the small shack built of bamboo and matting in which the boatman doubtless cooked and slept. Atop the rounding structure an ancient brass lantern made a point of light in the darkness. Slowly the Japanese swung his craft out from the tramp freighter; his bare arms moved with a swift rhythmic motion as, standing in the square stern, he sculled furiously in an effort to win his passenger's approval.

The boy dropped to a seat on a thwart and faced aft. "You understand English?" he anxiously asked. "Yes? Did you hear three shots fired at my ship?"

"Yes, mister."

"They came from a sampan lying off this side of us. Follow that sampan! I want to see who is in it—who fired those shots. Understand?"

"Yes, mister."

Though the man nodded in the gloom Stuart could not be sure that he fully comprehended; he might merely be assenting through a polite desire to comply with his fare's request. A faint suspicion took possession of the boy that the boatman knew only two words of English— "Yes, mister"—and that he used this phrase in response to every remark.

The Japanese, shipping his long sweep oar, stepped over a thwart to the mast. There was a creaking rustle as the square sail of straw matting swung aloft. When the sampan had drifted out from the lee of the *Nanking*, the sail caught the breeze and the little skiff gained headway. The boatman resumed his oar. Straight toward the breakwater sped the sampan.

Stuart rose and crouched over the roof of the deck house. Beads of spray dashed against his face. Eagerly he scanned the space of water ahead for a glimpse of the fleeing sampan. Only the darkness met his gaze; no sail was visible between his own skiff and the shadowy outlines of the steamers riding at anchor in the bay. A thought flashed through his mind. Perhaps the other sampan had sailed southward to elude pursuit; but the next instant the conviction came to him that in all probability the man who had fired those shots would have one desire only: to get ashore as quickly as possible. He would extinguish any light which might attract the attention of his pursuers and make with all speed for the passage through the breakwater.

The boy pulled his cap over his eyes. The wind whistled in his ears; from the arching prow of his sampan came the splash of waves against the planks. Soon another sound, louder, deeper, caught his attention. It was like the pound of a surf against a windward shore. Of course—the breakwater! They were approaching that long rocky jetty which, extending from shore, enclosed the inner harbour. The sampan turned to the right in a wide half circle, sped along for several hundred yards, and finally veered west through the passage.

They were in smoother water now. Through the darkness glittered the riding lights of the ships at anchor; the gleam of their portholes traced silvery paths on the surface of the water. Overhead stretched the arch of the Milky Way; and lower down and ahead was reflected the glow of Yokohama. Stuart's gaze swept the harbour. Where was the other sampan? Suddenly he gave a start; his fingers closed on the edge of the roof. Passing along the hull of the nearest steamer and blotting out her portholes was a shadow that merged into the surrounding obscurity. On the instant he knew that a sail had slipped between him and the ship.

"There it goes!" he cried. "Swing her more to the right!"

The Japanese leaned on his oar. Their frail craft

tilted as she veered on her new course. The sail flapped sluggishly for a second, then bellied out in the breeze again. On they swept in pursuit.

Stuart dropped to his seat. "Get as close as you can," he urged, peering round the sail at the man in the stern-sheets; "then pull up to the wharf alongside her."

"Yes, mister. My boat ver' swift."

At the words the boy gave a relieved sigh. Evidently the man understood. It was soon apparent to him, however, that the fleeing sampan was swift also. She rounded the black bow of the steamer and disappeared beyond. When his own boat reached that point he thought for a moment that he had lost his quarry. At length, by the lights at the steamer's accommodation ladder, he discerned the vague outline of the skiff racing shoreward. It was a large sampan with two men at the oars; it carried a lateen sail patched with a pale square of canvas.

"Straight ahead!" Stuart sang out. "We'll head her off from the docks."

In the offing lay a warship, doubtless Japanese, and toward this his sampan now moved through the calm water. The fugitive boat had vanished in the darkness near the warship's stern.

Through Stuart surged a thrilling sense of the chase. The man in the other sampan must now be aware of the pursuit; it would not be alone a question of the speed of their respective boats, but a matter of wits as well. Expectant, the boy leaned over the roof. He must not disappoint Captain Jarvis in this effort to track down the criminal!

Gazing about he saw that he was in the midst of innumerable ships at anchor in the harbour. To his immediate left rose the black hull of a tramp steamer, probably British; and far to his right lay a brilliantly lighted passenger liner. The warship was behind him now. He was sailing toward a two-masted brig which lay with sails furled, her anchor chain tugging at her bow. It was entirely dark here; no glimpse of the other sampan could be seen.

"Which way, mister?" The boatman spoke in his sibilant tone.

"Straight ahead," Stuart flung back at him. He was making a guess; he had no idea of the course taken by the pursued boat.

Five minutes later a flush of triumph spread over his cheeks when he caught another glimpse of the fugitive passing between him and the lighted deck of a small passenger steamer. It was still making for shore. Presently it dissolved in the night to one side of the vessel. Upon coming abreast of the spot he found that a dark stretch of open water lay beyond; perhaps half a mile farther on winked the string of lights along the Yokohama water front.

Where was the sampan? Was it still fleeing in the night toward the wharves? Stuart strained his eyes ahead. His own little boat was now faintly illuminated by the reflection of the steamer's lights. Abruptly, to one side of them, a shot cracked out. There was a soft tearing of the sail as the bullet ripped through the matting. The Japanese dropped to the flat bottom near the stern.

"No, mister—this enough!" he whispered, a tremulous note of fear in his voice.

Stuart sank to the thwart behind the deck house. "Get her out into the darkness! I'll douse this light, too—then they won't know where we are."

He waited until the reflection of the ship's lights had receded behind him, then he rose and, stretching his arms across the deck-house roof, opened the tiny door of the brass lantern. The oil flame guttered and flared in the night breeze. With a quick movement he took his cap from his head and pressed the cloth down upon the oily wick. Darkness closed around him.

"We're all right now," he whispered to the boatman. "Go a little to the left toward that tanker over there. The shot came from that direction."

Somewhat reluctantly the Japanese leaned on his oar. The sampan careened on its side. Eagerly Stuart listened. From the deck of the passenger steamer in the rear voices drifted across the water. The waves beat against the prow of the skiff; the sail creaked and groaned. As they swept on toward the dim outline of the tanker with its funnel rising from the stern he became aware that other small boats and sampans were plying between the docks and the ships at anchor. The chug-chug of a launch sounded behind him, and soon the red and green lights of a military motor boat passed in the gloom, headed for shore. Two sampans, emerging from the darkness ahead, went by with measured strokes from the oarsmen seated in the sterns.

A gasp of dismay escaped the boy's lips. The nearer he came to the water front the more numerous these boats would be—a better chance for this fleeing sampan to lose itself in their midst!

After a brief interval his skiff glided under the stern of the tanker. Stuart gave a start. The shadowy outline of a sampan was close against the steel sides of the vessel. As he swept past, he observed, high above, a dark form slip over the rail to the after deck of the tanker.

Stuart flung a whispered order back to his boatman. "Stop! This is the one." In the deep shadow of the steamer's side he distinguished a sail patched with a square of lighter colour. "Ask those sampan men if they have an American passenger—or if he has gone aboard the tanker!"

The Japanese swung his boat around; the sail flapped in the light breeze. A flow of guttural sounds came from the Japanese, answered in low tones by two of his fellow countrymen in the other skiff.

"No, mister," his boatman informed him a moment later; "these men say they got no passenger. They look for someone to go 'shore."

Stuart quickly reflected. The two Japanese were, of course, paid to put him off the scent. The man for whom he searched had climbed up a rope to the tanker's deck in the hope of avoiding capture. It might be the mate, or the chief engineer, or even the boatswain. Could he get aboard and investigate?

Pondering the best course of action he looked up at the ship. Above the black stern rose an after house with the funnel slanting up from the centre. Somewhere on her decks the fugitive was hiding—and only a glance at this man was needed! Impatiently he watched the sampan with the mended sail slowly draw out from the tanker's side, the two men rowing near the stern. There was no need to search that small craft; he was positive he had seen a man slip up to the deck above.

"Go close to this ship," Stuart ordered his boatman. "I'm going aboard."

"Yes, mister. I wait?"

"Yes—I'll be right back."

His skiff grated against the plates of the hull. Feeling in the dark along the riveted steel, his hands soon came in contact with a rope that trailed overside. He gripped it firmly, felt it hold his weight, and then like a sailor climbed upward, hand over hand. When his head was level with the bulwarks he reached over the edge and pulling himself up, jumped to deck.

He stood beneath an awning stretched between rail stanchions and deck house. Through an open passage lined with cabin doors he caught a glimpse of the opposite rail. As he considered his next move a seaman came round the corner near the taffrail.

"Whatcha doin' here?" the man demanded, stopping short in evident surprise.

Stuart hastily rose to the occasion. "Did you see a man climb aboard here a second ago? He's running from the police."

"Naw. I didn't see no one. An' what's more this ain't no place for you. Get off this ship—see?" There were distrust and annoyance in the man's tone.

"But this fellow is escaping," the boy remonstrated. "Let me look round your deck anyway, won't you?"

"Naw, I won't. I'm watchman here, an' if you don't beat it *pronto* I'll call the officer o' the watch!"

"Just give me ten minutes to look around," Stuart pleaded. "You come with me."

"Sure—I'll come with you, all right! I'll knock you overboard—see?"

The boy's gaze, roving the deck, abruptly stopped short. The figure of a man was scurrying forward in the gloom along the spidery grating that ran from the stern to the midship structure. "Look!" Stuart cried. "There he is now!"

With a muttered oath the watchman stepped forward. "I didn't see that blighter. But maybe he belongs here."

"No, he doesn't. I'm sure that's the fellow!" He spoke with conviction; yet so dark was the deck of the tanker that he had caught only a momentary sight of the running figure—and there was nothing about that form to distinguish it from any of the three men he suspected.

"Come on," grunted the watchman; "we'll take a look-see for'ard."

Stuart hurried after the seaman along the narrow walk which ran above the innumerable hatches of the oil tanks. In an alleyway abaft the wheel house they were met by one of the ship's officers. "Look here, watchman," came his complaining voice, "some strange bird just climbed overside into a sampan. I'm certain he wasn't a member of our crew."

"Yes, sir. He's running from the police. This here kid just came aboard an' told me, sir. Is the fellow gone?"

The three hung over the rail. Stuart could see only the dim shadow of a boat gliding shoreward. In dismay he realized that his man had eluded him, outwitted him. Doubtless the sampan had been ordered to go around to the other side of the tanker to await the passenger there.

He turned to the two men with a word of thanks. "I'll try to overtake him in my boat, seh. Sorry for this trouble." He swung about and ran aft.

With a glance over the rail to make sure that his sampan was still there, he slid quickly down the rope and dropped upon a thwart. "Hurry," he urged. "The fellow is gone. Get round to the opposite side."

A sense of futility came to him when he reached the leeward side of the tanker. Other sampans were moving to and from the shore; and the one with the square patch on its sail was now, no doubt, hopelessly lost in the confusion of the harbour.

"You go back to your ship?" the Japanese asked.

"Go back? No—we'll go on to the docks. We may find him yet."

Three hours later, tired and depressed, he returned to his ship. After paying the boatman he climbed the ladder to deck. There he discerned Captain Jarvis sitting in the darkness of number two hatch, still watching the accommodation ladder.

"Any luck, Alabam?"

Stuart went toward him. "I'm sorry, seh. He got away."

"Well, it was only a slim chance, anyway." The captain motioned him to a seat on the hatch. "That was their second attempt," he murmured, "and more daring than their first. When will they try again?"

CHAPTER XV

ANCHORS AWEIGH

THE SS. *Nanking* was scheduled to sail at noon the next day, but twelve o'clock found her still riding at anchor outside the Yokohama breakwater, with her decks deserted.

All that morning Captain Jarvis and Stuart had supervised the work of a group of coolies who hoisted, from a lighter moored alongside, great rolls of steel netting up to the forward deck. By the time the netting was stowed aboard only a few of the crew had returned from their night ashore. Stuart hung over the rail, watching each new arrival; he was searching for an expression of guilt or nervousness which might betray the man who had fired at Captain Jarvis. Two members of the Black Gang staggered up the accommodation ladder and lurched to their forecastle, where they threw themselves fully clothed into their bunks. The carpenter and the donkeyman were ferried unconscious to the ship by a sampan man, who immediately raised his voice for help; his fares were unable to navigate the steps to deck. Stuart went to their aid. Several others presently returned in a group, and were able to help one another to bed.

At one o'clock a hurried call from the American Consul informed Captain Jarvis that five members of the crew of the SS. *Nanking* were in jail as the result of a fight in a water-front café. The necessary money was sent, and the men were brought aboard an hour later. An S O S arrived from Toppy and Swede Jorgenson at two-thirty. The captain received the scrawled message from the hands of a Japanese ricksha runner; immediately such a torrent of oaths burst from the ship's master that the little Japanese grinned in delight. Toppy claimed that he and the Swede had been caught taking snapshots of a Tokio temple; they were arrested as spies and held at the central police station until their identity could be proved.

At three o'clock Shark Bashford and the chief engineer came aboard, arm in arm and singing boisterously. Soon after, the radio operator crept up the ladder, white and ill. Bill Sanderson, the steward, was carried to his cabin by two maudlin and sympathetic firemen who had picked him up at the American bar. Wu Sing arrived, voluble with excuses; but he was silenced by the captain's crisp remark that only four men aboard ship were able to eat, anyway, and those four had been so busy carrying the crew to their bunks that there was no time left for a social dinner hour. Wu, blinking impassively, hurried to the galley. At four o'clock Tony the Wop stepped from a sampan and turned on unsteady feet to assist Singapore Sam, whose face was taped and bandaged as if from a fistic encounter. "I hadda hold up the honour of the old U. S. A.," Singapore Sam, stumbling along the bulwarks, explained to Stuart. "I showed 'em who ruled the sea—an' the lan', too!"

Stuart gazed after the reeling seamen in dismay. Since noon a doubt had been stirring in his mind as to the value of the impression which these American seamen left behind them in Japan. He sighed with new comprehension. Wu Sing only had returned completely sober. At least half the crew now lay in their bunks in a drunken stupor. Others were either loudly proclaiming from the forecastle entrance the delights of Tokio or were berating the whole Japanese population for their unfriendly reception ashore.

As another sampan approached Stuart leaned over the rail, eager to see if the boatswain was coming aboard. It was Toppy and Swede Jorgenson, however, who staggered up the steps. The Swede waved a pocket kodak to prove the truth of their story, while Toppy clung to his comrade's arm, his little mouse-like face impudent and grinning.

"Gawd strike me bline," whispered the cockney as they lurched to deck; "there's the Ole Man over there starin' at us. Shut yer marf, now, Swede; lemme do the talkin'." He winked slyly at Stuart. "Yer missed a bloomin' good time, Alabam, by not goin' ashore."

The two seamen, clinging to each other, navigated a zigzag course toward the forecastle. Halfway across the deck Captain Jarvis blocked their way.

"What have you hidden under your coat?" he inquired casually of Toppy.

"Jus' dungarees, sir," the little cockney hiccoughed. "I thought—as 'ow I'd better buy——"

"Let me see them!"

"Wot!" Toppy's eyes grew wide in apparent surprise at this order. As the stern gaze of the captain remained focussed upon him, he fumbled under his coat and brought forth a package. "Ain't this a 'orrible end ter a perfec' day?" he mournfully sighed.

Captain Jarvis tore off the newspaper wrapped about the package, and disclosed a tin of Russian vodka. "Canned firewater! I thought so. You've brought plenty aboard inside yourselves without adding this." He tossed the can over the bulwarks.

Toppy gazed after it with an expression of intense pain upon his thin face. "Swede," he muttered, tottering to the rail, "we ain't 'ad nothin' but bloomin' bad luck ever since yer took those blarsted pi'tures. Throw that black box over, too."

Swede Jorgenson drew himself up. "Yah—it's bad luck."

The kodak followed the can of liquor into the water. Then, arm in arm, the two comrades went their reeling way toward the forecastle.

As Captain Jarvis walked aft, Stuart crossed to the discarded newspaper and picked it up. It was an American paper printed in Tokio. The boy, so long out of touch with the world of events, eagerly scanned the headlines. They comprised news of the civil war in China. The Nationalists were advancing upon Shanghai; the city was certain to fall. Nanking would be captured next. The northern troops were falling back in disorder with the Cantonese in pursuit. The International Settlement was preparing for a siege; English, American, and French gunboats were rushing to its assistance.

Stuart read with new interest now that he was nearing the scene of warfare. A missionary had been killed in Shantung; the American Minister was demanding a strict accounting from the Nationalists. Stuart turned the page. His eyes caught a familiar note: Army and Navy News. He gave a start. A name had leaped at him from the page. Breathless, he read:

Major Stuart Ormsby, United States Marines, formerly stationed at Washington, D. C., is proceeding to Shanghai on the transport *Château-Thierry*, which is bringing two thousand marines. Major Ormsby is well known in the East, having been stationed at Manila and Peking. . . .

The paper dropped from Stuart's nerveless hands. His father! And on his way to Shanghai! A cold sweat broke out over the boy. When the old tramp steamer tied up at her dock on the Woosung would his father be near, in the American cantonment, perhaps?

At the thought Stuart felt his pulse leap with joy. He forgot for the moment his own reason for leaving the States, his own disgrace at the Academy; he only remembered his father's smile, his expression of pride at his son's achievement in entering West Point. Almost immediately, however, came the full realization of his present position. He recalled the tall, stern figure of his father standing in Grand Central Station, and his own sense of panic. Could he face that older man now? Call on him—thus?

A tide of pain washed over the boy's bronzed features. His only clothes were blue shirts and seamen's dungarees; penniless, shabby, uncertain, his hair shorn by the inexpert hands of Toppy, he would present a deplorable figure beside the correct and immaculate Major Ormsby.

"Oh, Alabam! Come up and take over the wheel—we're pulling out."

The words of the captain pierced through his daze. "Yes, seh," he stammered. "Yes, seh."

At five o'clock, with the boatswain, two seamen, and a coal passer left behind, the *Nanking* weighed anchor and steamed for Uraga Strait. Seven days ahead lay Shanghai.

CHAPTER XVI

STUART MAKES A DISCOVERY

NOT until two nights had slipped astern were all the members of the crew able to take over their regular watches. Stuart and the morose and sleepy quartermaster, who had relieved each other every two hours at the wheel, were then given a day off; their places were taken by Toppy, Swede Jorgenson, and Singapore Sam.

By midafternoon the increasing heat drove the boy from his bunk. After a salt-water shower in the washroom he dressed and came on deck with a galvanized-iron bucket in one hand, his laundry in the other. Seating himself on a box in the scanty shade of the forecastle, where he could glance across the bulwarks, he went to work with soap and water on his socks and underwear. The ship was steaming through the Inland Sea beneath a cloud-banked sky. Off the starboard beam the Japanese mainland rose like an immense garden of flowers and shrubs. Green islands slid past. Fishermen in sampans moved slowly out of the freighter's course.

As Stuart bent over his bucket of suds Wu Sing emerged from the port alleyway and came toward him. Perched jauntily on the cook's shoulder was his pet monkey.

"How's Ming?" Stuart asked, looking up.

At the mention of his name the little creature slipped to deck and lurched on all fours to the boy's side. Stuart patted him affectionately; Ming showed his teeth in evident enjoyment.

Wu's yellow face broke into a smile. "Ming likee you, boy." He nodded approval. "The captain," he added, "tellee me he want see you when you wake up."

"Is the skipper still on the bridge?"

"No—he sick in his cabin."

Stuart walked aft with an oppressive sense of foreboding. The captain ill! That was a blow he had not anticipated. He found Captain Jarvis dressed and stretched on his bed. The man's whole body lay in an attitude of utter languor. His face, beneath its tan, was strangely pale; beads of perspiration stood on his brow. Though his eyes were tired and care-worn they gleamed with unusual brilliance.

"Sit down, Ormsby," he said in a listless tone.

"Nothing wrong, I hope, seh."

The captain's mouth twisted in a wry smile. "For two days I've been feeling sick. Well, I've suspected ever since their last attempt at Yokohama failed that something like this might happen. Somebody has been trying to poison me."

"Poison!" There was sheer horror in Stuart's voice.

"In Moji," resumed the man tonelessly, "I intend to lay in a supply of food for myself."

"It's the cook then, seh?"

"I don't know. Wu cooks most of my food, but the steward serves it."

"I've never thought of the steward, seh; he acts so dumb."

"One can't be sure of appearances, Alabam. I've just been looking into Tod's notebook which you found in the crow's nest. Bill Sanderson, it reminds me, has been on this ship for the last four voyages. I don't trust him —but in any case I shall eat no more food served either from the galley or the steward's pantry. I take my meals, however, with the chief engineer and the first officer—and perhaps one of them is responsible."

"With Shark Bashford!"

"Yes. But I'll eat alone after this—in my cabin."

Stuart moved uneasily. In vain he tried to throw off the sense of impending doom that weighed him down. "You've heard from Tod, seh?" he finally asked.

"Not yet. He was to radio only in case of necessity. We'll pick him up at Moji, though. That's why I wanted to see you." He wiped a hand across his forehead. "No one but the officers will be allowed to land at that port. I'd like you to follow the mate if he goes ashore there. He'll be sure to go to Sotoko's—probably a tea house— to meet his accomplices. Find out who is there—and look for Tod, too. Will you go?"

"Oh, yes, seh. Just let me know what to do."

The captain spoke in a lowered tone. "After Bashford leaves the ship, we'll get a sampan for you on the

Q. T. and let you slip ashore. If I were to go myself, it might arouse suspicions and defeat our plans."

Stuart looked anxiously at the captain. "And you, seh. Are you safe?"

Captain Jarvis smiled grimly. He clenched his hand, and the knotted muscles showed beneath the sleeve of his white shirt. "Do you notice that I'm locking my doors again? And no more food from the galley! I'm taking every precaution. To-morrow I'll have the deck crew start putting up that steel netting across the companionways as a barricade to the cabin deck, then the whole superstructure up here will be safe from sudden attack. All freighters and passenger ships have found this necessary when going up the Yangtse."

"But that won't protect us from an inside attack."

"No. We've got to watch that." He paused, a meditative look in his eyes. "I can't make out what they're up to. The thought that it might be illegal gun running threw me off the track. There are two cases now in the Federal courts in San Francisco against American cargo carriers for that crime. Machine guns were discovered packed in barrels of flour. But I've searched our holds carefully; there's no ammunition aboard."

Stuart looked up quickly. "Couldn't you force one of these men to tell, seh? Either the cook or the steward must know. Why don't you arrest them both?"

"I'm just waiting to catch them red-handed in some treachery—then I'll shove them into the brig.— Hush!"

A knock sounded on the door.

"Who is it?" called out the captain.

"Axin' yer pardon, sir," came a cockney voice from the passage, "the steward says 'e'd like ter see yer. 'E's so sick 'e cawn't move 'and or foot."

Captain Jarvis turned a startled glance to the boy. Without a word he rose from the bed and opened the door. "You say the steward is ill?"

Toppy stood there solemnly nodding. "Yes, sir. 'E says 'e's gettin' worse every minute, an' 'e'd like some medicine."

As the little Londoner moved away, Captain Jarvis, closing the door, swung about with a lithe movement. "The net is drawing tighter, Alabam! We're getting somewhere! Now we'll watch Wu Sing." He hesitated; his face lighted up. Under his close scrutiny, Stuart received the impression that those unusual eyes bored into his very soul. "I've got it," the man exclaimed. "This is our chance to put a watch directly over the cook. If Bill Sanderson is sick, we can turn his work over to you. How'd you like to act as pantryman?"

"Fine, seh."

"Very well, then. You'll take care of my cabins and bring my meals from the steward's pantry. You'll have to serve the chief and the mate, too. But your main work will be to watch Wu Sing. Come on—we'll go see poor Sanderson."

The boy's heart beat a little more quickly as he followed this broad-shouldered captain down the passage and around to the steward's cabin. From the open door came the purr of an electric fan. The captain entered; Stuart paused in the doorway.

"Yes, sir, I've been feeling pretty bad all morning, sir," spoke up the sick man in a weak voice. He lay outstretched on his bunk beneath a white coverlet. His body jerked and twitched as if from pain. "I don't know what's wrong with me, I mean I can't understand it, sir. Last night I didn't feel very well, and this morning I've been having terrible cramps. I'm afraid I won't be able to serve your meals to-day."

"Of course you can't, Sanderson," Captain Jarvis returned. "You just stay here in your bunk and get well. Don't worry about us. We'll get along."

"But your cabin, sir—and your salads and steaks what you like so well—who'll fix them like I do? I mean nobody aboard can broil a steak like I can, sir."

Captain Jarvis jerked his head toward the boy in the doorway. "I've brought this stowaway along. We'll let him take your place until you're on deck again. Just tell him what to do."

"Yes, sir." The steward was apparently somewhat doubtful.

"Oh, he'll do all right," insisted the captain. "I'll get you some medicine now from the sick bay. You'd better have some, don't you think?"

"If you'll be so good, sir."

Stuart remained behind. He sat on a chest by the bedside while the sick man went over his duties in minute detail. Bill Sanderson was voluble even in illness. His round face showed lines of worry about the eyes and mouth; he stopped talking every now and then as a spasm of pain went through him. He groaned audibly.

Captain Jarvis soon returned with a small glass containing a clear thick liquid. "Here, take this. We can't have you left behind in the Seamen's Hospital in Shanghai."

As the sick man made a grimace of disgust over the medicine glass the boy left them. Inwardly elated that this new aspect of the situation confirmed his suspicions, he descended the companionway to the after deck. He had been right all along! Wu was the culprit for whom they searched. All that remained for them to do was to catch the cook in some act of treachery; then this sly Oriental would be trapped.

In the port alleyway the boy halted outside the galley, where the heat smote him like the abrupt opening of a furnace door. Yet in that sweltering galley the cook, dressed in spotless white, was bending over his bread board, making cinnamon rolls, probably for the petty officers' mess.

"I've been given a new job, Wu Sing," Stuart called out.

The cook turned. "You gottee new job, boy?"

"You bet. The steward is sick in his bunk, so I'm to take his place for a day or two."

Wu's yellow face broke into a broad grin. "No can tell—but that steward drinkee too muchee booze ashore. Sabbee?" He began kneading his rolls again. "You gottee good job now, boy—belly good job."

Stuart swung about and went forward to the pantry. He was determined to carry through this new assignment to the best of his ability. At noon he donned the white coat that hung in the pantry and set the table in the officers' saloon. Half an hour later the first mate and the chief engineer entered and slumped into swivel chairs before the table. They both looked up with a questioning glance when Stuart turned toward them from the sideboard.

The boy placed a salad before them somewhat self-consciously. He had opened a can of pineapple, laid a slice upon lettuce, and topped this with cream cheese which he had found in the cold-storage locker. It was his first attempt at a salad, and he was proud of the result.

"What the devil do yuh call this?" growled Shark Bashford, as he gazed in distaste at the dish. His red hair fell over his forehead; a scowl deepened the corners of his mouth. "Where's the steward, anyway?" he added.

The boy stumbled on his reply. "He's—he's sick, seh."

Mr. Rankin smiled knowingly. "Yoko was too much for him—eh, Bashford?"

The mate continued to scowl; his wide red eyebrows drew together. The two officers ate in silence for a few minutes. Behind them the electric fan purred softly.

Stuart had returned from the galley with a plate of cold roast meat when the chief engineer looked up. "Where's the skipper, young man?"

"He's sick, too, seh."

Mr. Rankin and Shark Bashford exchanged glances. The boy scrutinized them closely. The chief's stocky form and dark bearded countenance marked him as a man who ruled the engine room with a fist of iron. By Cæsar, the boy said to himself, he was mighty glad he wasn't working under that fellow! Across the white cloth the mate sprawled in his chair, his long legs outstretched beneath the table. As he bent his head low over his food he impressed one as a man of fiery temper and erratic actions but altogether lacking the cold brutality of the engineer. In any case, Stuart decided, he wouldn't care to work for long under the driving fury of either of these men.

Did he only imagine now that the mate, in spearing a slice of bread, was endeavouring to keep back a grin of satisfaction at this announcement of the captain's illness? The man's hand, covered with a mass of freckles, trembled unmistakably as he raised the bread to his lips. The boy crossed to the sideboard; his breath came faster. Was it Shark Bashford who was guilty?

"Are yuh goin' ashore at Moji, Chief?"

"Naw! These blamed Oriental ports are too dirty to suit me."

No further conversation was passed across the table. The mate soon rose and wiped his mouth with the back of his hand. "Comin' into my cabin for a smoke, Chief?"

Mr. Rankin grunted an affirmative as he hastily gulped down a glass of water. A moment later they were both gone. The boy cleaned up the cabin, then returned to the galley to discuss the next meal with the cook.

At five-thirty that evening he again served chow to the two officers. Scarcely a word was said in his presence. Wu Sing also gave him no cause for suspicion. When Stuart went above to the captain's cabin with a glass of milk and a meat sandwich the master of the *Nanking*, swinging about in his chair, regarded him inquiringly.

"No news, seh," Stuart announced.

"Keep your eye peeled this evening, Alabam. We tie up at Moji to-morrow."

"Yes, seh. Feeling better, seh?"

The captain nodded. "I'm laying low here just to quiet everyone's suspicions. Let 'em think they've got me running before the wind. But I'll be fit as a hawser in the morning."

Toward eight o'clock, when the day's work was finished and the table set for breakfast, Stuart, coming into the alleyway, spied the cook disappearing up a small inner staircase that led above to the boat deck. The boy stood for a moment pondering. The ship had quieted down for the night; the passageway was empty. Wu Sing, he knew, was berthed in a cabin opposite the galley. Then where was he going now?

Stuart followed. Entering the door to the stairway he

heard the soft scuff of slippers climbing above. Eager to carry out the captain's orders he tiptoed after the Chinese.

When he came out under the stars the boat deck was deserted. A cool breeze blew from the south. He crossed to a stokehole ventilator and, halting, looked about. A dim glow shone from the wheel-house window. Just abaft the ventilator rose the ship's funnel, from which issued a steady hissing breath. To starboard the lifeboat lay in its cradle; and on the after edge of the little deck stood the radio shack, its dark bulk pierced by gleaming portholes. The Chinese cook, Stuart told himself, had entered either the wheel house or the radio shack.

In the darkness the boy moved silently aft until he drew up before the door of the wireless cabin. From within, voices came to him low yet distinct.

"Sure I'll send it." It was Sparks of the wireless speaking. "Didn't I put the last one through all right?"

The reply carried a cool note of authority. "Very good, young man. Send this at once."

Stuart gave a start. That voice! Whose was it? Certainly not Wu Sing's, for there was no trace of pidgin English; rather was it the clear enunciation of an educated man giving orders to a subordinate.

Sparks spoke again, quietly, "You want me to get the same station?"

"Yes—Shanghai."

Shanghai! A shiver of dread went through Stuart. All during the voyage that name had been sounded like the recurrent knell of an impending doom. The closer the old tramp came to the China coast the more sinister grew its import. Over the boy swept the swift conviction that the final events of this mystery were about to occur. This unknown person in the radio shack would disclose the secret of the problem. With fast-beating heart he stood on tiptoe and gazed through the porthole.

At what he saw a breath of sheer amazement escaped his lips. The radio operator sat at the table before his instruments, his face half turned to the visitor. And leaning toward him, proffering in one long yellow hand a roll of bills, was Wu Sing, speaking in faultless English

CHAPTER XVII

THE RADIOGRAM

THE instant realization that it was Wu Sing who stood there conversing in the voice of a cultured gentleman, that it was Wu Sing who was dispatching secret radiograms, sent Stuart's thoughts whirling. His own suspicions were justified! The Chinese cook must be the leader of this conspiracy aboard the old tramp freighter; in all probability he was also guilty of those attacks upon the captain's life. But now he was caught—caught in an underhanded attempt to transmit a message without the knowledge of the captain. Stuart, with a sense of elation, told himself that he had now only to get possession of one of those messages and his evidence would be complete. Those communications would no doubt reveal the hidden motive for the mysterious happenings aboard the *Nanking*.

At the sudden opening of the door of the radio shack Stuart slipped back into the deep shadow of the starboard lifeboat. There he crouched, peering forth with eager eyes. He clearly discerned the white form of the cook pass forward and disappear down the companionway. When the boat deck was again quiet Stuart stole round the wireless cabin and flung open the door.

197

The radio operator glanced up from his instruments in startled surprise. "Want something?" he asked, a barely perceptible tremor of fear in his voice.

Stuart closed the door firmly behind him. The boy's jaw was squarely set, his eyes flashed in anger. "Yes," he articulated slowly, "I've got something to say to you."

"Shoot then, kid. I'm busy." The young man's slender fingers shoved a folded paper beneath his radio call book; then, swinging about in his chair, he took the receivers from his ears.

Stuart stepped forward; his hands were clenched at his sides. "Oh, I'm well aware, Sparks, that you're busy to-night—busy sending secret messages for Wu Sing."

For a moment Sparks stared at him in amazement. His eyes widened, his cheeks grew pale. "What—what do you mean?" he stammered.

"Mean? Just what I say. You've been sending messages for the cook, messages that may endanger the captain's life."

"Aw, cut this stuff, kid! Pipe down." The radio operator rose and stood with one hand resting on his table. "You got me all wrong—see? I never did anything——"

"Oh, you didn't? Well, I saw you through the port taking money from Wu Sing." There were both scorn and disgust in the boy's tone.

"Don't bother me. I'm busy, can't you see?" He dropped to his seat and, swinging round to his desk,

with his back to Stuart, began fingering the antennæ
throw switch.

Stuart moved forward to the table. Sparks, he knew,
was endeavouring to maintain his composure in the face
of this unexpected attack, was striving to find an explanation which had not yet come to him. But Stuart
was prepared for this. He leaned over the table and
spoke in a tense voice.

"Sparks, I'm not sure whether or not you know all
the trouble we've been having aboard this tramp. The
first mate and his gang are trying to get rid of Captain
Jarvis; three murderous attacks have been made
against his life. Are you going to help those men? Are
you throwing in your lot with those blackguards?"

The young operator's hand trembled as he rested it on
the transmitter. When he looked up Stuart saw that
his face was working spasmodically. "Listen, kid; I
didn't intend to do anything to hurt the skipper. He's
too good a sort for that. All I was doing was sending a
few messages about a shipment of silk from Shanghai—
that's all."

"A shipment of silk!" Stuart laughed drily. "Maybe
you think that's what they're about—but I know better.
If you were so sure that those messages were harmless,
then why did you take a hundred-dollar bill as a bribe
from Wu Sing?"

Sparks leaned over the table, his head hidden from his
accuser. "They weren't hundred-dollar bills," he said
in a low voice; "they were fifties."

Stuart felt a thrill of triumph go through him at the man's confession. But as he gazed down at that bowed head before him a swift feeling of pity, of commiseration, swept away his anger. Sparks was evidently a fellow who did not go deeply into his own acts; he was apparently willing to send Wu Sing's messages and accept the money without once questioning his own sense of right and wrong. Stuart saw at a glance that the young man had not realized the seriousness of this affair. It was obvious, too, that he was not yet closely allied with the cook and the mate.

When Stuart again spoke his voice had lost its ring of scornful accusation; it carried instead a hint of friendliness. "Listen, Sparks—if you're not yet in league with these men take my advice and keep clear. You're running into dangerous waters. Now act like a man! Come with me to the captain's cabin and tell him what you know. Take him copies of those radiograms."

Sparks turned a twitching face to Stuart. "And if I do?" he questioned.

"You'll be O. K. with the skipper then. If you don't —you'll have to take the consequences."

"But I promised Wu——"

Stuart cut him short. "Who comes first on this ship —the cook or the captain?"

"I know—I know!" His voice trembled with emotion. "I've pulled a bonehead stunt. If I turn over these messages to the Old Man, the Chink will probably knife me in the back." Slowly he got to his feet. His fingers slipped the folded paper from beneath the call book. "I'll come," he added in a whisper.

The boy nodded. "All right, Sparks. Don't worry. But you'd better also bring along copies of Wu Sing's other messages."

"I threw them overside. Wu made me promise to do that."

"Never mind, then. You probably remember what they were about?"

Silently Sparks nodded.

"Come on." Stuart led the way.

When he knocked upon the door of the captain's cabin, he waited impatiently while he took in with sympathy the pale, set face of his companion. He heard the key turn in the lock; the door swung back, revealing Captain Jarvis standing on the threshold.

"Oh, it's you, Alabam!"

"Yes, seh. Sparks and I wanted to see you, seh."

The captain stood aside to let them enter. "Have a seat. Now, what's up?" He looked at them inquiringly, and Stuart noted that his body seemed to have dropped its former languor; once more he was the captain in command.

"It's Sparks, seh," Stuart brought out; "he wants to tell you something about Wu Sing."

"Oh, I see." Captain Jarvis turned his searching eyes upon the huddled figure of the radio operator on the settee. "Well, Sparks, out with it!"

"Yes, sir." Sparks gazed at the rug on the floor; his

hands twitched on his knees. His throat moved with a convulsive effort. "I—I didn't mean to do anything—disloyal, sir. I sent some messages for Wu Sing."

Captain Jarvis stood with his hands thrust into his trouser pockets. "Messages? Was there anything underhanded about that?"

"Only that he paid me, sir—paid me good money not to let you know."

"Who did you send them to?"

"To someone in Shanghai, sir."

"Shanghai!" Captain Jarvis brought out the word with a quick intake of breath. He took a step forward. "Where are they? Have you copies?"

Sparks looked up; his lips moved tremulously. "I—I've got the one he gave me to-night—but the others I destroyed."

"Let me see it."

Sparks handed over the folded paper. Captain Jarvis spread it out in his hands and silently gazed at it for a full minute. "What were the others about, Sparks?"

"The same thing, sir. Just a shipment of goods."

"And you thought that these messages that Wu Sing paid you so well to transmit were nothing more important than they appeared to be?"

"I wasn't sure, sir."

"You weren't sure! Did you notice who they were for?"

"Some Chink. That's all I noticed."

"This is to be forwarded to Chang Tso-lin!"

"Yes—I think that's the name they all went to."

"And you don't know who he is?"

Sparks looked up, evidently nonplussed. "No, sir."

"Then I'll tell you. Chang Tso-lin is the war lord who rules all of northern China. He is the general who is fighting to keep the Nationalist troops from advancing upon Shanghai. Do you think he is interested in a shipment of silk?"

The radio operator shook his head. "I don't know, sir."

Captain Jarvis threw a glance of exultation at Stuart, then he turned back to the young man on the settee. "Listen here, Sparks; you've let yourself in for trouble —how serious this is you probably don't realize. Now, I'll give you one chance. Go back to your job and say nothing about this to Wu Sing. If he gives you any more messages, take them. Say you'll send them as he desires. But instead, each and every one comes to me. Understand?"

"Yes, sir." Sparks rose with a relieved sigh. "I didn't know they were important, sir—really I didn't. I'll do anything you say."

"That's all right." The captain waved him to the door. "I can trust you?"

"Yes, sir. Oh, yes, sir. And here's the cook's money. I don't want it."

"Put it on the desk there. We'll give it back to him later. Remember, don't let him know by your manner that you're not sending his radiograms. Have any replies come?"

"Not one, sir."

"Very good, then. That's all." Captain Jarvis opened the door to the passage, and Sparks slipped out, a woebegone figure of humiliation.

"Well, that's that!" muttered the captain, closing the door and turning to Stuart. "You did some good work there, Alabam. I suppose you got friendly with the radio operator and he told you about this?"

"Hardly that, seh. I followed Wu Sing above and saw him pass that message with some money to Sparks. And the cook's pidgin lingo is all a sham, seh, just as you suspected. He speaks better English than most of the men aboard this ship."

The captain nodded, a smile on his lips. He was looking intently at the message in his hand. "This, of course, is a secret code. On the surface it tells of a shipment of silk to be sent to the States; it's all a matter of freights and cargoes and tonnage. I doubt if I'll be able to work this out, because it probably translates into the Chinese."

"But you've got Wu just where you want him, seh," Stuart eagerly put in. "You'll lock him up?"

"No—I don't think so." The words were uttered with thoughtful deliberation. "We've got a watch over the cook; and you have certainly proved that you know your business. I believe we'll gain more if Wu Sing doesn't know that we suspect him. He may walk right into our trap. When we drop anchor off Moji to-morrow you'll go ashore there as we planned. That's where I expect to find the key to this whole problem—and it's up to Tod and you, Alabam, to bring me that knowledge. Are you equal to it?"

Stuart's face lighted up in eager anticipation. "You bet I am! Just let me get to Sotoko's Tea House! I've got a hunch, seh, that things are going to happen there."

CHAPTER XVIII

SOTOKO'S TEA HOUSE

AT MOJI, the next evening, Stuart went ashore alone. Seated in a sampan with a Japanese boatman at the tiller he watched, across the widening water, the round lights of the freighter recede behind him.

Dusk had already fallen when the *Nanking* dropped anchor in Moji's landlocked harbour and began discharging cases of gasoline into a small lighter alongside. Only two men went ashore—Shark Bashford and the chief engineer. Five minutes later the captain threw a Jacob's ladder over the taffrail, and Stuart let himself down into a waiting sampan. He had his orders; he was eager to set foot on land, eager to explore this foreign town.

From his seat in the stern of the little boat he now looked ahead. To one side of the bamboo sail he could see the lights of Moji rising from the dark shore. Halfway up the hillside they dwindled away in the velvety blackness, and beyond them rose the sombre outline of a range of mountains against a star-strewn sky. When the sampan drew up at a wooden jetty, Stuart sprang out with an order to the boatman to wait for him.

He moved noisily across the gloomy water front, his body still swaying with the motion of the ship. How his shoes resounded on the pavement! A feeling of enchantment and adventure surged through him. On land again —and in Japan! By Cæsar, this was worth the whole voyage out! As he entered a cobbled street that mounted the hill he looked about him in wonderment. Flanking both sides were stores still open for business, and above these were the homes of the shopkeepers. In the doorway of one of the stores the boy halted. A paper lantern, hanging from the ceiling, threw a greenish light upon dried fish stacked on a counter, upon shelves lined with canned goods. The proprietor came toward him.

"Can you tell me where Sotoko's Tea House is?" Stuart asked.

The little Japanese showed his teeth in a broad smile. "Yes, mister," he replied in broken English. "Turn corner at next road. You see Sotoko's there—but it is not good place."

Stuart turned away with a word of thanks.

"Many sailor go to Sotoko's to-night," continued the Japanese.

The boy whirled. "You mean two men just ahead of me?"

"No, mister. One hour ago a seaman jus' same you— young fellow—stop here and ask where is Sotoko's. I show him." The man lowered his tone. "I tell you jus' same I tell him—Sotoko's is not good place."

Stuart brushed aside the advice and left. This third seaman must have been Tod. He'd better hurry.

Up the little crooked street he continued; it was well lighted here and very clean. Suddenly the impression seized the boy that he was the object of many eyes. He looked about him quickly. Two Japanese fishermen passed, wearing straw raincoats. A shopkeeper and his family went by in kimonos and wooden *getas*. The clackety-clack of their footsteps sounded above their low laughter. Stuart watched them draw up at a doorway and exchange their wooden shoes for grass slippers before entering the house. Save for them the street was deserted. In a dwelling directly opposite, an open bamboo screen gave him a view of the interior, where a family sat upon the floor around a tiny charcoal stove; a steaming pot of food sent a faint aromatic odour to his nostrils. He stood there, with mounting interest watching them eat with chopsticks by the light of paper lanterns. Their merry chatter drifted out to him. Observing this peaceful scene Stuart shrugged. He mustn't imagine things. He climbed on.

Above him a new moon rode high in the heavens. Its pale glow impressed him with a sense of unreality. Surely this was a make-believe fairyland through which he walked, and these Japanese in their gay kimonos sitting in becoming attitudes on the floor were merely wooden figures in a puppet show.

Presently he turned into a road that led to the right.

Just ahead, the lighted doorway of a tea house invited customers to enter. He paused in the shadow before the doorway and surveyed the interior. His heart dropped in disappointment when a quick glance assured him that no American seamen were within. Instead he noted that a dinner party was in progress; seated on pillows on the thick matting of the floor, three men in kimonos of sombre hue and two women in brilliant robes were being served by a young girl.

Stuart glanced about him swiftly, then stepped to the door. An elderly Japanese woman with an elaborate coiffure came toward him. "Yes?" she said with an intake of breath.

"Is this Sotoko's?" he questioned.

"Yes—this is my café, known to sailors from Frisco to Singapore. You wish a meal, perhaps?" Her voice was harsh; her knowledge of English amazing. She was an old crone of a woman; her piercing eyes and protruding teeth gave her face a sinister expression that repelled the boy.

"I—I was looking for some sailor friends of mine," Stuart continued. "I understood——"

"Oh, they eat in the garden. You will find them there." The long trailing sleeves of her black kimono moved in graceful folds as she made a gesture toward a vine-covered gate a few feet farther along the street. From her expression the boy realized she feared he might enter the café in his Western shoes, to the detriment of the heavily matted floor.

He hung back. "Not ship's officers! A seaman like myself."

Sotoko shook her head. "No—only three Americans are here."

"Just bring me some tea and almond cakes," Stuart said, turning toward the gateway.

He swung back the bamboo lattice and looked about. Stone lanterns dimly lighted a path which wound between pools and rocks where grew ferns and purple lilies. Following the direction of this path he saw that it led to a group of small houses with low overhanging roofs and paper walls through which a yellow glow filtered into the surrounding darkness. Cautiously Stuart moved forward. He crossed a bridge like a half circle which spanned two connecting pools, where mullet and carp were swimming. As he drew near to the first tea house, he moved more slowly. The sliding panel, drawn back at the front, revealed a deserted interior with a lantern burning above a low table in the centre of the room. Two dwarfed pines in blue jars stood like sentinels at the entrance.

Suddenly voices struck Stuart into immobility. The sound issued from another tea house only four or five yards along the path. Quickly he stepped back into the shadow of a camphor tree. He heard Shark Bashford's high voice raised as though in maudlin humour with his companions. Of course they were drinking, Stuart told himself—probably warmed *saké*, the potency of which he had heard the men discussing in the forecastle.

Let them get hilariously drunk; in such a condition they would be less likely to discover his presence. But where was Tod? A flash of apprehension went through Stuart at the thought that his friend had possibly met with disaster on the train from Yokohama; for certainly it would be no small task to escape the eyes of the boatswain. And if the oiler had come here, where was he now?

Stuart silently pondered the situation. Crickets chirped near him; frogs croaked from the mullet pond. Fireflies made darting points of brilliance around the shrubs. A sense of peace hovered over the garden and brought to the waiting boy a feeling of quiet security. Surely it was impossible that in this secluded retreat men could be planning death or dishonour to the captain aboard the *Nanking*.

Abruptly he turned, his gaze directed upon the tall form of a Chinese coming down the path from the café. This new arrival was dressed in Chinese clothes of black brocaded silk; the boy noted that he carried himself with a proud air of assurance. This was no coolie; in his own country he was doubtless a person of authority. As he came to the second tea house the man paused, drew back the sliding door, and surveyed the interior.

"Lee Chong!" It was the first mate's voice, loud and jubilant.

In the brief interval during which the tall form of the Chinese was silhouetted in the doorway Stuart noted a small satchel in the man's hand. When the panel slid to, obscuring the scene within, the boy was overwhelmed by a desire to peer into the room. Slowly, and with the utmost caution, he crept closer. He circled a rocky eminence of ferns and felt his way in the deep shadow of the bamboo fence until he came to the rear of Shark Bashford's tea house. The paper wall was luminous. Voices came to him distinctly.

"Yuh got the money, Lee Chong?"

"Yes. You are prepared to carry out your part of the agreement?"

"Sure we are! We got everything fixed. Yuh don't have to worry, Lee Chong."

"You are helping a great cause. Our troops will soon be in Shanghai. The government at Peking is tottering —and then, when it falls, your help will be remembered."

"Oh, we're satisfied, Lee Chong. Ain't it the truth, Chief?"

"It sure is," replied the chief engineer.

"And your captain agrees, too? We must not run into trouble with the American gunboats on the Yangtse Kiang." There was a faint note of distaste in the voice of Lee Chong, as though he disliked this company which the exigency of war had forced upon him.

"Oh, sure," agreed the mate. "The skipper is all fixed."

"On the Woosung River, then."

"Sure thing—yuh don't have to go into that here.

Somebody might be listening. Just let me count this coin."

Stuart moved close to the wall. Remembering his pocket knife, he opened the blade with trembling hands. With the greatest care he inserted the sharp steel into the paper where it joined the wooden corner. A second later he was gazing into the room. His eyes opened wide in amazement.

Onto a small table the Chinese, Lee Chong, was pouring handfuls of gold coins which he took from the black bag on his knees. The boy flashed a quick glance round the room. Three men were there—the mate busily stacking the coins, the boatswain gazing with covetous eyes, the chief engineer swaying, half drunken, with a *saké* cup raised to his lips. But where was Tod? A sudden conviction swept over him that his friend had been discovered. In vain he attempted to throw off this thought. Perhaps Tod was now hiding in the garden. Stuart stepped back and turned to survey the shrubbery.

He found himself looking into the beady eyes of Sotoko.

"Hai!" The woman's shrill cry pierced the stillness.

Stuart tried to brush past her, but her fingers, strong as steel, gripped his wrists. "You listen?" she hissed. "I thought you came for no good, so I follow. Help— help!" Her voice rose to a scream. "I hold this fellow!"

The boy heard a sudden rush of feet within the house, the sliding of a panel. He flung himself backward against the wall to escape those clutching hands. There was a tearing noise in his ears; he stumbled, lost his balance, and fell through the paper wall into the tea house.

Flat on the floor he lay. Terror stricken by this accident, he cast a frightened glance round the room.

An oath came from Shark Bashford. "Get him, Boats!"

As the boy struggled to his feet, muscular arms closed about him. "Keep quiet, youse little devil," snapped the boatswain. "We got youse—youse can't git away now."

Stuart faced the men, pale, defiant. Lee Chong stood to one side, as though taking no part in this affair. Shark Bashford was stooping over the table to shield the coins. "Well, Boats," he said, looking up, "this is the second one we got, huh?"

The second! Stuart felt his heart drop like a leaden weight. Tod was caught, then, just as he had surmised. And here he was, sent by Captain Jarvis to help, to discover the secret of these men, and he, too, was now a prisoner. He had failed—failed dismally. Why hadn't he been more cautious—why hadn't he suspected Sotoko!

"Yeah," grunted the boatswain. "The blamed oiler followed me all the way from Yoko—no foolin'. An' I didn't know it till to-day. Whatcha think o' that?" He laughed deep in his throat.

Shark Bashford turned his angry eyes on the boatswain. "Shut yer jaw! Yuh acted like a jackass, lettin' that oiler foller yuh here. An' now we got this kid to deal with."

"Leave him with me." It was Sotoko speaking in her rasping voice. So quietly had she entered that Stuart was surprised to find her now standing in the doorway, her waxen face aglow with malice.

The boatswain tightened his grip on the boy's arm. "That's the only thing to do, Bashford," he agreed. "Sotoko will hold them till the ship pulls out, then let 'em loose. They can ship home from Nagasaki—if they're lucky."

"No, you won't!" Stuart cried. "I'm going back to my ship."

"Yuh little fool," broke in the mate, "don't yuh know when yuh're in luck? Better keep off the *Nanking*."

"Sure," agreed the chief, his voice thick with liquor. "You oughtn't to butt in like this. Can't we have a quiet little meal without someone spyin' on us! What do you mean, anyway?"

"What do I mean?" The boy raised his head; his eyes flashed in anger. "That's just what I'd like to ask you. You and Shark Bashford have been trying to get rid of the captain ever since the beginning of this voyage. You're up to some dirty work. When you explain that, we'll let you alone. But not till then."

The boatswain heaved a deep sigh. "It ain't no use, Bashford. Youse can see for yourself he's gotta be left behind."

"Yeah," said the mate with an uneasy glance at Lee

Chong, who stood impassively to one side, his face a mask of tranquillity. "This kid's got us all wrong. Ain't it the truth, Mr. Rankin?"

"Sure it is." The chief engineer nodded agreement.

Stuart laughed shortly. "I suppose," he nervously broke in, "that you know nothing at all about the attempts on Captain Jarvis's life?"

"Naw, we don't. An' what's more——"

The mate abruptly swung about at the sound of running footsteps on the garden path. Sotoko turned and, stepping aside, allowed Singapore Sam to enter.

The seaman was out of breath; his face was flushed and excited. "I got news for you, sir," he announced to the mate. "The third just sent me to tell you."

Shark Bashford quickly rose and stepped to the door. "Just a minute, gentlemen," he said.

Singapore Sam followed him outside and Stuart heard the murmur of their voices, low and tense. A moment later the mate returned alone. At the expression of triumph on his face, Stuart trembled. The man was radiant; the muscles of his face twitched with suppressed emotion.

"Everything is O. K.," he declared exultantly. "Let's finish our business, Lee Chong. And you, Boats, take care o' that boy. Just throw him in with the other kid. Sotoko will show you. We'll be ready to sail by midnight."

CHAPTER XIX

"WHO ARE YOU?"

"WHERE are you taking me?" The question came, muffled, from Stuart's lips.

"Aw, youse don't have to worry, kid. Sotoko's got a nice little place where she hides sailormen who wanta disappear for awhile. Youse just gotta stay there till we weigh anchor—then youse can beat your way to Yoko or Nagasaki and ship out on another boat."

Stuart was too depressed to ask more questions. With the boatswain gripping his arm, he was forced to follow the Japanese woman across the garden. They entered a door in the rear of the café, went down a long passage dimly lighted by a single lantern, and turned into another corridor. There Sotoko, coming to a halt, pointed to a brass ring in the floor boards.

"Open!" she said.

The boatswain nodded to Stuart. "Go ahead, Alabam, an' lift up that trapdoor."

Stuart knelt and pulled on the ring. The door swung up on its hinges without a sound, disclosing a dark cellar below.

"Now git down there like a nice li'l' boy," ordered the boatswain. "Sotoko will let youse out to-morrer."

217

"Then I'll go straight to the police!" Stuart challenged.

Sotoko's wrinkled face broke into an evil grin. "And do you think they will believe you? I will say you were drunk—like all sailormen who come to Moji."

As the boy looked about him helplessly, his mind desperately striving to evolve some method of escape, the boatswain gave him a sudden shove. He half fell, half stumbled down the ladder-like steps into the obscurity of the cellar. A faint odour of sour wine assailed his nostrils. Above his head the trapdoor thudded into place; impenetrable darkness closed about him

"Alabam!"

Stuart leaned trembling against the steps. Tod's well-known voice, coming from a far corner of the cellar, brought with it a feeling of infinite relief. "Where are you?" Stuart called. "Can we get out?"

"Stay there, Alabam. I'll come—I know this place now."

Footsteps drew near; his friend touched his arm. "We can't get out," Tod said close to him. "I've been going over this hole for the last hour. It's a wine cellar with several locked rooms filled with *saké* and *Ng Ka Py*. But how'd you get here?"

Stuart somewhat ruefully related his experiences. "We've only got to wait until morning," he ended hopefully.

"But the *Nanking* will be gone then!" There was fierce resentment in Tod's tone. "That will leave Captain Tom on board alone with those cutthroats. We've got to get out before dawn, Alabam. Otherwise we'll be too late."

"Tod, she's sailing at midnight.'

"How do you know?"

"I heard the mate say so. Singapore Sam brought him a message telling him to get back at once."

"That's strange," Tod murmured thoughtfully. "Captain Tom told me in Yokohama that he was scheduled to lie overnight in Moji and shove off at dawn."

Stuart sat down on the steps. "What brought you here, Joe Macaroni?"

"Oh, I was a big fool," Tod confessed in a resigned tone. "You see, I went to the station in Tokio and waited there in the hope that one of the officers would take the train for Moji. I expected Shark Bashford to come—instead, the bo'sun appeared. I followed him in the crowd to the ticket window and heard him pay his fare to Nagasaki. Then I bought a ticket for the same place and got into the coach behind the one he was in. And who do you think I saw sneaking round the station, peering in at the bo'sun?"

"The chief engineer?"

"No—Wu Sing! I spotted him through the train window before we pulled out. He saw the bo'sun, I'm sure; but I don't think he discovered me there, too."

"So you followed Boats all the way here?"

"You bet I did. And everything was all right until

to-day. This morning in Nagasaki he went to a big hotel and met a Chinese there. I don't know who the Chink was, but you could tell he was a person of some importance."

"Lee Chong," Stuart put in.

"Perhaps. I didn't hear his name. Anyway, after the bo'sun left the Chinese at the hotel he took a tram for the station—and then I lost him. I decided that it didn't make any difference, though, because he was probably on his way to Moji. So I came here on the first train; I thought I'd pick him up again. Well, I did—but he saw me first." Tod paused as though he disliked to face the memory of that incident.

"The bo'sun," he explained, "must have got a glimpse of me in Nagasaki, for he had this Sotoko take me along that passageway above. Before I knew what was happening Boats darted around a turn in the passage and knocked me through this trapdoor, which was open. By thunder, he was hostile! I fell all the way down these blamed stairs. I tell you I was sore in more ways than one. Anyway, I'd been here an hour before you were so kind as to come and keep me company." Tod laughed, but there was very little mirth in the sound.

The minutes dragged by while the two boys discussed every possible means of escape. The mate and his gang, they knew, must now be on their way to the ship. Perhaps they were already aboard. Soon the anchor would be drawn up through the chock to the forecastle head, the propeller would beat the waves astern, the

Nanking would steam through the night for Shanghai. By morning she would be hull down upon the horizon of the China Sea. And they would be left behind! It might be weeks, perhaps even months, before they learned what had happened aboard the old tramp. Suppose, too, they were not fortunate in getting a berth out of Nagasaki. In that case they might have to face the degradation of a beachcomber's life in these Oriental ports of the Pacific. Their talk dwindled with long moments of silence intervening.

Presently footsteps in the corridor above made Stuart look up. "Someone's coming, Tod," he whispered.

"That's Sotoko! I know her step."

"It can't be more than an hour since I was put down here," Stuart said, puzzled. "We weren't to be let out until morning. What can it mean?"

Tod touched his shoulder. "Maybe, Alabam, it's Captain Tom!"

Both boys rose quickly to their feet. The door above slowly lifted, and the dim rays of a lantern filtered into their prison. Two faces peered down at them—Sotoko's, her protruding teeth showing in a grim smile, and Wu Sing's, like an impassive mask.

"Wu!" Stuart cried out the name in surprise. Stepping back out of the pale light he pulled Tod with him.

"Come up at once," said Wu Sing in his faultless English, which he evidently donned like a robe for certain occasions. "I learned of your presence here just in time. We shall find it necessary to make all speed to our ship."

"What—what do you want?" Stuart demanded. "We're taking no chances, Wu Sing!"

Wu laughed pleasantly. "Don't you see that I am your friend? It happens that this Sotoko is known to me—yes, well known." He glanced at the Japanese woman, who visibly quailed under that direct gaze. "She is sincerely eager to do my government a good turn. Come up at once! Our ship sails at midnight."

Tod stepped forward. "Come on, Alabam," he insisted. "We've got to trust Wu now."

Somewhat reluctantly Stuart followed his friend up the steps. Once more in the passage, he scrutinized Wu narrowly. Somehow the Chinese appeared changed. He now wore his shore clothes of dark-blue satin. The poise of his head, the aristocratic carriage of the body marked him as a person of superior position in his own country. And Stuart, observing Sotoko, saw on her wrinkled face a look of respect and fear. She was unmistakably grovelling before this man.

As they went down the corridor past the café, Wu spoke to the woman. "The Peking government will notify Tokio of your assistance. And you need a good word or two—eh, Sotoko?"

Sotoko bowed low in obeisance. A moment later the two boys stepped out under the stars again, where three jinrickshas were drawn up in the roadway. Stuart gazed at these man-drawn carriages with interest.

"Get in," ordered Wu as he climbed into the first.

The boys clambered eagerly into their respective rickshas. Stuart, sinking back in his narrow seat, was almost pitched into the road, for the runner, without warning, had picked up his shafts and started after the other two carriages. The man ran easily; the two wheels bumped and jolted over the cobbles, so that Stuart sometimes found himself in the seat and sometimes in the air. By Cæsar, this was surely a dangerous method of travel.

The rickshas turned the corner into the narrow street and swept down the hill toward the water front. Desperately the boy clung to the handles at each side of his seat. To the best of his ability he was trying to remain in his ricksha and at the same time ponder the problem of Wu Sing's identity. Who was he? He had followed the boatswain to the Tokio station; he had sent the secret code messages. Why? The Peking government, the boy knew, was friendly to Japan, who looked with alarm at the successes of the Nationalist troops which were sweeping up from the south with their cry of a new China, a free China unfettered by any foreign concessions. If Wu Sing sympathized with the Peking government then he must be an enemy of Lee Chong, who was assisting the southern troops; an enemy, too, of the mate and his gang aboard the *Nanking*. How much had Wu been able to discover of the plans of Shark Bashford?

Stuart was still mulling over the problem when the

rickshas reached the water front and drew up at the jetty. The boy descended to the ground with a sigh of thankfulness. Wu tossed some coins to the panting runners. "Come quickly," he said to the boys. He led the way across the wooden pier. "The ship may leave at any moment."

The three jumped into a waiting sampan, the boatman shoved off, the sail swung aloft. As the breeze sent them out into the dark harbour, Stuart anxiously looked ahead. The lights of the *Nanking* still shone a mile offshore.

Tod, seated next to Stuart in the sternsheets, raised his voice to Wu in the stem. "Wu Sing, you saw Captain Jarvis before you left?"

"Yes," the Chinese answered. "He had just sent Toppy ashore for a doctor. The steward was much worse." Wu remained silent for a moment, then he resumed, "To-night I decided that I must throw in my lot with you and the captain. He is reliable? He is not to be bought?"

Tod's tone, when he replied, expressed irritation at this slur on the captain's honour. "Captain Jarvis is fighting these men! The first mate and the bo'sun and the chief are all against him."

Stuart leaned forward intently. "Wu Sing," he asked, "who are you?"

The Chinese replied without hesitation, "I am an agent sent out by the republic at Peking. We are fighting with our backs to the wall against this uprising of southern China. I represent Chang Tso-lin." He uttered the name of the northern war lord with reverence.

"And the mate?" Stuart pursued. "Do you know what he is planning?"

"Not fully. My government suspected collusion between the officers of this ship and a Nationalist general; I was ordered from San Francisco by our consul there to get aboard the *Nanking*. Last trip we went to Singapore, not stopping at Shanghai. When we returned to Frisco the captain was left ashore and his place taken by this Captain Jarvis. I was afraid that he was in league with the mate. Now I know better. When we get aboard ship we shall go to the captain's cabin and lay all our cards on the table—then perhaps we shall learn enough to defeat these enemies aboard our ship."

Stuart's thoughts flashed back with new understanding to that foggy night on the forecastle head. He pressed his hands in excitement against his knees. "Have you ever heard of wreckers' lamps?" he hastened to ask.

"Wreckers' lamps!" Tod echoed. "What are they?"

Wu Sing did not reply. The sampan was drawing close to the *Nanking*. On the fore deck men were moving about at the top of the accommodation ladder, evidently ready to hoist it up to the deck.

"Wait!" called Wu across the intervening water. "We come aboard."

The prow of the sampan grated against the little platform. Wu sprang out, and the two boys followed him.

Stuart, in the lead, hastened up the steps. His heart beat madly. It was good to be back on the tramp freighter, to feel the decks once more beneath his feet. Why, the old *Nanking* was almost like home!

Suddenly he stopped short and stepped back against the bulwarks. Shark Bashford blocked his path. In the light of the electric globe Stuart saw the mate eye him in shocked amazement.

"Where'd yuh come from?" the man blurted out.

Wu and Tod moved to the boy's side. "I find them in street," the Chinese explained in a suave voice, "so I tellee them to come back with me."

"Oh, yuh did!" The mate's eyes narrowed to points of fire. "Well, I'm not sure that these boys will want to stay aboard—now. Yuh two better go ashore an' find another ship to the States."

Tod raised his head defiantly. "No, sir—we're staying here with the captain."

The mate threw back his head and laughed. "I'm the captain now," he said.

Stuart stared unbelievingly. He saw Shark Bashford slowly take his officer's cap from his red hair, saw him wipe the visor with his sleeve. Then the boy realized the implications of that movement. On the first mate's cap was sewed a master's emblem.

Tod's hands trembled. "What—what do you mean?" he gasped. "Where is Captain Tom?"

Shark Bashford's wide mouth slid into a grin of triumph. "Your former captain has slipped his cable and left the ship. That's what. I dunno where he is. I guess he got afraid—huh?" He hesitated and glanced round at the boatswain, who stood near by. "Get in that anchor, Boats! We're pulling out."

Tod, with blazing eyes, stepped forward. "If Captain Jarvis has gone ashore, Mr. Bashford, you've got to wait for him!"

"Oh, he's gone for good," the mate returned, "an' now I gotta take command. Ain't it the truth, Chief?"

The chief engineer came into the circle of light from the starboard alleyway. "Yes, sir. Jarvis took all his gear with him, too. There ain't none of his clothes left in his cabin."

"Hear that?" exclaimed the mate. "He disappeared from the ship when we was at Sotoko's. The third mate got worried an' sent Singapore Sam with the news. —Well, this is your last chance. Are yuh goin' ashore?"

Wu touched Stuart on the arm. "We stay here," he whispered.

Tod swung about, and in his eyes Stuart saw a look of deep entreaty. There was no need to voice that desire. Stuart understood. "We'll stay, Joe Macaroni," he said.

Shark Bashford raised his voice to the third mate on the bridge. "Get under way at once! Chart the course for Shanghai. . . . *Full speed ahead.*"

PART FIVE

WRECKERS' LAMPS

OVERDUE AT SHANGHAI
July 10

SS. *Nanking* — 4258 tons; Trans-Pacific Steamship Co. Last reported off Tsungming Isl. in Yangtse River with First Mate Bashford in Command.

North China News.

CHAPTER XX

FLOOD TIDE FOR SHARK BASHFORD

THE freighter *Nanking* pushed her blunt nose through Shimonoseki Strait and, swinging southwest, steamed by slow degrees down the Latitudes. On the second day out, the heat of the China Sea became almost unbearable. The volcanic sun beat down upon the steel decks with a pitiless intensity that drove the night watch from their bunks in the stifling forecastle. The men, cursing the sea, the ship, and the whole ship's company, climbed the ladder to the forecastle head, where they threw their mattresses upon the deck; there beneath the awning they lay, naked and sweating, through the long afternoon in a vain endeavour to sleep.

Men of the engine-room gang dragged their weary

legs up the iron ladders and across the grating to the ice-water fountain outside the galley, and then dared only to moisten their parched lips with the cooling liquid which gushed forth like a miracle to soothe them. Firemen, stripped to the waist, their glistening bodies black with coal dust, staggered up the stokehole fiddley to gasp for breath in the alleyway. Before again going below they would pause to gaze wistfully ahead across the metallic surface of the sea toward that hazy horizon which never drew near.

Shark Bashford, acting as captain, drove the deck crew at times with relentless fury and at times secluded himself in the master's cabin for hours on end. The boat-swain, however, saw that the men did not lag in their work. The barriers of steel netting covering the ap-proaches to the upper decks were now nearly com-pleted.

Upon this work Stuart toiled during the broiling hours in the sun; for Bill Sanderson was well enough to take his place once more in the pantry. "I'm glad to be back on the job," he told Stuart. "I mean it seems good to be able to make a dessert again, even though it ain't for the captain, but Shark Bashford ain't as bad a skipper as you might expect. But I kinda liked Captain Jarvis because, if he hadn't sent ashore at Moji for that Jap doctor, I wouldn't be here now."

Stuart was too preoccupied to listen; he was trying to figure out Shark Bashford's motive for continuing this work planned by Captain Jarvis. If the former mate was

really in league with the Cantonese troops, then why
was he barricading the superstructure against an attack? The boy wondered if this could be a blind, if these
apparent precautions were only an effort on the man's
part to divert suspicion from himself. In any case, if
disaster met the *Nanking* on her passage up river to
Shanghai, the person in command would have to face
an inquiry conducted by the insurance underwriters and
the officials of the Trans-Pacific Steamship Company.

By an order from the chief engineer Tod Moran's
watch had been changed, with the result that the two
friends had little opportunity to see each other. On the
second afternoon out from Moji Stuart, desperate and
lonely, came to a firm resolve: he would descend into the
engine room and attempt to get in touch with Tod.
Choosing the evening mess hour as the best time to
carry out this decision he waited impatiently until the
Filipino mess boy had beat his triangle. When the men
had taken their accustomed seats at the long table he
slipped down the alleyway to the engine-room entrance
and stepped quickly over the high casing.

Immediately he was enveloped in a blast of fiery air
that swept up to the open skylights. With one hand on
the steel rail, he walked carefully along the grating and
down the steep ladder to the middle platform. Here the
terrific vibrations smote his ear drums with a deafening
throb. He made his way past the cylinder heads and
swung down the next ladder to the steel plates of the
flooring, just over the bilge. The third engineer stood

at his station between the gauges and the telegraph dial with its indicator at *Full Speed Ahead*. The man favoured Stuart with an inquiring glance, but the boy passed by without a word.

Near the ventilating fan he paused to look about for Tod. His friend was nowhere to be seen.

The third engineer raised his voice above the pulsing tumult. "Hey, whatcha doin' down here?"

The boy whirled. "I'm looking for Moran. Isn't he on duty?"

"The oiler's in there." The man jerked his head toward the stokehole.

Stuart went forward and, stooping slightly, entered a dark tunnel between two boilers. He could hear the steady draught of the furnaces, the sharp scrape of a shovel on steel, the clang of an iron door. A moment later he came out into the stokehole, a narrow, high compartment running athwart the ship.

A flaming light dazzled his eyes. On the black bulkhead forward leaped the grotesque, long-legged silhouette of a stoker shovelling coal into the fiery mouth of a furnace. Stuart turned to gaze with pity at the three men who toiled like moles here in the depths of the ship. They were stripped to the waist; their shoulders glistened with sweat and coal dust; their muscular chests rose and fell as they breathed heavily in the stifling atmosphere.

A stocky Chilean, feeding the two fires beneath the starboard boiler, touched the forced draught check on number one furnace and, swinging open the square iron door with the tip of his shovel, sent coal flat upon the glowing clinker within. Before the port boiler a giant Negro leaned exhausted against the bulkhead; in the centre, near Stuart, Tony the Wop was breaking up the clinker of number three furnace with a long slice bar. To escape that scorching heat which flared outward, the boy stepped back beneath the ventilator opening. Flames licked hungrily at the edges of the furnace doors. The draught roared. Shovels scraped the steel plates of the flooring.

Stuart momentarily forgot his search for Tod as he took in with curious eyes this first glimpse of the fire room. By Cæsar, how could these men stand it here in this sweltering hold encased in steel? Four hours of work like this each watch—four hours of toil and torture! Thank heaven, he was on deck and not a member of the Black Gang.

Turning to the Italian, he shouted above the roar of the draught, "Is the oiler around here?"

Tony the Wop looked up from his pile of coal. Before replying he took a dirty sweat rag from his belt and mopped his face and chest. "Yeah," he explained at last, "he go up feedley to geet ice water for us. He ver' good fellow."

At that moment a black flood of coal came clattering down a chute in the bulkhead and spread in a cone-shaped pile on the plates. The unseen coal passer, at work in the dim bunker compartments above, had sent a barrow of fuel sliding down to the stokehole. A cloud of black dust rose toward the two electric lights which burned behind wire screens.

A friendly hail from the fiddley caught Stuart's attention. He looked up. In the deep obscurity he could discern a familiar figure descending the lowest of the three perpendicular ladders which led down from the starboard alleyway. It was Tod. He was carrying a bucket in one hand.

Before the oiler reached the last rung the firemen eagerly crowded about the ladder. "Don't drink too much," Tod warned the Italian.

Tony smiled wearily. "Me? I don' geet seeck. The chief tell me, 'Tony, you the bes' stoker we got. Your fires always clean!' Jus' take look at those fires o' Chile Con Carne. Huh!" He snorted in disgust, then raised the bucket to his lips.

Stuart saw the Chilean fireman regard Tony with a look of deep hatred, and the boy realized with surprise that these men evidently took the condition of their fires to heart.

"Hello, Alabam," said Tod, drawing Stuart forward. "Come on into this tunnel where it's quiet. It leads up to the bunkers."

Halfway up the incline the two halted. In the gloom beyond, the black figure of the coal passer went by, wheeling his iron barrow.

"How'd you get down here, Alabam?"

"Through the engine room. I thought I'd chance it while most of the men were at chow. I only hope the chief isn't around."

"They're trying to keep us from seeing each other," Tod blurted out in anger.

"I know it. Any news?"

"Not a thing."

"Joe Macaroni, how do you figure out the captain's disappearance?"

"Something has happened to him—something terrible!"

"Then you don't think he went ashore at Moji?"

"No. I wish I could, though; then I'd feel he was safe." Tod lowered his voice. "I managed to talk with Wu Sing to-day. He told me to lay low—not to let any of the officers see me near the galley. He doesn't want them to suspect that he's a secret agent of the Peking government. . . . Hush!"

Tod raised his hand in warning as voices, loud and wrathful, issued from the stokehole. Stuart looked down the incline. The chief engineer stood near the centre boiler, pointing accusingly at the gauge above his head.

"Don't you swine see that the steam's down ten points?" the man shouted. "Git busy! Can't I even eat a meal without havin' an anvil chorus callin' me below?" His voice was lost in the sudden scrape of shovels and the clang of furnace doors.

Stuart put his hand on Tod's shoulder. "Joe Macaroni, are those stokers apt to side in with the chief?"

"With that slave driver? I should say not! They hate Mr. Rankin."

"Then there are some men on board who are loyal to Captain Tom?"

"You bet there are. But they don't know one another as the mate's gang does. And they're hardly the kind of men you could rely upon in a pinch."

"If we could get them together!" Stuart mused.

"Here, get back," Tod warned in a whisper. "The chief's coming this way."

Stuart moved swiftly up the incline toward the 'tween decks. Before he could reach the bunkers the voice of Mr. Rankin called out after him, "Hey, you birds! What d'you think you're doin' up there?"

Tod turned. "I was just taking some ice water to the men," he explained.

"Ice water!" The chief laughed in his beard. "Hell! Who told you to waste your time doin' that? These swine drink too much, anyway. That's why they've been sick since we left Moji. Come back here."

"Yes, sir."

Tod led the way down to the stokehole. Mr. Rankin, in blue jumper and overalls, met them with a leering smile. "Oh—ho! So you're talkin' to your stowaway friend, eh? Gettin' quite chummy, I s'pose, talkin' about your officers."

A crash of coal sliding down the chute interrupted his speech.

"My friend has never seen the glory hole before," Tod went on to explain.

"Aw, pipe down. I'm on to you two. Lookin' round to find the former skipper, ain't that it? Well, young man, he won't appear as suddenly as you did outa nowhere. Yeah, that was a nice way to set the crew a-talkin'—comin' aboard at Moji just as if nothin' had happened. Where was you, anyway?"

Tod looked the man in the eye. "I imagine, sir, that Mr. Bashford could tell you about it."

"Like hell he could! He don't know any more than I do. You get back to your oiler's job *pronto*, see?"

"Yes, sir."

As Stuart started to move aft with his friend, the chief put out a hand. "You just stay here a minute, kid. I want to talk to you."

Stuart stopped short. Glancing over the officer's shoulder he saw that Tod had halted in the tunnel leading aft to the engine room. With this knowledge heartening him he turned his eyes once more to the chief.

"Now, young man, I've got a question to put to you."

"Yes, seh."

"Who sent you to Sotoko's Tea House?"

"Captain Jarvis."

Mr. Rankin emitted a sarcastic grunt. "Oh, ho! So the skipper sent a boy there when he didn't dare go himself!"

Stuart bit his lip to keep back a heated retort.

"Did you know, young man, that the oiler would be there, too?"

Stuart's mind worked quickly. Should he lie? With a sudden surge of anger he decided to defy this man. "Yes, seh. I expected him there."

"Oh, you did! And where was he comin' from? Do you know?"

"Yes, I know. But Captain Jarvis is the man to question—not me."

The chief looked Stuart over with his beady eyes. "The captain? What a chance!" His face relaxed; a smile flitted across his bearded countenance. "Well, you don't belong to the Black Gang. I guess I better turn you over to Captain Bashford. I'll send him word you want to see him right away. Go up to his office at once. That's all."

"Yes, seh."

Stuart stepped to the fiddley ladder. Climbing up the iron rungs into the gloom he ran over in his mind the questions which he would probably have to answer. Captain Bashford? First mate Bashford! He'd never call that man captain. How high this ladder was! The draught of the furnaces dropped away below him. Sweat stood out on his brow. The higher he climbed, the hotter grew the ladder to his touch. Was the chief already at the speaking tube telling the mate to question him? Well, he wouldn't lie. Yet he'd better use discretion.

When finally he reached the last platform, he swung eagerly up the few remaining steps. Just a breath of fresh air! He stepped over the casing into the alleyway.

Ahead of him the door of the captain's cabin swung open. Shark Bashford stood on the threshold. Stuart's heart pounded madly. He was in for it now!

"So yuh've been explorin' the ship! Just come in here a minute."

"Yes, seh." Reluctantly the boy entered the saloon cabin.

The mate closed the door behind him. "Well, what's this the chief's been tellin' me? What was yuh doin' down below?"

"Nothing special, seh. I just went down to see an oiler friend of mine."

"Yeah—that Moran. Talkin' over the skipper's disappearance? Ain't it the truth?"

"Yes, seh."

"An' did yuh discover anything?"

"No, seh."

"Well, yuh won't. Yuh never will."

Stuart regarded the man narrowly. "What do you mean, seh?"

"Simply that Tom Jarvis has loosed his cable and gone for good. That's what. He's finished as far as ships on the Pacific are concerned. He'll probably have his master's licence revoked. But, kid, I don't know no more about him than yuh do, see?"

Under the boy's direct gaze, the man's eyes never wavered. Stuart drew a deep breath. Could it be possible that the mate spoke the truth? If the first officer did not know what had happened to Captain Jarvis where could he and Tod turn for evidence?

"Naw," went on the man, solemnly nodding his red head. "An' it sure ain't my fault if the skipper deserts his ship. I'm goin' on with his work aboard, anyhow, puttin' up those barricades in case we have trouble goin' up the Yangtse."

Stuart's mind leaped to a quick conclusion. This must be the reason the mate had called him in here. In the event of an investigation no one on board would be able to report any inefficiency on the man's part. Apparently every precaution would have been taken. But was Shark Bashford clever enough to plan this? The boy doubted it. But if not the mate's, then whose mind had conceived this flawless conspiracy?

"An' remember," the man resumed, "that I am now in command of this here packet. No more sneakin' round these decks at night. No more pryin' into business what don't concern yuh. I run this ship my own way without help from anybody. Understand?"

"Yes, seh."

Shark Bashford leaned toward the boy. "If there is any more interference from the like o' yuh there's liable to be another little disappearance. Nobody would miss yuh—yuh wharf rat! Ain't it the truth?"

The boy's eyes narrowed; a misty haze obscured his vision. "Is that all, seh?" he asked in a voice tremulous with emotion.

The mate threw back his head and laughed. "Yes,

yuh can go. I got nothin' against yuh. But yuh're so damned inefficient that yuh better not plan on goin' back to the States on the *Nanking*. I gotta have real seamen."

"Yes, seh." Stuart turned toward the door.

He opened it slowly and went out to the fore deck. The sun was low in the west. At the bulwarks he stopped to look overside and breathe in deeply the cool fresh air. This, he realized, was flood tide for Shark Bashford. The mate was flushed with success, certain of victory. But after the flood came the ebb tide. Would it come in time to save Tom Jarvis?

CHAPTER XXI

A SLIP OF PAPER

THE next evening, as Stuart stepped from the salt-water shower in the seamen's washroom, he found Tod looking down at him from the entrance.

"Hello," said Tod. "Haven't seen you all day." He spoke in a depressed and weary manner.

Stuart, dripping wet, a bath towel in his hand, climbed to deck to dry himself in the cool of the evening. His feet were thrust into straw slippers, for the steel plates were still hot from the heat of the day. "Any news?" he asked.

"Nothing."

Without further words the two moved to the bulwarks. Twilight was deepening; off the port beam a half moon rode low in the luminous blue of the sky.

"We're already in the Yangtse River," Tod remarked.

Stuart drew a deep breath. Since early morning he had noticed that the old tramp was ploughing ahead through yellow water, yet he knew that this great muddy river spread its silt for miles into the China Sea. There was no shore visible to indicate that they had already entered the wide mouth of the Yangtse Kiang.

244

He fancied, however, that the faint breeze blowing up from the south brought a hint of land with it, redolent of the tropics. "Then to-morrow," he murmured, "we'll be in Shanghai."

"We'll never make Shanghai!" Tod spoke with bitter emphasis. "We can be sure that Shark Bashford will never allow that."

"Not so loud, Joe Macaroni!" Stuart looked about with a nervous glance. Though the fore deck was dark and deserted, voices floated down to them from the forecastle head where the men were stretched for the night.

"If Captain Tom were here!" Tod brought out at length.

At mention of the captain's name a sudden warmth of feeling went through Stuart; as he realized how low the tide of their fortunes had ebbed, he leaned on the rail in despair. Through misty eyes he watched the sluggish water scud along the blistered flanks of the ship.

"I've looked in every cranny I could find," Stuart said in a low tone. "I can't think what more to do. At every turn I make there's always the bo'sun or Shark Bashford following me with their eyes. We're prisoners, Joe Macaroni—prisoners!"

Tod snorted. "They haven't been so busy watching me to-day. But what good has it done? I haven't discovered a thing."

"Let's go see the cook," Stuart suggested. "I'll slip into a singlet and dungarees. Wait a minute."

He was soon back at Tod's side, and together they went aft. In the starboard alleyway they met Shark Bashford, garbed in the white pajamas and slippers that he had worn for the last two days. The new master of the *Nanking* favoured them with only a beady glance as he passed into the captain's office.

Through the open door of the galley they glimpsed Wu Sing still busily at work; but fearing that the former mate might be observing them they continued aft to the open deck without attracting the cook's attention. When fifteen minutes had gone by they slipped forward again to the galley.

Wu looked up from the meat bench. "You boys hungry?" he asked, quickly going to the opposite door to glance down the alleyway. Evidently finding it clear he turned with a nod of encouragement. "Come with me. It is not safe here."

He stepped across the starboard passage and threw back the thick heavy door of the cold-storage room where beef hung on hooks from the deckhead. Pausing to switch on the lights he waited while the boys darted into the room ahead of him; then he closed the door and swung about to them with a smile. "It is better here. No one can overhear our conversation."

The coolness of the room brought a welcome chill to Stuart's face, though the odour of beef and green vegetables overwhelmed him with a sickening sensation. He looked at Wu with eager eyes. "Anything new?" he asked.

The Chinese shook his head. "It looks as if the mate were right in saying that Captain Jarvis had gone ashore. He can't be on board."

"Yet he told me," Stuart affirmed, "that he intended to stay aboard ship. Toppy said yesterday that the skipper sent him ashore to get a doctor for the steward; he didn't see him again. Swede Jorgenson was standing watch at the accommodation ladder, and he says that the captain didn't leave that way."

"He must be aboard," Tod insisted.

In the pause that ensued Wu looked at them closely. "Have these men," he said, "got rid of him—killed him, you think, while we were in Moji?"

The words, voicing their unspoken fears, struck the boys into an attitude of consternation. "No—no! I can't believe it," Tod brought out vehemently. "Captain Tom was suspicious; he was always ready for an emergency. He couldn't have been caught unawares."

"I don't see who could have done it," Stuart pursued. "The mate, the chief, the bo'sun were all ashore. The steward was so sick in his bunk that he would have died if Toppy hadn't brought that Japanese doctor. None of the ringleaders were aboard ship at the time."

"You mean," said Wu with emphasis, "so far as we know."

Stuart looked away from Tod's gloomy countenance. "Just what are you thinking about, Wu?"

"Simply that we cannot be sure of anyone. What of Singapore Sam and three or four other members of the

crew? And are we absolutely certain that Captain
Jarvis disappeared while his officers were at Sotoko's?
We have only the mate's word for it. True, you tell me
that Singapore Sam brought an important message
from the third officer; but do we know what that message was? Is it not possible that the three men returned
to the ship just ahead of us and caught the captain in an
unguarded moment?"

"It's possible," Stuart acknowledged; "but Singapore
Sam was so excited that I'm willing to believe——"

His words were cut short by a peremptory gesture from
Wu Sing. The Chinese swung about toward the door.
"Hush!" he whispered. "Someone is there."

Stuart and Tod looked at each other in apprehension.
Had Shark Bashford seen them enter the cold-storage
room and then crept down the alleyway to lock them
inside? Breathless, they listened.

There was a faint scratching at the door.

Wu sprang to the long handle, pushed it up, and
shoved his weight against the door. Slowly it swung
outward. The cook's pet monkey was dancing there in
the passage, eager to join his master.

"Ming!" Wu cried in exasperation. A low singsong
murmur came from his lips as he spoke to the little
beast in Chinese.

Ming hurled his small form into the room, rose on his
hind legs, and blinked at the boys.

"He thinks he'll get some food—a banana, perhaps."
Wu once more tightly closed the door.

"What's he got in his hand?" Tod inquired. "Look— it's a slip of paper."

"He always picks up everything he can find and brings it to me. He makes a regular garbage deposit of my cabin." Wu reached down and took the paper from the monkey's grasp. He unfolded a crumpled fragment not more than three inches wide, evidently torn in haste from an envelope. The cook eyed it blankly. "I don't understand," he murmured. "It has some writing on it."

Stuart stepped closer. As he saw the letters scrawled across the face of the paper, he felt his heart give a sudden leap. "Tod," he blurted out, "look!"

The two boys bent over the writing in Wu's yellow hand. On the paper were two names written in pencil: *Joe Macaroni—Alabam.*

Tod caught his breath sharply. "Captain Tom's handwriting!"

"Are you sure, young man?" Wu's face lighted up with sudden interest.

Tod nodded without a word. Indeed, there was no need of explanation. That hastily scrawled message was a cry for help, written by someone who was stricken down, whose only hope lay in the chance that it might reach the owners of the names and that they might understand.

"It's Captain Tom's! I'm sure of it." There was a ring of excitement in Tod's voice. "He's on board this ship—a prisoner, hidden away some place. But he's alive, Alabam—alive, and calling to us for help!"

"Where can he be?" Stuart mused. Abruptly he looked at the Chinese. "Wu, could Ming take us to the place where he found this paper?"

Wu remained silent a moment, pondering. "This may be an old note which was written perhaps days ago."

"No," Tod hastily remonstrated; "Captain Tom wouldn't have written like that. That's his handwriting all right, but it shows how desperate he is. Look at the torn envelope, the letters as large as a child's. It was probably written in the dark. He's a prisoner on board —and he's trying to get us word. He may have slipped this out of a port."

Wu knelt and took the monkey's forepaws in his hands. He spoke in a quick, incisive tone to his pet. Ming, blinking, turned his head away. Wu finally looked up. "If Ming has just found this, there is a chance that he may be able to take us to the spot. If the note is a day or two old, there's no hope. Let us see."

He placed the paper in the monkey's paw and pressed the little creature's finger-like claws around it; then, rising, he opened the door and pointed out into the alleyway. Ming glanced uncomprehendingly about for a moment. At length he lurched on all fours out of the door.

Breathless, eager, Wu and the two boys followed.

CHAPTER XXII

COMMAND

MING did not go far. He stopped short at the door just next to the cold-storage room, fumbled for a second with the crumpled message in his claws, and, crouching low, shoved it as best he could through the crack beneath the door. His actions told better than words that he was trying to return the paper to the spot where he had found it.

Stuart gave an excited exclamation. "Captain Tom must be there."

"The door's padlocked," Tod whispered. "Wu, I thought you used this bunker every day. Doesn't it contain coal for the galley range?"

"No, I use coal from the port side. This one is empty as far as I know. Because it is so near the galley we never suspected!"

"We must be certain." Tod knelt down and, taking a screw driver from a back pocket of his dungarees, tapped sharply twice on the heavy door.

Stuart, crouching tense and anxious beside his friend, felt the silence beat in waves about his ears. Then, faint yet distinct, came the answer to their wordless message: *tap, tap—tap, tap.*

Wu's voice broke in upon them. "Get into my cabin —quick! Someone is coming." He caught up the monkey in his arms.

As approaching footsteps sounded around a turn in the alley the three darted through the galley and across the opposite passage into the cook's cabin. There Wu closed the door behind them with a smile of triumph.

"A close escape," the Chinese confessed. "But I very much doubt if more than one or two men on this tramp know that the captain is hidden there. We dare not attempt to open that door now."

"But we've got to," Tod hastily declared. "Captain Tom is in need of help. We can't wait, Wu!"

The cook eyed the boy sternly. "Young man," he said, "you must have patience. That door is securely padlocked. Do you think we could open it in one minute? No—it will take time to file that lock."

"I can't wait—I can't!" Tod persisted.

Stuart put out his hand and touched his friend's shoulder. "Listen to reason, Joe Macaroni. There's somebody passing through that alleyway every minute or so. The ship won't quiet down until after ten o'clock."

Wu nodded. His eyes narrowed, his high cheek bones glistened in the light. "We'd better wait until after the watch changes at midnight."

Tod made a gesture of resignation as he dropped to a seat on the bunk.

"Wu, what's that empty bunker like inside?" Stuart

turned an anxious glance toward his friend as he put the question.

"It's a steel compartment with only one porthole. There's a ladder that leads up perhaps fifteen feet to the door in the alleyway. Anyone hidden in there might never be found—or even heard. I wonder, now, who put him there."

"I don't care about that," Tod brought out nervously. "By thunder, I want to get that door unlocked."

Stuart dropped to a seat beside his friend. "We've got to plan this carefully, Joe Macaroni. If Captain Jarvis is there—and we have every reason to suppose that he is—we must plan his escape so that no one will know. We can't allow ourselves to make a mistake now."

Wu flashed Stuart a look of commendation. "You speak wisely for so young a man," he said, seating himself on a locker chest. "Let us decide upon our actions."

Tod looked up hopefully. The three conversed in lowered tones, their heads close together. At one o'clock, they decided, they would make their effort to free the captain.

Presently Wu rose. "Now go to your bunks," he said quietly, yet in an unmistakable tone of authority. "Act as if nothing had happened. Let no one suspect! When you hear one o'clock strike on the bridge come back here. These alleyways should then be deserted."

Tod slipped out the door first, and after five minutes

Stuart followed. He reached the fore deck without encountering anyone. Under the stars the night was dark. The ship was steaming up the Yangtse Kiang; but so wide was the river that neither shore was visible. He climbed to the forecastle head, made his way amid the recumbent figures of the men, and reached his mattress next to the windlass drum. Throwing himself down, dressed as he was, he looked about him. Two men near by were discussing in lowered tones the coolness of the evenings along the Bund in Shanghai and the fine chow served at the Astor Hotel, where they'd have a real meal for a spree. Another seaman was furtively smoking a cigarette with the glow concealed in the cup of his hand. Low breathing all around told the boy that many of the men were already asleep.

Sleep, however, was not for Stuart. His brain was working madly. Was Captain Jarvis injured? Had he lain there in the utter darkness of that coal bunker without food or drink for three days? Was there sufficient air in the place to ease his suffering? With a nervous movement he rose on one elbow and glanced past the stanchions of the rail to the black river. A light was passing to leeward—some Chinese junk probably. By morning, he knew, when they left the Yangtse and turned south into the Woosung River toward Shanghai, the stream would be swarming with junks and sampans. Gunboats would be there, too—American, British, French, and Japanese, sent by their respective governments to protect the foreign settlements. With a pang he thought of his father, perhaps on one of the American destroyers.

Four bells struck on the bridge. Only ten o'clock! Would the hours never pass? A squall blew up; rain pattered on the canvas awning above his head. The men who lay near the rail rose with muttered curses and, grumbling, took their mattresses below to the fore-castle. Then six bells struck. Seven—eight bells. Midnight! Now the watch was changing.

Was Shark Bashford taking over the command on the bridge, or would he sleep in the captain's cabin and let one of the mates take his place? Twelve-thirty. The rain stopped; two members of the eight-to-twelve watch slipped up to the beds near him. The silence grew profound. Two bells struck clearly on the bridge. The watchman in the bow answered with quick strokes on the bronze bell—*one, two!* Stuart sat up.

Stealthily he rose, looked about in the darkness at the sleeping men, and then, barefooted, stole silently across to the ladder and down to the main deck. He breathed more freely now. When he came to the door of Wu's cabin, he glanced about. The dim light in the alleyway showed him that it was deserted. The door yielded to his touch. Tod and the cook awaited him with eager faces. Ming, he noted, slept atop a shelf on the wall.

Tod's face glowed with excitement. "Here's Alabam! Come on, Wu. We're ready."

Without another word the three passed quietly through the galley to the starboard alleyway. Each understood what he was expected to do. Tod, with a file and a small bottle of oil, stopped before the steel door of the empty coal bunker. Wu slipped out to the after deck, there to guard the passage, and Stuart went forward.

The boy took up his position in the darkness just outside the alleyway entrance. High above he heard the officer of the watch pacing the bridge, and at length a few words spoken to the helmsman in the wheel-house window. It was Shark Bashford's voice. Otherwise the decks were utterly quiet. Only the faint throb of the screw pulsated through the night. The watchman, he knew, must be in the bow of the ship, on the lookout for possible shoals or sand bars. Off the port bow a cluster of lights drew near, and Stuart knew that the river was narrowing here; it must be a Chinese village which they were passing on their way upstream. He waited until it had drawn abreast of them and slowly slipped astern before he walked out into the darkness and peered down the alleyway.

The door of the padlocked room was now open. Two figures emerged—Tod leading the way, and Captain Tom Jarvis walking unsteadily but apparently uninjured. As Stuart stood there watching, his muscles tense with anxiety, he came to himself with a start of dismay. Behind him footsteps sounded on the steel deck.

Remembering on the instant that he must be careful not to arouse suspicion, he walked as casually as possible into the alleyway. Tod looked about. Stuart raised his hand in a warning gesture. At once Tod quietly closed the heavy door and, with the captain, disappeared into the galley.

Stuart continued aft. When he reached the seamen's messroom he entered and sat down on the bench at the table. He was busily engaged in making a meat sandwich when the steward went by with only a glance thrown at him through the doorway.

As the minutes slowly passed he continued to sit there. Presently Wu appeared in the door, a cup of coffee in his hand. "You have a sandwich ready? Very good." He came close and whispered, "He is weak, but that is all. He needs food." He took the plate of bread and meat and turned back toward his cabin.

Ten minutes more passed. True to his share in the plan, Stuart remained there on watch. As nothing disturbed the peace of the ship he finally rose and, slipping into the port passage, went forward to Wu's cabin. He knocked softly.

The door opened. Tod greeted him with shining eyes. "We're O. K., Alabam," he whispered, closing the door. "The captain is feeling better already, though he was as weak as a jellyfish. I've told him all we know. He's ready to storm the bridge."

Captain Jarvis was seated on the bunk, finishing his meal. He glanced up at Stuart with a half-mocking smile. His face, beneath its streaks of coal dust, was pale and drawn. Stuart noted the knotted muscles of his arm; as the man raised his coffee cup to his lips, the blue snake, tattooed upon the white skin, coiled and writhed over the huge biceps. He was dressed in duck trousers and a singlet once white but now a dirty gray. "Oh, I'm all right, Alabam," he said softly. "Just let me get these hands on that mate up there in the wheel house!" He clenched his great fist as he spoke.

Wu came close to Stuart. "I suppose you are eager to learn what happened to your captain? Well, on the night that we were in Moji, someone must have hit him a terrific blow on the head as he was going down the alleyway. When he woke he found himself a prisoner in the darkness of that hole. He doesn't know who his assailant was, so swiftly came the attack."

"Captain Tom," Tod questioned, "what are wreckers' lamps?"

The captain raised his head from a basin of water in which he was washing his face. "Where did you hear of that?" There was intense interest in his tone.

"Alabam heard the mate mention it, that's all."

"Well, they are false lights put out by Chinese pirates on river bars or on the coast here in the Orient to lure unsuspecting ships on the rocks so they can be looted. Good heavens! You don't suppose—" he stood erect; his great height seemed to dwarf the little cabin—"you don't suppose that my officers are planning to use that trick to turn over the ship to the Nationalist troops?"

In the silence that followed Stuart looked with

widening eyes at the man. Was this the explanation? Was this the agreement that Shark Bashford had entered into with Lee Chong? The boy was well aware that predatory bands of marauding troops had been carrying on a guerrilla warfare along the Yangtse Kiang, a warfare fraught with as much danger to the native villagers as it was to Europeans.

"There should be help awaiting us somewhere along here," said Wu. "I sent a radiogram to Chang Tso-lin asking him to have a gunboat look out for us when we entered the Yangtse."

The captain whirled in dismay. "A radiogram! And I held it up. Wu, it was never sent."

"Then everything depends upon us. But we are ready."

"Quick!" Captain Jarvis flung out the word with an oath. "We haven't a moment to lose. If they are using wreckers' lamps the old *Nanking* may run onto a sand bar any minute now. We must be nearing the mouth of the Woosung River." He glanced hastily at his three supporters, two of them no more than youths, the third a Chinese secret agent. "We'll carry out our plan to storm and capture the bridge; but it must be done without noise. None of the crew must know yet. Listen carefully:

"I'll slip into my cabin and up the inner staircase. Ormsby, you'll go up to the boat deck and plan to enter the rear door to the wheel house. Joe Macaroni, you and Wu creep up the forward ladders to the bridge.

When I give the signal—a shrill whistle—rush the doors to the wheel house and cover the men inside. There should be only Shark Bashford in charge, and a quartermaster at the wheel. We'll get control of the ship! Is it plain?"

"Yes," Tod replied in a tense whisper; "but what of guns?"

Wu Sing moved forward. "Look here." He unlocked a chest which lay beneath his bunk and brought forth two automatic pistols and a revolver. "You take these," he urged. "I have a knife." He passed the automatics to Captain Jarvis and Stuart and the revolver to Tod. From beneath his white apron he drew a Chinese dagger with a curved blade. "I can use this in an emergency," he said with a barely perceptible smile.

"Very good," acknowledged Captain Jarvis. "Are you all ready? Remember my whistle. One at a time. Come on!"

The captain led the way. Stuart went aft to the open deck, and in the darkness of the night quietly climbed the ladder. A barricade of steel lattice work blocked his way to the cabin deck. This was familiar to him, however, as he had assisted the boatswain and Swede Jorgenson in fitting this very door across the companionway. His fingers encountered an open padlock hanging by its shackle in the crosswork of the netting. As he slowly swung back the door, the hinges grated softly, and he stopped in sudden terror; but as no inquiring voice was raised from the dark cabins near by he shut the barricade and went on. His bare feet made no sound on this hardwood deck. He circled the cabins, climbed the companionway, and found himself on the boat deck. There, in the deep shadow abaft the hot funnel, he paused. No lights now gleamed from the radio shack; the whole superstructure was utterly still. In the wheelhouse window that opened aft he saw a reflected glow of the binnacle light. In there, he knew, stood Shark Bashford and the quartermaster. Slowly he crept nearer.

He was now at the foot of the three iron steps that led up to the rear door. With his hand resting on the steel rail he waited. His heart beat so loudly in his ears that he wondered that the men within did not sense his proximity from the intensity of his excitement. Was Captain Jarvis now in his old cabin? Was he already ascending the inner staircase? And Tod and Wu Sing? They must be climbing the ladders to the bridge, waiting as he was for the whistle that would send them into action. What if one of them should make a slip, a noise that might attract the mate's attention! In vain he tried to quiet his quickly mounting pulse. Nervously he fingered the automatic in his hand.

Suddenly a whistle pierced the stillness of the night. Stuart flung himself against the door. It swung open to his touch.

At the helm stood Singapore Sam, staring over his shoulder in shocked surprise. Shark Bashford was slowly retreating into a corner near the locker; before him stood the huge form of the *Nanking's* master. The mate was fumbling in the back pocket of his trousers for a weapon.

"Hands up, Bashford!" Captain Jarvis spoke the words in a sharp tone of command. "We've got you both covered."

The door of the bridge swung outward, and Tod and Wu Sing stepped into the cabin. Tod's pistol swung up toward the mate.

"What's this mean?" Shark Bashford snarled. There was a hint of fear in his tone; Stuart saw his hands tremble as he raised them above his head.

"It means," said Captain Jarvis with emphasis, "that I'm here to take command. Quartermaster, keep her on the course. Ormsby, search the mate for a gun."

"Yes, seh." Stuart stepped forward, slipped his automatic into a dungaree pocket, and ran his hands quickly over Shark Bashford. From the man's trouser pocket he drew forth a weapon that dimly glistened in the gloom.

"An automatic, seh. I've got it."

"Good. Give it to Wu. Now, Bashford, I intend to get the truth out of you at once. Just what are you planning with this ship?"

The mate stepped back against the wall. His eyes narrowed; his mouth twisted into sullen lines. "I don't know nothing," he slowly articulated. "I got nothin' to say—see?"

Captain Jarvis spoke in a low, tense tone. "Joe Macaroni, keep your eye on the helmsman. I've———"

Singapore Sam broke in volubly. "I don't know anything about this, sir." There was a whine in his voice. "I'm just carryin' out Mr. Bashford's orders."

"Pipe down! We'll tend to you later. Tod, see that he keeps quiet."

"Yes, sir."

"Now, Bashford, I'm ready for you." Captain Jarvis lowered his weapon. His face was stern, unyielding. His eyes glittered above his high cheek bones. "You're going to answer my questions—or you won't live through it."

The mate crouched back against the wall. "No, sir. I don't know nothin' about what happened to yuh, sir. I was at Sotoko's in Moji when somebody hit yuh on the head. Ain't it the truth?"

"Ah! So you know that somebody slugged me, do you? Well, I'll strangle the truth outa you. Come here."

Under that compelling gaze, Shark Bashford quailed. Step by step he stumbled forward until he was opposite the open door to the boat deck. Stuart, taking in the man's position, mentally made a note of it. He raised his automatic again in case the mate might attempt to escape.

"You realize," continued the captain, "that I'll lock you in the brig, and to-morrow, when we reach Shanghai, I'll have you arrested for attempted murder."

"Murder! No—no!" In the mate's voice was a distinct note of fear.

"You're guilty as the devil, and you know it."

"No, sir. I'm not—I'm not! Maybe I have been

trying to clean up a little money with some other members of the crew, but I didn't try to murder yuh. I'm not guilty o' that."

"Then who is?"

Stuart leaned forward expectantly. Would Shark Bashford tell? Would they now learn who had shot at Captain Jarvis, who had murdered the former masters of the *Nanking?* He saw a look of ruthless cunning creep over the mate's face.

"An' if I tell," began Shark Bashford, moistening his lips, "will yuh see that I get off?"

Stuart turned away in repugnance from that face before him. Shark Bashford, to earn leniency for himself, was willing to confess the name of his accomplice.

"I make no promises, Bashford. But if you're not guilty of murder you'll not be charged with it."

The mate wavered. He cast a hunted look about him as though seeking a chance of escape; his eyes travelled over his shoulder to the open door to the boat deck, then across to the automatic that Stuart held, and on to the weapon that Wu kept trained on his tall form.

"All right—I'll tell." The man brought out the words with an effort, evidently realizing that there was no likelihood that help might come from his confederates at this hour of the night. "The man who is guilty—who murdered Captain Buckard trip before last and planned this whole thing—has kept well in the background. He's a sly one. Yuh wouldn't suspect him. But I'll tell."

Suddenly he broke off. A pistol shot sounded from the

boat deck. Close to Stuart, so close that he heard the whine of the bullet as it sped on its way, whizzed a shot. Shark Bashford's face took on a look of surprise and bewilderment. He staggered, swayed for a moment, while the men gazed at him, astonished. "He's—he's got me, too!" The man's lips moved silently. His hands went up to his heart. He whirled and fell to the floor in a heap.

Captain Jarvis stepped forward. "Where'd that shot come from?"

"From the boat deck, seh. It whizzed right past me."

Wu dropped to his knees beside the prostrate form of the mate. "The man we want—the ringleader—fired that shot." He looked up and spoke more slowly. "Shark Bashford will never tell now. He's been shot through the heart!"

CHAPTER XXIII

AMBUSHED

"WE'VE searched the boat deck, and there's no one there." Captain Jarvis flung out the words as he and Wu slipped into the wheel house. "Whoever fired that shot has gone below. It was a fiendish method of stopping Shark Bashford's confession. I felt sure that the mate was not the leader in this conspiracy. We have yet to discover our man. However, we haven't a moment now to lose. Alabam, take the helm! Wu, you lock Singapore Sam below in the brig."

"I ain't guilty o' nothin', sir."

"You can prove that later. Go ahead, Wu."

"Very good, sir." Wu raised the mate's automatic and pointed it at the man. "Come on, sailor!"

Stuart sprang to the wheel. "Keep her straight ahead, seh?"

"Yes." Captain Jarvis looked over the boy's shoulder. "See that dark line of shore half a mile to port? Don't get any closer. I'll be with you in just a moment."

"Yes, seh."

"Joe Macaroni," went on the captain, "we'll take the mate's body down to my cabin. After that I want you to go forward and find Toppy and Swede Jorgen-

266

son. Tell them we need their help. Then see that the padlocks are all clamped shut on the barricades to the companionways. We'll have these upper decks secure before the chief or the crew know what's up."

"Yes, sir."

With the body of the mate between them the captain and Tod disappeared down the inner stairway; Stuart was left alone at the helm. He threw back his head and drew a deep breath. The ship was theirs. They had only to keep her headed upstream till they hit the Woosung River soon after dawn; some time later they would tie up at the dock in Shanghai. In vain Stuart tried to keep his mind on the thought of their destination; always piercing through his imagined picture of the Bund or the narrow crowded streets of the Chinese city was the pale, stricken face of Shark Bashford as he fell.

Captain Jarvis presently leaped up the steps to the wheel house. "Now for the course." He stood gazing over Stuart's shoulder, apparently puzzled by something. "How long have you noticed that light off the port bow?"

"Just a minute or two, seh. It seemed to come on all of a sudden." Stuart let his gaze sweep out to the left, where the pale yellow gleam of a distant light was slowly drawing nearer.

"I don't remember that light just there," murmured the captain. Suddenly he raised a startled head. "Good heavens, Alabam, are we running into their trap? Can that be one of their wreckers' lamps?"

At once he sprang to the telegraph dial. Quickly he pulled down the indicator to *Half Speed*. Stuart felt the old tramp lose headway as she slowly nosed her way upstream against the ebbing tide. Behind him he was aware that the captain had swung about to the shelf in the rear; he could hear the man hurriedly turning the pages of a pilot book.

"There's another yellow light, seh, drawing near—off the starboard bow."

"It must be one of those islands off Tsungming," the captain jerked out. "We surely can't be approaching the Woosung yet."

Stuart swung the wheel slowly to port. His gaze was fastened upon that soft gleam which was drawing abeam of them on their left. He could make out in the darkness the half mile of water between them and the shore, the low land lying off to port. Suddenly his eye caught a long dark reach of sand ahead of them.

"Captain Jarvis!" His tone was vibrant with fear. "Look—a sand bar ahead!"

In a second the man was at the telegraph dial. The indicator curved to *Stop*, then to *Full Speed Astern*.

Stuart breathed with relief. In the stillness the two stood waiting to feel that steady vibration beneath their feet cease, and after that the quick jar as the propeller beat the water astern with a reverse movement. But no cessation came, no backward movement. Instead the steamer leaped ahead at full speed. The boy felt the wheel strain as the tramp surged straight toward that dark stretch of sand.

"Chief—chief!" Captain Jarvis was at the speaking tube that communicated with the engine room. "Full speed astern! Do you hear? Astern!"

Evidently there was no response, for the man dropped the tube and flung himself upon the wheel. He whirled it to port in a furious effort to swing the bow clear of that obstruction in the stream ahead.

Cold fear struck at Stuart's heart. In that stirring instant he realized that they were too late. From the stem of the *Nanking* came a soft grinding noise as the ship shoved her bow high on the sand bar. She trembled; the forecastle head slowly rose with a quivering movement; the bridge listed perceptibly to starboard.

"They've done it!" The words came, stifled, from the captain's lips. For a moment he seemed to look about him helplessly as the old tramp came to a stop. Her engines jerked spasmodically for a second, then trembled into silence. The deck beneath them was utterly quiet.

The captain was again at the speaking tube. "Is this the second engineer? The chief? Full speed astern, man! We've run her bow on a sand bank."

Stuart remained motionless at the wheel. So used to the regular vibrations of the engines had he become that this unexpected cessation overwhelmed him with terror. Were those engines to fail them in this moment of dire need?

"What! Out of order? . . . Man, get them going at once! Yes—this is Captain Jarvis speaking. Jarvis—do you understand? I'll give you exactly one minute to get them going."

He dropped the tube. His voice was low, tense. "Alabam, those engines are all right. This has been carefully planned. The man who fired that shot at the mate must have gone below deck and warned the chief. They are carrying out their part of the bargain, even with the mate gone. Get out that gun. We'll need it. They may rush the bridge."

Stuart let his hands drop from the wheel. As in a dream he felt himself fumbling for his automatic. He looked toward the inner staircase as Tod came running up to join them.

"I've locked the whole superstructure, Captain Tom! Toppy and the Swede and Wu are on the cabin deck, guarding the fore and aft companionways. Are we aground?"

In the gloom Captain Jarvis nodded. "See those lights? They're wreckers' lamps, I'm sure. Yet we would have made it past this sand bar if the engine room had obeyed my signals. What are they planning? To loot this ship?"

As the man threw open the door and stepped to the bridge, Stuart leaned out the window. Abruptly the ship's search light, in the master's expert hands, sent a great cone of light pouring down upon the fore deck. Stuart's fingers closed upon the sill in a vise-like grip.

He felt the blood drain swiftly from his face. Over the bulwarks, in the glare of that immense light, swarmed a dozen Chinese. From the darkness of the river several sampans filled with countless others were moving into the glowing white circle.

Captain Jarvis's automatic barked in rapid succession. Stuart saw the Chinese, dressed in nondescript clothes, waver for an instant. Answering shots pattered like rain against the bridge.

"Fire at them, Joe Macaroni! They don't expect any resistance. This is our chance to make them flee—before they can attack in force."

Stuart and Tod flung themselves out of the door to the bridge. Their weapons made points of light in the darkness. Below them the Chinese scurried out of the glare of the search light.

"We've got 'em running. Keep it up." There was a ring of triumph in the captain's voice.

Suddenly the search light winked out. Darkness, more complete than before, closed down on the deck below them.

Captain Jarvis swore. "The chief's fixed the dynamo. Quick, Joe Macaroni! Get to the wireless shack and see if you can send out a call for help."

"Yes, sir." Tod ran aft to the boat deck.

"Get inside the wheel house, Alabam," ordered the captain. "I'll go down to the cabin deck. Toppy and I'll keep them off the bridge. You watch here—but take no chances."

Stuart took his place near the wheel. He could hear the captain's footsteps echoing on the stairs; after that silence descended upon him. Evidently the Chinese were surprised at the sudden attack from the bridge; they had apparently expected no resistance from those on board. Stuart wondered if they were holding a conference, planning perhaps, with the help of the chief engineer, to capture the bridge by strategy.

The air was heavy with suspense. The boy's pulse drummed in his ears. In the east a faint hint of dawn was in the sky. Would daylight come in time to save them? Abruptly he started. A soft scuff of feet sounded on the companionway to the bridge. He slowly tiptoed to the door, swung it open, and stepped out. Cautiously he peered down the companionway. Was someone creeping up the steps? In the darkness he could not be sure.

From a porthole below him a shot cracked out. A body plunged downward. "Blimey, I got 'im!" It was Toppy's excited cry.

Stuart dropped to the narrow deck in the shelter of the port wing. There behind the canvas wind dodger he was safe from searching eyes; and yet he could defend the two ladders which led up to him. Peering from behind the canvas, he tried to make out what was happening forward. Near the forecastle he heard guttural cries and muffled comments from the men. Stuart surmised that the crew, caught asleep on the forecastle head, were being securely locked in their quarters. With the engine room held by their confederates the attackers had only to seize the superstructure, and the ship would be completely in their hands.

Thudding blows soon sounded below. The marauders were trying to break through the steel netting that enclosed the companionways to the upper decks. Two shots rang out in rapid succession. The blows stopped. Stuart shivered. How long would this last? He glanced toward the east.

The sky was lightening. Streaks of gray slowly spread across the heavens; but the river and the ship still remained in shadow. Of a sudden the boy crouched low. A shot hit the deck near him. In surprise he looked up. That shot had apparently come from overhead. Of course—the crow's nest! One of the attackers had climbed the rigging and was now securely hidden in the basket-like structure on the main mast. The man evidently knew of his presence on the bridge.

Gradually, as dawn spread, the crow's nest took form; it stood dimly outlined against the sky. An object moved above the rim of the basket. Stuart took quick aim and fired. The head disappeared, but a second later another shot struck the canvas to the left of him.

Stuart raised his automatic. Shot after shot hurled itself toward that blot against the sky. He was riddling mast and canvas with bullets. A second later he stopped as a dark form slipped from the basket and slid down the ladder. Stuart let the man escape in safety. With the crow's nest empty he had no more fear from that direction.

"Alabam!" The cry came from below in Tod's voice. "They're getting ready to storm the bridge. Hold 'em. I couldn't radio for help. The blamed thing is dead; but Sparks is here, helping. Wu is bringing us ammunition. Carry on!"

Stuart lowered his weapon. How many shots had he left? Perhaps two or three. He must aim with care; he mustn't waste a shell.

Perhaps five minutes later the attack came with a quick rush of feet. He heard guttural cries, shots thudding against the superstructure, blows crashing against the barricades. Winged death leaped from the portholes to meet the assailants. Shrill screams tore through the air. On the deck below, points of light flashed as the attackers riddled the companionways with bullets. Stuart fired downward till his automatic was empty.

The violence of the attack diminished; the Chinese fell away. The boy realized that perhaps these guerrilla troops were unwilling to risk life and limb in an effort to gain possession of a steamer which their leaders had paid good money to receive. The door of the wheel house opened, and Stuart looked up to find Captain Jarvis standing there in the entrance.

"Come inside, Alabam, before it gets too light," he said in an undertone. "The Chinks are holding a counsel of war, I imagine. With day coming on our chances are growing better."

Stuart slipped inside. "What do they want this steamer for?" he asked.

"Probably for a drive up the river. With the troops hidden below deck this old tramp could slip up to any village wharf without arousing suspicion. Of course, no leader of the Nationalists would dare acknowledge complicity in this manœuvre; they'd say some of their men got out of hand. That's their excuse whenever any American is killed or any foreign settlement raided. This is the reason why the United States is rushing marines to Shanghai."

"Look!" Stuart cried, stepping to the forward window. "There's a vessel coming down river."

In the gathering light a ship could be seen far ahead. The river spread out on both sides of the *Nanking*, now lying slightly tilted upon the sand bar. A swarm of sampans was close under the flanks of the old freighter.

"Do you suppose, seh, that it's a Chinese vessel? A gunboat?"

"We'll soon see. Even if it is Chinese, it'll have to come to our assistance. They wouldn't dare refuse to aid an American steamer."

Tod rushed into the wheel house from the boat deck. "The American flag that was flying at the taffrail is gone," he announced from the doorway. "There's a Japanese flag there now."

Captain Jarvis pondered for a moment. "I begin to see their plan. If that approaching vessel is an English or American gunboat her officers would be sure to investigate if our flag were flying at the stern; but with a Japanese flag there she is liable to pass us, merely thinking we're on a bank and will float off when the tide comes in."

"Couldn't I sneak aft——" Tod began.

"Under fire of those men below? No. I'd never allow it."

The three stood silently gazing ahead. The approaching vessel was taking form. Stuart gave an exclamation of joy.

"It's an American destroyer! I've seen my father on them too often not to know." The boy uttered the last words without thinking. He turned to Captain Jarvis and raised a face radiant with hope. "Even if the wireless is dead, seh, we can get a message to that vessel. Have you any semaphore flags?"

The captain nodded. "In the locker there."

"I know the two-arm code," Stuart continued eagerly. "I'll send a message to them as they pass."

"Under fire?" Tod protested.

"We can do it!" There was a ring of enthusiasm in the captain's voice. He crossed to the locker, threw up the lid, and searched around inside. When he turned, there were two small red-and-white flags in his hands. "Alabam, you take your place atop this wheel house. It's growing lighter now, and that ship will see you. I'll keep the forecastle covered with my automatic. Tod, you get out to the boat deck and cover the stern. *If anyone attempts to stop Alabam, fire without mercy.* Understand?"

"Yes, sir."

"We'll wait just a minute or two. Perhaps that destroyer will come closer to make an investigation."

But as the moments passed it became evident to them that the American vessel was merely going downstream and in no way interested in a tramp steamer lying half a mile to starboard. Day had come. In the east the sky was thick with rosy clouds. The river sparkled like silver in the early light. The low, slender destroyer, with an American flag at its stern, was now drawing abeam of them.

"Are you ready, Alabam? The only decent thing Shark Bashford ever did was to bring you aboard. Ready?"

"Yes, seh."

"Get to the boat deck, Joe Macaroni. I'll stand in this window." The captain suited his action to his words. His automatic rested on the sill, pointed toward the forecastle.

Stuart slipped out of the rear door after Tod. He became aware for the first time that the air of morning was slightly chill. Two gulls circled over the *Nanking's* stern. He stuck the flag staffs in his belt, jumped to the rail of the little steps, and climbed up to the flat roof of the wheel house. Glancing forward, he could just glimpse the forecastle head, apparently deserted; but he knew that behind the windlass, under cover of the awning, a man might be in hiding.

As he stood upright on the small square roof, he gazed to starboard at the passing destroyer. Quickly he raised both arms, let the flags unroll from the staffs and felt them quiver in the faint breeze. He knew the signal. That meant: *attention*. Was someone watching from the gunboat? Did the officer of the watch, perhaps, see him here, outlined against the eastern sky?

A shot suddenly whizzed by him. It had come, he knew, from the forecastle head. But he did not falter, for an answering shot sounded from the wheel house. Captain Jarvis had seen his man.

Though no sign came from the destroyer, Stuart quickly went through the code. Thank heaven he had learned this at West Point, learned it doggedly while he doubted that he would ever have any need of the knowledge. He flung his right arm outward, straight from the shoulder; his left went down obliquely—the letter S. The letter O quickly followed—his right arm upraised at a slant, his left across his body. Then the letter S again. *S O S—S O S*. His arms moved with rapidity as he went through the familiar code. *Chinese— troops—attacking—American—steamer—Nanking*.

Once, aft of him, he heard Tod fire. A moment later a shot whined by with a hissing breath, and he saw that a sampan had been shoved out into the stream; someone was firing at him from the boat. But Captain Jarvis's automatic soon enforced silence from that direction. As he finished his message he dropped to deck, where he was out of range of the rifles below.

"Hurt, Alabam?" It was the captain calling in an agonized tone.

"No. I'm all right. I signalled for help, but they haven't answered yet."

"Lay low for a minute."

Stuart's eyes were fixed upon the destroyer. Already it was slipping past them. Desperate, he rose again. His flags came up. *S O S—S O S*. He stopped. From the stern of the destroyer a sailor was flagging an answering message.

Eagerly he read: *We are coming closer. Hold on.*

He saw the destroyer slow down, saw her sharp prow veer to the right. Suddenly a puff of smoke went up from a gun amidships. The shot exploded just ahead of the *Nanking's* bow.

Shouts were flung across the old tramp's fore deck. He heard the scurrying of innumerable feet. Another shell thundered astern of them. Stuart peered over the edge of the roof. Sampans were wildly making away from the steamer, heading for shore. And standing at the bulwarks were the chief engineer and the boatswain, pleading in vain with the Chinese to be taken along.

"Come down, Alabam!" The captain's deep voice boomed out from the bridge. "You've saved the day! They're running like rats. Come down!"

CHAPTER XXIV

THE INQUIRY

I'M HOLDING this inquiry," began Captain Jarvis an hour later, "in order to lay the charge of murder against one man only—the man who is guilty of First Mate Bashford's death."

He paused and glanced round the saloon cabin at his officers and men. "Our ship," he resumed, "will have to remain on this sand bar for several hours; at high tide we'll be able to float her and proceed upstream. Every man here is under the surveillance of twenty marines from that American gunboat, which will convoy us up river to Shanghai. When we arrive there the eight men who assisted these guerrilla troops will be lodged in jail. But of the graver charge of murder only one man is guilty. And that man I intend to discover right now."

A stir went round the circle of men sitting against the cabin walls. Stuart, seated next to Tod Moran on the settee, looked up. Opposite him, in the doorway to the passage, stood a marine garbed in the light khaki uniform of the tropics; his rifle butt rested on the floor between his feet, both hands gripped the barrel. Four other soldiers of the sea stood about the cabin with their eyes fixed upon the members of the crew. In a swivel chair at the centre table was Captain Jarvis. Stuart noted the masterful poise of the man as he sat there in his white uniform; his flashing glance bespoke a purpose even stronger than his words. He was looking round the circle, wondering, Stuart fancied, which man was guilty.

The boy followed his gaze. It passed over Tod, over Toppy and Swede Jorgenson, and rested for a moment on Tony the Wop, who sat on the end of the settee. It quickly moved on to the first chair, in which was Wu Sing with his pet monkey in his arms; then to Singapore Sam, the steward, the radio operator, the chief engineer, and finally the boatswain. One of these men was guilty. But which one?

"I'll call Wu as the first witness," announced the captain. He made a gesture toward the chair across the table.

Wu rose soundlessly, dropped Ming into Tod's lap, and took the appointed seat. "You wish me to tell why I came aboard?"

"Exactly." Captain Jarvis leaned back in his chair.

Wu Sing's words came with slow distinctness. "I am a secret agent of the Peking government. Some months ago my chief learned that the tramp steamer *Nanking* was doing business with our enemies, the southern troops, who call themselves Nationalists. Officers on this ship were smuggling opium into the States, and in return were bringing small consignments of arms and ammunition to our enemies. I was ordered from San

Francisco, where I was born and educated, to investigate this steamer. I procured the job of cook two voyages ago. So cunningly was this illegal traffic carried on that I was unable to secure evidence. Soon after we started on this voyage, however, I began to suspect that a deeper mystery lay behind the actions of these men. On the second night out from Vancouver I discovered a secret meeting on the fo'c'sle head, held there in the dense fog of that night."

"Can you name the men who were there?" The captain put the question in a low tone.

"Yes. The first mate, the chief engineer, the steward, the boatswain, Singapore Sam, and three or four others of the crew. I was unable to learn their plans in detail, but I gathered enough to suspect that they plotted to turn over their ship to certain troops who would use it in making a drive up the Yangtse against my government." Wu stopped and raised his eyes to the captain. "Any questions, sir?"

"Yes. Did you see anything of the fireman called Slim Morgan?"

"No, sir."

"Have you any reason to suspect that one of these men you have named is guilty of murder—of the murder of this fireman and the first mate?"

"I have no evidence."

"That is all," murmured the captain. His gaze left the Chinese and travelled on to Tony the Wop. "Tony, will you please take the chair?"

"Yes, sir." Tony reluctantly rose. He rubbed his blue jowls thoughtfully as he sank into the seat.

"Tony, can you tell us the identity of the man who knifed Slim Morgan?"

"I don' know heem, sir. I hear Slim Morgan scream out, and then somebody grab me, somebody not ver' tall." The Italian's eyes focussed upon the boatswain.

"You can't say for sure?"

"I don' like to, sir."

"Very well. That's all, Tony. Ormsby, you'll be the next witness."

"Yes, seh." Stuart dropped into the chair vacated by Tony, and in a slightly tremulous voice began to recount his experiences on that foggy night. As he went on his voice grew steadier, more assured. He told of his being relieved by the first mate, of his hearing the words "wreckers' lamps" spoken in an undertone. From that point he plunged into his adventures in Moji, where he had seen the mate, the chief, and the boatswain receive money from Lee Chong, one of the Nationalists. As he related this part he was aware that two of the men mentioned stirred nervously in their seats. One of the marine guards casually lifted his rifle.

"You saw money pass between them?" asked the captain, leaning across the green baize of the table.

"I did."

"Did you hear any remark to the effect that they intended to get rid of the ship's captain?"

"None, seh. I heard them tell Lee Chong that the skipper was willing to play his part."

Captain Jarvis turned his piercing gaze upon the chief and the boatswain. "Evidently, then, they gave this Chinese Nationalist the impression that I was in league with them?"

"That was what I took it to mean, seh."

"Very good. Tod Moran, you are the next witness."

Stuart went back to the settee, and Tod took his place at the table. His story was quickly told. He recounted his experiences when he followed the boatswain by train from Tokio to Nagasaki; he described the man's meeting with Lee Chong at the hotel in the latter city, and then his own mishap at Sotoko's café. He told of Stuart's joining him in the cellar as a prisoner, of their escape with Wu's help, and their race to the ship, only to discover upon their arrival that the captain had disappeared and Shark Bashford was in command.

"You heard nothing that might lead you to suspect which of these men was guilty of attempted murder— which one was so desperate that, when he heard the chief mate about to betray him, he shot the man to stop the confession?"

"Nothing, sir."

"That is all for the present, Moran."

Tod went back to his seat. Captain Jarvis pondered for a moment. Abruptly he looked up. "When I took the command of this ship I was told of the strange series of misfortunes that had occurred to the three captains who had preceded me. So at once I considered all possible precautions. I had new Yale locks placed on my cabin doors; when we entered Oriental waters I ordered barricades put around the companionways to the upper decks, such as all passenger ships now carry on the Yangtse Kiang. Three attempts were made upon my life. The first was an effort to knife me in the back; the second was a shot coming from a sampan outside the Yokohama breakwater; the third was the lowest, most cowardly attempt of all—poison!"

He ceased speaking and looked about the cabin. Every man there, Stuart saw, was intent upon the captain's story. Even the marines gazed at him with heightening interest.

"I was not the only one, however," resumed the captain, "who ate this poisoned food. My steward, eating from the same pantry, came near death, too. Mr. Sanderson, will you please take the chair?"

The steward stepped forward. His round face seemed paler than usual as he looked across the table at the captain. "You want me to tell how I got sick, sir?"

"Yes. Did you suspect poison?"

"Oh, no, sir! I mean I didn't think of anything like that, sir. I had been ashore at Yokohama, and I thought as how I'd ate something in one of those Jap restaurants what didn't agree with me; but when that doctor at Moji saw me an' I told him all my symptoms, he said right off the bat, sir, 'Mr. Sanderson, you appear to be suffering from slow poisoning!' His very words, sir! An'

I tell you I was that surprised that I couldn't say a thing."

Stuart smiled to himself. Somehow, he couldn't imagine Bill Sanderson ever at a loss for words.

"You have no idea who put this poison in our grub?"

"Oh, no, sir. I can't understand—I mean——"

"That will do, Sanderson." Captain Jarvis raised his hand. "Of course I realize that you've been making a little money on the side, eh?"

"Oh, no, sir! I don't know what you mean, sir."

The captain's tone grew lower, more incisive. "I know you were in deep with the mate; and I also know that you've been making a rake-off on the grub money. Don't lie, now."

The steward's glance faltered; finally a faint smile played about the corners of his mouth. "Isn't it done on most ships, sir? A little pin money, you might say?"

"That's all, Sanderson. Take your seat. . . . Bo'sun, have you anything to say? Do you know who shot Mr. Bashford?"

The boatswain squirmed in his chair. "No, sir, I dunno nothing!" His hairy hands twitched on his knees.

"You mean you refuse to tell?"

"But I don't know what youse mean, sir."

"Very well. Now, Mr. Rankin, can you help us?"

The chief engineer glanced up with a glowering expression upon his bearded face. "I got nothing at all to say."

"Very well." Captain Jarvis's eyes took on a deeper

glitter. His fingers drummed on the green baize. "We'll just go over that first attempt upon my life," he resumed. "I was sitting with Moran and Ormsby in my little cabin above this one when a knife whizzed through the forward port. The force of the throw embedded the blade in the table. Leaving it there, we went on deck, first making sure that the door was locked. Isn't that true, Ormsby? I asked you to be sure the cabin door was locked."

"It was, seh. The catch was on so that it locked itself when we went out. You remember you had to open it with your key when we came back."

Captain Jarvis nodded; he leaned forward intently. "Yet when we got back the knife was gone. How can we account for that?" His gaze swept the cabin, but no one spoke. "Every door securely locked, only the portholes open because of the heat. No man could enter and take that knife—and no man was hiding there."

Abruptly he rose, stepped to his desk in the corner and, opening a drawer, brought forth the knife in question. A second later he was back in his seat, leaning over the green baize. With a quick movement he drove the knife blade into the table. Stuart felt his pulse mount. That quivering steel against the green brought back the scene to his memory.

"Wu." The captain spoke only one word. The eyes of the men turned to the cook. Wu was gazing impassively ahead, the monkey still in his arms. Suddenly he loosed his hold. Ming stood upright, jabbering profusely, his solemn eyes fixed upon the knife; then, as if with a quick resolve, he jumped to the floor.

Stuart stared. Would his plan work? For it was his plan that Ming should be brought here. Ever since that day of the typhoon when he had found the monkey in the crow's nest and the knife there amid the refuse, the theory had taken form in his mind that it was Ming who had stolen the weapon from the locked cabin. But would the monkey play his part? Would he point the way to the discovery of the guilty person, to the boatswain, whom he and Tod suspected? Stuart watched in an agony of suspense.

Ming sprang to the table at a bound, lurched across to the knife, and shook it back and forth till it came loose in his clutch. With a profusion of chattering sounds he next swung himself to the floor, sprang past Tod on the settee and caught hold of the rim of the porthole. There for a moment he hung before drawing himself up, as though he meant to make his exit by way of the open port.

The little creature turned abruptly, however, and looked back into the cabin. His beady eyes circled the group. It was a tense moment when at length he dropped to the floor again and lurched by Tod and Swede Jorgenson. He passed Tony the Wop, passed Wu Sing, passed Singapore Sam, and at last came to a full halt before the steward.

Raising his fore paw with the dagger tightly clasped he offered it to Bill Sanderson.

There was utter quiet in the cabin. Captain Jarvis did not move; his gaze never left the steward's face.

Bill Sanderson smiled wanly. "Ming brings me everything," he rasped; "I mean he's a friend o' mine because I always give him candy an' nuts. Ming don't mean anything."

"Perhaps not." Captain Jarvis nodded. He swung about in his chair to one of the marines. "Sergeant, will you keep your eye on that man?"

"Yes, sir." At the sergeant's bidding two of the marine guards moved to either side of the steward.

"We'll go on with our inquiry," said the captain "Toppy, will you take the witness chair?"

"Me, sir?" Amazement blazed in the man's wizened face. "Blimey, I dunno—— Yes, sir." He rose and slid into the chair; his hands moved nervously.

"I want you to tell what happened when you came aboard with the Japanese doctor in Moji. Did you see me at that time?"

"Gawd blimey, sir, yer wasn't 'ere. The third mate, 'e just went aroun' the deck arskin' if anybody 'ad seen the skipper. Yer 'ad gone!"

"Did you take the doctor ashore?"

"No, sir. 'E went in a bloomin' sampan with a Jap boatman."

"Did you have any conversation with him before he left the ship?"

"Yes, sir. I arsked 'im 'ow the steward was makin' it, an' 'e says ter me it was a blarsted peculiar case, 'cause he couldn't find nothin' wrong with the blighter."

"That's all."

"Yes, sir." Toppy took his seat with a relieved sigh. With a look of interrogation he turned his surprised eyes upon Stuart.

"Moran, will you please take the chair again?"

Tod moved over to the appointed seat.

"Now, Moran, I want you to tell us what you found when you searched Mr. Bashford's dunnage."

"Yes, sir. I went as you ordered to look through the mate's belongings. I found nothing, sir, until I began to search the body. Around the waist was a leather money belt. In it were five hundred dollars in gold and a written memorandum."

"Yes, I have it here." The captain passed a small slip of paper across the table. "Tell us what is written on it."

Tod looked down at the paper. "This is evidently a financial statement kept by the mate. He has noted here twenty-five hundred dollars received from Lee Chong. A thousand dollars is subtracted from the amount, leaving fifteen hundred. This fifteen hundred is divided into three parts of five hundred each."

"Good. That is all. Sergeant, did you search the two officers?"

The sergeant of the marines came to attention. "Yes, sir. The bo'sun had five hundred upon him. Chief Engineer Rankin had his five hundred concealed in his cabin."

"Have you searched the steward?"

"No, sir."

"Do so at once."

"Whatcha mean?" The steward was on his feet. "Just because——" He stopped short as the two marines pinned his arms to his sides.

The sergeant quickly ran his hands over the man. "He's got a money belt around his waist, sir."

"Get it."

The steward squirmed in helpless rage. "Whatcha want my money for?" he shrilled.

"Just to see, Sanderson, how much of Lee Chong's money you received. I have an idea that the man who got twice as much as the other three is the man who is guilty of this murder."

"Just because that monk brings me a knife——"

"No. Not only because of Ming. I began to suspect you when you told me you were sick and I gave you that big dose of castor oil. You made a wry face, but you swallowed it. I wondered then—just a vague thought not put into words—if you were not pretending sickness. When I sent Toppy ashore for that doctor I wanted to see if he would tell me that nothing was wrong with you—that your illness was merely a pretense. *And you knew that I suspected!* Your cunning game was up if that doctor ever saw you and gave me his report. You were the man who knocked me unconscious and locked me in that empty galley bunker! You were desperate, Bill Sanderson."

As the sergeant stepped forward with the money belt the steward's eyes narrowed to points of glinting light. An expression of intense hatred spread over his round face.

"Will you count the money please, Sergeant?"

"Yes, sir."

Utter silence descended upon the cabin. Only the clink of gold coins came from the table. The sergeant at length looked up. "There's a thousand dollars in gold here," he said.

A barely perceptible sigh came from the circle of men.

"I thought so," acknowledged the captain. "This is another link in the chain of evidence against you, Sanderson."

"Oh, no, you don't," the steward snarled. "You can't fix murder on me just because of whatcha might call circumstantial evidence!"

"Very well." Captain Jarvis rose to his full height. "We'll let a court of law decide who is guilty. For my part"—and he gazed squarely at the boatswain, the chief engineer, and the steward—"I intend to charge you three men jointly with murder—with the murder of First Mate Bashford!"

"What!" The boatswain struggled to his feet. In vain the chief engineer tried to pull the man down into his seat again. "No, youse don't. I got my share of Lee Chong's money all right, but youse don't charge me with murder. I ain't guilty—and the steward is."

"You lie!" Bill Sanderson struggled impotently in the hands of the two marines.

"Go on, bo'sun," said the captain. "How do you know?"

"Last night I got feeling that somethin' was up when my cabin mate, the oiler, didn't turn in. So I gets up and climbs above to the boat deck. It was almost morning, I guess, and I heard voices comin' from the open door of the wheel house. Then I hears a shot. It came right from beside the lifeboat, and I sees Bill Sanderson standin' there with a pistol in his hand. That was enough for me. I runs down again. But I ain't goin' to let that skunk try to get me mixed up with murder. He's the one! He's guilty as hell."

"You are willing to swear that in a court of law?"

"You bet I am."

The captain motioned to the sergeant. "Have your men lock Sanderson in the brig. When we reach Shanghai I'll swear out a warrant charging him with murder."

A furious stream of oaths came from the steward's lips. "I'm glad I killed Shark Bashford," he cried shrilly. "He was willing to be a stool pigeon—the muck, the swine! If I get a chance at the bo'sun——"

"That will do, Sanderson. We've got you at last. You'll be in the Shanghai jail within four hours. Sergeant, take charge, too, of the bo'sun and the chief. ... The inquiry is ended."

CHAPTER XXV

SHANGHAI

BLIMEY, listen ter those blarsted beggars down below. 'Ear 'em arskin' fer eats!'' Toppy, standing precariously near the edge of the deck, grasped the tarpaulin of the starboard lifeboat and leaned overside.

Stuart looked up from his bucket of water. The *Nanking* lay in stream off the Shanghai wharves, and he and Toppy and Swede Jorgenson were holystoning the boat deck. All three were barefooted, with their dungarees rolled up to their knees. Their heads were bare; and the sun beat relentlessly down upon their necks and arms, unprotected by their scanty singlets.

"Whadda they want?" asked the Swede, stepping to Toppy's side. Stuart followed. On the muddy water far below, bumboats and sampans were milling about the flanks of the freighter. Each small boat carried a bamboo cabin amidships in which could be seen numerous ragged children. In the stern of the sampan directly beneath the three seamen a sweating, half-naked coolie dragged on his oar. In the bow his wife held up a long pole with a fishing net at its end; she stretched this up toward the steamer's rail, while an incessant whine came from her lips.

"Are they talking English?" Stuart asked.

"They thinks they are," Toppy grunted in disgust. " 'Ear that?"

From the jabber of cries issuing from the sampans Stuart soon distinguished a singsong refrain repeated over and over: "No mamma, no papa—no brudder, no sister—no chow-chow. Wah-a-a-ah!"

"Can yer beat that?" Toppy, turning his wizened face to Stuart, raised his voice in derision:

> "No mommer—no popper;
> No brudder—no sister;
> No chow-chow.
> Wahr-a-a-ahr!"

The cook was evidently answering this petition of his people, for at that instant a sudden waterfall of refuse went overside from the galley. With cries like swooping gulls the beggars dipped their poles into the slimy water to retrieve potato peelings, apple cores, and remains of uneaten food.

Stuart turned away from the sight. "Let's get back to work," he said gruffly. He sluiced his bucket of water across the hardwood deck.

"Oh, Alabam!" Tod stepped from the wheel-house door. "The skipper is in his office with the major of marines. They want to see you."

"Me?" Stuart looked up in surprise.

"Yes; Captain Tom sent me up for you. The major wants to see the fellow who sent that semaphore message under fire. He says you're just the sort that the marines would like to have join them."

Stuart smiled. "Oh, I'd rather not go down there, Joe Macaroni. Can't you fix it up so I won't have to?"

Tod gave him a questioning glance. "Captain's orders, Alabam. And Major Ormsby is dead set on seeing you."

The boy's face grew white. "Major who?"

"Ormsby—the same name as yours. Better come along."

A ground swell of terror pulled at Stuart's limbs. He leaned against the lifeboat for support. His father! . . . Did he know that it was his son who had sent that message?

Tod moved closer. "Come on, Alabam."

With a look of decision upon his face Stuart drew his friend to one side near the funnel. "Listen, Joe Macaroni," he hurriedly explained; "that man is my father! Yes—don't be surprised. Now you can realize why I don't want him to see me like this." He glanced down ruefully at his dungarees and bare feet. "Fix it up for me, won't you?" There was an eloquent appeal in his voice.

"All right." Tod shot him a glance, deep, warm, and sympathetic. "I understand. I'll do what I can, Alabam."

As his friend moved toward the companionway Stuart went back to his work. But his mind was not intent upon the swabs and holystone.

"Yer a crazy bloke not ter go down," Toppy reproached him. "Yer might get an easy job."

"But I don't want one, Toppy. This suits me. I want to go back to the States on this tramp."

Toppy heaved a deep sigh. "Well, it won't be so bloomin' bad with a new set o' mates and a few new seamen." Abruptly he raised his head. "'Ere comes Wu Sing."

The cook emerged from the companionway garbed in shore clothes; and Stuart realized that Wu was once more taking his place as an agent of the Peking government. The Chinese came toward them with a wide grin on his ivory countenance.

"I have just signed off the *Nanking*," he said. "Yes, I leave to join Chang Tso-lin. This means good-bye."

"You're really going?" There was deep regret in Stuart's tone.

"It is necessary. My work here is finished, and I am called by my government to take up another case." His Oriental face softened as he gazed at the three seamen. "We have sailed through dangerous waters with our captain, and we've come through to safety." He held out his hand. "May you likewise always make a happy port!"

Stuart wrung the strong, slender hand. "Good-bye, Wu. I can't begin to tell you what it's meant to me to know a Chinese like you."

Wu raised his eyebrows slightly. "Me? I am only a poor specimen of my race. If you could know Chang

Tso-lin!... Good-bye. I only pray that in my next case I find comrades like you men aboard the *Nanking*."

When he had gone Toppy leaned for a moment on his swab. "Fer a bloody Chink 'e ain't so bad arfter all. But fer me, Alabam, I prefers my friends to be w'ite."

Stuart, who was kneeling at the faucet filling his bucket, looked up with a grin; but as his gaze left Toppy and passed across to the companionway the smile suddenly left his face.

Captain Tom Jarvis had come up to the boat deck, and following him was another man—a man in the immaculate uniform of an officer of the United States Marines. There was no need for Stuart to look closely. That slender military figure with that compelling gaze was his father.

"Oh, Alabam!" It was Captain Jarvis calling. "Come here just a moment. Major Ormsby wants to meet you."

"Yes, seh."

Slowly, with his heart pounding in his throat, the boy got to his feet. Wiping his dripping hands on his dungarees he went forward. His eyes, travelling from the captain to his companion, met the direct gaze of his father.

"This is the young man," said Captain Jarvis. "He sent that message under fire—the bravest deed I've ever seen!"

Major Ormsby's glance never wavered. Neither by sign nor intimation did he show that he recognized his son. Only his voice, when he spoke, indicated that he was making an effort to control himself. "I wanted to see you, young man—and if the mountain won't come to Mahomet, Mahomet will come to the mountain." A faint smile touched the corners of his mouth. "You are just the sort of person we'd like to have join the marines. Would you care to consider the proposition?"

With a quick sense of relief Stuart caught the tone which his father had evidently set for their interview. "Thank you, seh," he slowly answered; "but I intend to be an officer in the marines."

"You do?" There was a hint of surprise in the Major's voice. His lean bronzed face grew intent.

"Yes, seh. You see, seh, I flunked out of the Academy at West Point—and then I got mighty scared at the thought of meeting my father. You—he had always wanted me to graduate—as he did." Stuart looked down for a second. Then he raised his head; his words rushed forth. "I'm going back now, just as soon as I reach the States. Oh, it can be done, all right—if I get another appointment and start all over again. Two years ago a fellow did it—and I reckon I can, too."

Captain Jarvis nodded. "Not a bad idea—eh, Major?"

There was a gleam of approval in Major Ormsby's eyes. "My son," he said, "I'm proud of you."

Stuart's glance faltered. Through misty eyes he looked across the river, crowded with junks and sampans, to the wharves; slowly his gaze travelled downstream to the teeming life along the Bund.

"Yes, Captain," went on Major Ormsby, "this is my vagabond son. However, he's not such a bad sort, after all."

"Bad sort!" boomed Captain Jarvis in his deep voice. "Major, I feel like congratulating you. You haven't heard half the story yet. You see, after the luck I had two years ago in unravelling the mystery on the steamer *Araby* the Trans-Pacific Company asked me to take command of this old tramp. Every passage out something always happened to the master, and the Company sent me to solve the riddle, if possible. If it hadn't been for your son and Tod Moran and Wu Sing, I would have been a failure. In fact, I owe them my life. Now you understand how grateful I am."

"I'd like to hear more about it, Captain. How about a little dinner aboard my ship to-night? Bring along young Alabam and his friend Moran, too. We'll have a quiet talk, eh?"

"Very good, Major. We'll have to see that this young fellow gets another appointment."

"Indeed we shall. . . . Oh, Stuart!"

"Yes, seh?"

"Would you like to go home on a transport? I can arrange for your passage. It would be quicker—and perhaps less work."

Stuart turned his radiant face to his father. At the man's well-remembered tone of affection his fears had fallen like a leaden weight from his shoulders. "Thank you, seh, but if you don't mind I'd rather go back on the

Nanking. It was my fault that I flunked out of West Point—and I'd like to get back on my own. I've got friends aboard, too."

"If the captain will have you, my boy . . ."

"Have him?" Captain Jarvis chuckled. "You don't get a seaman like Alabam every day, Major."

"Good. Then I'll see you three to-night." Major Ormsby turned away, then hesitated. "You are certain, Stuart, that you want to start over?"

"Yes, seh." The words were low yet distinct. "I'm going back to West Point."

The boy stood there in silence, watching the two men go down the companion steps. Through him surged a swift feeling of happiness; for the first time since leaving the Academy he could look the future steadily in the eye.

Toppy's derisive cries brought him back to the present. While the little Londoner holystoned the deck a whining refrain issued from his lips:

> "No mommer—no popper;
> No brudder—no sister;
> No chow-chow.
> Wahr-a–a–ahr!"

THE END